CRUFFINS AND CONFESSIONS

PERIDALE CAFE
BOOK 33

AGATHA FROST

PINK TREE PUBLISHING LTD

WANT TO BE KEPT UP TO DATE WITH AGATHA
FROST RELEASES? *SIGN UP THE FREE
NEWSLETTER!*

www.AgathaFrost.com

You can also follow **Agatha Frost** across social media.
Search 'Agatha Frost' on:

Facebook
Twitter
Goodreads
Instagram

ALSO BY AGATHA FROST

Claire's Candles

Head to Northash to join Claire as she solves mysteries from her candle shop...

1

"*A*bout time!" Katie Wellington-South declared, clapping her hands together as she leaned against the counter in Julia's Café. "We missed summer, autumn, and Christmas, but after all these months of planning delays and building setbacks—and the *mild* bat infestation—the Peridale Community Square is opening tomorrow. I couldn't have done it without you, Julia."

Julia South-Brown smiled as she sprayed the display cabinet with glass cleaner, the January chill outside tempered by Katie's enthusiasm—and the café's bubble of radiator warmth. The overhead lights glinted off the bright pink power suit Katie wore, a striking choice against the yellow hard hat on the table behind her. The café was quiet, save for a few regulars nursing their last cups of tea as closing time approached.

"You're giving me far too much credit," Julia replied, wiping down the front of the gleaming cabinet housing the day's sweet leftovers. "You're the one who did all the heavy lifting. I just provided the tea and cakes."

"As always, you're too modest." Katie waved her hand, her giant diamond ring catching the light—she was technically Julia's stepmother, but they were almost the same age. "You were at every planning meeting, and the builders would have downed tools weeks ago if it weren't for you ferrying trays across to the building site every hour. You were our morale machine."

Julia blushed under the praise, her fingers fiddling with the pink cloth. Katie's words touched her; truthfully, she was just as excited as anyone about the new square's grand opening. Not only was the square—with a market, playground, public allotment, and gardens—on the field behind the café, but Katie had given Julia the first refusal of a stall, which she had gratefully accepted.

"Credit to both of you," Dot announced, placing her empty teapot on the counter with a satisfied thud. "I don't think anyone thought you had it in you to manage a project like this, Katie, but I always knew you could do it." She pushed up her short curls at the back, and Julia bit her tongue, knowing her gran had been one of Katie's longtime detractors. Dot's husband, Percy, followed close behind, dabbing at his shiny head with a napkin. "Haven't I always thought Katie was capable of big things, Percy?"

"Yes, my dear," Percy said, beaming at Dot, still in love as ever. "Quite capable. I do hope someone's selling pies at the market launch tomorrow."

"And I hope my gnomes will fly off the shelves of my

little stall," Ethel White added from the table nearest the counter—the unlikely trio were as attached at the hip as ever.

"If they don't, it'll be because those gnomes are as ugly as you, dear," Dot muttered under her breath, eliciting a chuckle from Katie and Julia. "I'd say they were uglier, but nothing can be."

Before Ethel could fire off a comeback, the door flung open with a clatter, letting in a blast of icy air and a woman shouting into her phone. She marched to the counter, acknowledging no one, her voice slicing through the café's comfortable hum.

"I don't care what's going on. Just sort it. I want my money," she barked into her phone. Her sharp tone drew every gaze in the room, but she didn't seem to notice or care. She squinted at the menu board above the counter while continuing her loud rant. "I've given you plenty of time, and as I have to keep reminding you, it's not my fault the school wasn't successful."

Julia stepped forward, her customer service smile in place. "Can I help you?"

The woman lowered her phone just long enough to snap, "I need something strong."

"Strong?" Julia asked, taken aback.

"Coffee?" The woman rolled her eyes with an exaggerated sigh, dropping her handbag on the floor. "This is a café, isn't it?"

"Last time I checked," Julia replied, unable to help herself. She smiled wider and said, "A strong coffee, coming right up. We have lattes, cappuccinos, or—"

"Yeah, whatever. Just hurry—I don't have all day."

3

"Excuse you!" Dot exclaimed, planting her hands on her hips. "Manners?"

The woman shot Dot a warning glare while Julia prepared a cappuccino with two espresso shots, hoping to diffuse an argument from the customer carried in on the bitter winter wind. She continued her phone tirade, berating someone about 'people not taking her seriously.' Julia handed over the cardboard takeaway cup, and the woman looked at it like she didn't know what it was.

"Food?" she demanded. "What have you got?"

"It's a little late in the afternoon for that," Julia said, offering the display cases. "But there's still plenty of lemon drizzle left and a slice of Victoria—"

"No," she barked, glancing with disinterest at the cakes revolving around. "Diet." She lowered her phone long enough to wave it near the card reader to pay. She took a sip of the coffee and grimaced. "Ugh. I asked for it strong. Whatever…"

The woman and her two espresso shots stormed out, letting the door slam behind her.

"And good riddance!" Dot declared, reclaiming her seat. "What was her problem?"

"I've felt like her a few times with all these building delays," Katie said, though the wrinkle forming between her immaculate pencilled-in eyebrows suggested even she knew she'd never been that brutish. "She was rather mean."

"She was," Julia agreed, frowning. "Did she seem familiar to anyone else?"

"I might have seen her in the post office a few days

ago," Percy suggested, wagging a knowing finger. "Yes, I'm certain I did."

But Julia hadn't seen the woman in the past few days. Something stirred deep in her memories, and she wished she could pinpoint where.

Her gaze dropped to the floor by the counter, where a sleek leather handbag lay abandoned. Her heart quickened—half with alarm, half with a bubbling sense of intrigue. She scooped it up, tempted to look inside for some form of identification for the woman. But she couldn't—she wouldn't.

"She's left her bag," Julia announced, though no one was listening.

Dot was mid-rant about switching dog food brands for Lady and Bruce, and they all seemed oblivious to the rain pattering against the window. Julia hesitated, glancing at the door.

The woman would come back for it eventually. But did Julia really want her back in the café? If she never darkened the doorway again, it would be too soon.

A nagging voice in her mind told Julia to hurry after her with the bag. Before she could argue with herself, she and the bag pushed through the door. The bell jingled faintly behind her as she stepped out into the drizzle.

Up by The Plough, she spotted the woman clutching the coffee cup, her pace brisk against the rain. Despite all her griping earlier, she'd walked past two bins without throwing the cup away. Julia tightened her grip on the bag and quickened her steps.

"Excuse me!" Julia called, breaking into a jog. "Wait!"

The woman slowed but didn't stop, glancing over her shoulder with an irritated glare.

"What?" she snapped. "I paid, and don't tell me my card declined because I know it didn't."

Julia forced a polite smile as she held up the handbag. "You forgot this."

The woman stopped, her sharp gaze snapping to the bag in Julia's hands. Her expression softened for a fleeting moment, though the warmth never reached her eyes.

"Oh. Right," she said flatly. She stepped closer, snatching the bag as though Julia might change her mind. "Is there something else?"

Julia hesitated, gulping. Her hands twisted together as she blurted, "I know you, don't I?"

Without missing a beat, the woman rolled her eyes, a humourless laugh escaping her lips. "I don't think so. Maybe you saw me on TV."

She turned on her heel before Julia could answer, her boots clicking against the polished stone pavement as she marched off.

Julia stood frozen, her hands still hovering where the bag had been, a strange chill settling over her, and it wasn't from the January drizzle. She knew that woman —she was sure of it.

A few moments later, Julia slipped back into the warm safety of the café, her mind racing with half-formed memories. Dot and Ethel's familiar bickering blended into the background until Ethel's voice cut through her thoughts.

"Ugly as a gnome, eh?" Ethel crowed, giving Dot a

light swat with the back of her hand. "That's rich, coming from you, Dorothy South, with a face as frosty as this miserable weather."

Dot sniffed, adjusting her brooch with exaggerated precision. "I could have been a model, I'll have you know. Back in my younger days."

"On tins of dog food, maybe," Ethel shot back with a sly grin, her voice more teasing than biting.

And just like that, the café was back to normal, but Julia's thoughts lingered on the woman.

It wasn't just her rudeness. There *was* something familiar about her—she was sure of it. She'd been brunette, around Julia's age in her early forties, and dressed like someone with a professional job, but Julia couldn't quite place it.

"Right, I should get to the market," Katie announced, scooping up her hard hat with her perfect manicure. "Still lots of last-minute things to fix. Vinnie needs picking up from his after-school club, your father wants to take me to The Comfy Corner for dinner to celebrate, and I've got two late-night nail clients at the salon." She let out an exhausted sigh. "Someone needs to invent extra hours in the day."

Katie's girlish laugh—bordering on delirious—lingered as she disappeared through the beaded curtain to the kitchen. Before the beads rattled back together, Jessie appeared, already in her jacket, her backpack slung over one shoulder, pulling out her wireless earbuds.

"Am I alright to head off early, Mum?" she asked, tucking the headphones into their case. "I've finished the washing up, but that new food critic for the paper is already at the office. Veronica wants me to meet her before the grand launch." She rolled her eyes, her lingering teenage edges never too far from the surface, even at twenty-two. "Veronica won't stop going on about her. Are you still having that market stall for your cruffin thingys?"

"My cruffins will make their debut," Julia replied, her voice distant as her mind wandered back to the stranger. "Of course, love. You head off."

"You alright?" Jessie peered down her nose, tilting her head. "You look like you've seen a ghost."

Julia blinked, snapping back to the present.

"I think I might have," she murmured. "It's nothing. Go on. The weather has kept this place quiet all day— I'll manage the clean up." She took Jessie's apron from her and said, "Don't forget dinner at the cottage tonight. Your dad's cooking."

Jessie sighed. "Does he have to?"

She kissed Julia's cheek and headed through the front door, rattling the bell and leaving Julia with the regulars.

At the table by the window, Evelyn from the B&B and Shilpa from the post office took turns with *The Peridale Post*'s crossword. Next to them, Amy, the church organist, got on with some knitting, though from her unsteady handling of the needles and the lumpy mess she was making, her New Year's resolution to 'be more crafty' wasn't going so well.

"Don't look so glum, dear," Dot said, her voice brimming with optimism as she began helping herself to a fresh pot of tea behind the counter. "The new square will sort out this quiet January. People will come from far and wide for the market. Mark my words; it will put Peridale on the map."

Julia hummed her agreement, deciding not to bring up the woman again. If her gran had recognised her, she wasn't the type of woman to keep her thoughts to herself. Perhaps Julia had seen her on TV—that felt as unlikely as seeing her in the post office.

She made herself a cup of her favourite peppermint and liquorice tea as the rain turned from drizzle to a full downpour, but the familiar minty sweetness did little to comfort her as the memory hovered just out of reach.

A flash of a classroom kitchen, the scent of powdered sugar, and the sound of a bitter laugh all jumbled together. *Where* did she know that woman from?

With a soft shake of her head, she set the cup aside and resumed her cleaning, but the unease lingered. She didn't know why, but the woman's voice, like the memory it stirred, made her want to crawl up in a ball and hide.

2

*J*essie took the metal steps two at a time, her Doc Martens clanging against the wet fire escape as she rushed towards her second job. The rain had dampened her dark hair, droplets sliding down her leather jacket. Above Katie's Salon, warm light spilled from the frosted windows of *The Peridale Post's* office.

Pushing through the door, Jessie stopped short. Veronica was perched on the edge of her desk, her spiky grey hair wilder than usual and her electric blue glasses slipping down her nose as she laughed—a rare, almost disarming sight that made Jessie pause.

Beside her was a brunette in an expensive cream blazer. Her perfect nails curled around a familiar takeaway coffee cup, and a sleek black bag hung over her shoulder.

"Ah, Jessika!" Veronica straightened, gesturing between them. "Perfect timing for introductions. This is

Wendy Michaels, our new food critic that I've been telling you all about. She's quite the catch for our little paper."

"Please, call me Wendy." The woman's smile was bright, but something flickered behind her eyes as she extended her hand. Her grip was a touch too firm. "Veronica was just filling me in on the funny story of how you got here." She gestured a finger at the framed front pages lining the countryside mural walls. "Seems like the locals put up quite the big fight for that little patch of grass, so I'm looking forward to seeing what all the fuss is about."

"It's more than a patch of grass to people around here." Jessie shrugged off her damp jacket, noticing how Wendy's fingers drummed against her coffee cup. "But yeah, everyone has been getting ready for this for months. People are excited."

"I hope it doesn't disappoint." Wendy's laugh held a frosty edge. "Though I admit, I'm a little nervous about diving into print journalism. Newspapers are so... different from television. I've always thought of them as quaint."

"'Our doubts are traitors, and make us lose the good we oft might win, by fearing to attempt.'" Veronica waved away the concern, a Shakespeare quote never too far from the retired English teacher's lips. "We're lucky to have someone of your calibre joining us. And Jessika's excited to show you around tomorrow."

The tapping of Wendy's fingers against the cup grew more pronounced, as though listening to Veronica irritated her. The sickly smile never wavered.

"That would be lovely, though I'm not new to the area," Wendy said as she nodded in a vague direction. "I grew up on a small estate near here. Fern Moore?"

Jessie arched a brow. "We've heard of it." Wendy was as far from Fern Moore as they came. "When did you move away?"

Veronica stared in a way that let Jessie know her less-than-excited tone was landing her in hot water. But Jessie couldn't warm to the woman.

"Just after college," Wendy said, clearing her throat before finishing her coffee. "I got into working on TV soon after, and I never looked back until... now." She placed the cup down, and Jessie noticed a shake in her hand. "Is this door for the bathroom?"

Veronica nodded. "Help yourself."

When the bathroom door clicked shut, Jessie moved closer to Veronica's desk. "What's got into you?"

"I could ask you the same thing." Veronica slid up her blue glasses. "You're so prickly today."

"And you're fawning over her like she's special or something."

"She is... or was. She had her own cooking show back in the day. *Culinary Delights*, or something like that."

Jessie wrinkled her nose. "Never heard of it. And if she's so famous, why was her first email to us begging for a job? We're her backup plan."

"It's about time we expanded." Veronica's expression hardened. "You're far too distrusting, Jessie. You've been bored because we've just had a slow news year, and this is how we spice it up for the new year. Not everything is about saving villages from developers and twisted tree murder cases."

"I'm not bored, I'm just..." Jessie slumped against the desk. "*Bored*."

Veronica laughed. "See?"

The toilet flushed, and Jessie sighed. "Maybe I don't like the idea of a critic ripping apart the new market on the first day."

"That's not what she'll be doing. It's a fluff piece. People want to know what's on offer, and a little celebrity sparkle will bring in readers. Slow news doesn't just mean bored journalists—it means less circulation. We couldn't ride on the wave of bringing down Greg Morgan and James Jacobson forever. *This* is the proper work." Veronica straightened some papers before wheeling her chair closer to her computer, cast in the pink neon haze of the salon sign glowing through the window. "So, can you show Wendy around? Point her to The Comfy Corner and The Plough?"

"And tuck in her bib while cutting her steak?" Jessie folded her arms. "She's from round here—she already knows where everything is, and I'm having dinner at the cottage. Barker's cooking."

"You'd rather your dad's cooking?" Veronica shook her head. "I still haven't recovered from those soupy beef leftovers you brought in last week." She squinted over her glasses. "What's got into you?"

"This woman just... doesn't match our vibe, that's all."

"Then give her a chance to 'vibe.'" Veronica peered over her glasses like they were back in the classroom.

"Get to know her and stop trusting your gut instinct so much."

"Isn't that the opposite of what you told me when I joined the paper?"

Veronica turned to her computer screen, engrossed in whatever was on it. Jessie rolled her eyes and headed for the door. As she passed the bathroom, she caught snippets of Wendy's voice, harsh and demanding over the sound of a running tap.

"This isn't a game, Conrad. If I don't see that money tomorrow, you *will* regret it."

Jessie hesitated outside the bathroom door, her curiosity pulling at her. But she shook her head. Whatever Wendy was involved in, it wasn't her circus or monkeys.

∼

Barker glanced up from his laptop as Olivia's crayon skittered across his old papers, her tongue poking out in concentration. The soft overhead lamp cast a warm glow over the wood-panelled walls of his basement office, highlighting the private investigator case notes she'd decorated with pink and purple scribbles.

Above, Julia's footsteps creaked across the café floor as she stacked chairs and swept. The harsh buzz of the doorbell interrupted the familiar rhythm of closing time. Finally. He'd been waiting all day for this delivery.

"Come on, Liv." He scooped her up, her latest masterpiece floating to the floor. "Want to see Daddy's new book?"

She nodded, clutching her crayon as they climbed the stairs. The vestibule light flickered on, illuminating a plain brown box on the damp doorstep. He heard the delivery van rumble away through the puddles in the narrow alley between the café and the post office.

His fingers itched to tear into the package. After months of editing and rewrites, *The Man in the Field* was here. The yard gate creaked open just as he crouched to retrieve the box. A glimpse of the new community square's fairy lights twinkled beyond.

"Need a signature?" he called, expecting the delivery driver.

Instead, a diminutive figure shuffled through the gate. Layer upon layer of mismatched clothing engulfed her slight frame: a moth-eaten cardigan over what appeared to be several dresses topped with a man's overcoat. Her weathered face peered out from beneath a woollen hat pulled low.

"It's a socket I need," she said in a breathless voice.

"Socket?" Barker shifted Olivia's weight, studying the strange woman more closely.

"A plug socket." Her voice carried the weariness of a long journey. "I'll pay you for it."

Before he could respond, she began rummaging through the deep pockets of her oversized coat. Objects emerged one by one, pressed into his free hand: a damp slice of Christmas cake wrapped in a holly-patterned napkin, recipes scrawled across the backs of what looked like old bus tickets, and a handful of paperclips and drawing pins.

"Ah!" She produced an old pound coin, its edges

rounded, unlike the newer angular ones, and thrust it into his palm. She followed it with an old plug hanging on by exposed wires.

Barker peered around the gate, trying to trace where the wire led. The woman sighed, his curiosity testing her limited patience.

"I'm here for the market opening," she explained. "It appears I'm a day early."

He glanced around the new village square as Katie darted between builders, still directing last-minute preparations in the darkness. The newcomer seemed oblivious to the late hour and the unfinished state of things.

"Prudence White," she announced. "Now, be a good man and plug that in, would you?"

Leaving his box of books on the doorstep for a moment, Barker dragged the mysterious wire down to his office. He sat Olivia on the cracked leather sofa in the corner before reaching for the nearest socket.

The wire trailed up the basement steps like a snake disappearing into the growing darkness outside. Barker shook his head, bewildered by how long this peculiar arrangement might last, but his attention returned to the box waiting on the doorstep. He rushed upstairs, snatched up the box, and returned to his office to place it on his desk.

"Look, Liv—Daddy's new book is here!" He traced his palms across the edges of the box, heart racing as he sliced through the packing tape. Olivia abandoned her crayons, toddling over to investigate.

The cover emerged from its cardboard cocoon: a

stark photograph of an empty field at twilight, skeletal trees silhouetted against a bruised sky. Bold white letters proclaimed *The Man in the Field* across the moody landscape. His hands trembled as he lifted out the first copy. It represented a year of work piecing together the cold case of Sebastian Morgan, whose bones had been unearthed in the field where the market would open tomorrow.

With reverent fingers, he cracked open the spine— and froze. The text swam before his eyes, inverted. Heart sinking, he grabbed another copy. And another. Each book revealed the same disaster: the pages had been printed upside down.

"No, no, *no...*" He slumped in his office chair, running his fingers through his salt-and-pepper-edged hair. "The launch is tomorrow..."

Olivia tugged at the box. "More paper?"

"Yes, sweetheart." He managed a laugh that bordered on hysteria. "More colouring paper for you."

The sound of *Close to You* blasted from above, making them both jump. Abandoning the printing catastrophe, Barker followed the mysterious wire out into the night. It led him to a battered red camper van tucked behind the post office, Karen Carpenter's voice booming from within.

He rapped his knuckles against the window, and Prudence's pruned face appeared between the threadbare curtains.

"Do you mind?" she snapped. "I'm entitled to some privacy!" The curtains snapped shut with surprising force.

Barker stood in the darkness, wondering what on earth he'd got himself into.

∼

In the dining room of their cottage on the outskirts of the village, Julia pushed her shepherd's pie around her plate. Steam curled up from the untouched portions before her family, except for Olivia, who was far more interested in feeding imaginary bites to Mr Waddles, her treasured penguin.

"And then we went swimming," Olivia told her stuffed companion, making whooshing noises as she demonstrated with her fork. "Didn't we, Mr Waddles?"

Julia exchanged glances with Barker, who seemed preoccupied with his own thoughts. Jessie hadn't touched her food either, her phone face-down beside her plate—a rare sight indeed.

"So…" Julia ventured, breaking the heavy silence. "Who's going first?"

"You," Jessie said without hesitation.

Julia sighed, pushing a piece of carrot across her plate. "Nothing much has happened. Just slight nerves about the market opening tomorrow." She paused, setting down her fork. "I need an early night to get an early start for the cruffins."

"That'll be easy for you, Cake Lady," Jessie replied, some animation returning to her voice. "And I'm helping, and Sue. You've had months to perfect them, so… what else?"

Julia's fingers traced the rim of her water glass. "Just…

a feeling." The memory of the sharp-tongued visitor surfaced again. "A woman came into the café today. I know her. I *know* I know her, but I don't know where from." She sighed, forcing a smile as she reached for her glass. "It's not important. Barker?"

Instead of answering the question, Barker reached into his messenger bag and retrieved a copy of his new book. The glossy cover caught the light, the title embossed in silver.

"They arrived!" Julia's excitement bubbled up, pushing aside her concerns. She reached for the book, but her smile faltered as she flipped it open. "Oh, Barker... it's upside down."

"I had noticed." He prodded at the grey mound on his plate. "Five hundred pounds down the drain and a ruined book launch for tomorrow. I have nothing to sell unless they're acrobats who don't mind craning their necks."

She took another dutiful bite. Beside her, Jessie was making similar progress with her portion.

"And Jessie?" Julia turned to her daughter, hoping to shift the mood. "Does it begin with *Peridale* and end in *Post*?"

"New food critic." Jessie set down her fork. "Veronica didn't even interview this woman—didn't even ask what I thought. She just handed her the job because she used to be on TV."

Olivia offered a bite of shepherd's pie to Mr Waddles. "He doesn't like carrots," she declared, drawing a faint smile from Julia.

"What show?" Julia asked, trying to steer the conversation away from Veronica's decision. She understood Jessie's hurt at being left out of the process, especially given how close she and Veronica had become.

Jessie's forehead creased. "*Culinary Delights*... or something? Never heard of it."

"Oh!" Julia straightened. "I used to watch that with Mum when I was little. It was hosted by—oh, what was her name—Prudence?"

"*Prudence*?" Barker's head snapped up. "The same woman staying in that van?"

Julia frowned. "What van?"

"Prudence White," he said. "She's got her camper plugged into my study. Didn't give me much choice in the matter."

"That's her." Julia beamed. "She's still around?"

"Sort of," Barker replied. "She seems a little all over the place."

"Not Prudence," Jessie said, shaking her head. "The woman at the paper is called Wendy."

The name hit Julia like a stiff wind, raising goosebumps along her arms as the cottage's dining room walls seemed to stretch away from her, leaving her adrift in a void where only the steady drumming of rain remained. Her throat constricted as memories flooded back—that cold, cruel laugh echoing through the college corridors, now attached to a face she'd tried so hard to forget.

"W-Wendy... what?" The words scratched past her lips.

Jessie's brow furrowed in thought. "Michaels. Do you know her?"

Julia's fingers found the edge of the table, gripping until her knuckles whitened. "I suppose she married Conrad Michaels."

"You know her," Jessie stated, leaning forward. "I heard her talking to someone called Conrad on the phone. What's up, Mum?"

Rising from her chair, Julia gathered the plates of uneaten shepherd's pie. Her movements felt robotic, detached, as if her body had taken over to avoid the storm brewing in her mind. She carried the plates into the kitchen, her breathing shallow. The mush of leftover gravy and mash met her fingers as she scraped them into the sink, watching the heap rise with each plate emptied.

She turned on the tap, letting the water rush in. The food began to bob and swirl, rising and falling as the waterline climbed. Julia didn't know why she hadn't scraped the plates into the bin; she couldn't think straight. Her hands trembled as she twisted the tap off, and she gripped the edge of the sink to steady herself. The sound of the dripping water filled the silence.

"Julia?" Barker's voice broke through the fog, gentle with concern.

She didn't turn, her focus fixed on the murky water.

Doc Martens padded closer. "Mum?"

Taking a deep breath, Julia forced herself to let go of the sink and face them. "That's how I know that woman," she said, her voice strained.

Barker and Jessie exchanged a glance.

"What woman?" Jessie's tone held a note of irritation.

"A woman came into the café," Julia explained, her words halting. "She was rude, dismissive... and that's how I remember Wendy." She swallowed hard, trying to force the lump in her throat away. "But she looks different now. She was blonde back then, for one, and she..." Her voice caught. "I was almost kicked off the patisserie and baking college course because of her."

Her words seemed to hang in the air as she returned to the sink, gripping the counter once more. The memories she had buried clawed their way to the surface, threatening to spill out with the tears stinging her eyes as she stared into the dark garden.

"Mum?" Jessie pressed, her voice softening.

"She spent almost two months making my life hell," Julia continued, her voice trembling. "And if she's going to be the food critic at the market tomorrow—"

She didn't finish the thought as a sharp rap at the front door cut her off, the sound ricocheting through the cottage like a clap of thunder. Before anyone could move, the lock clicked, and the door swung open, bringing in a gust of cold evening air and the familiar jingle of dog collars.

"Ah, there you all are!" Dot bustled into the kitchen, Lady and Bruce padding at her heels. Her cheeks were flushed, and wisps of grey hair had escaped her pristine curls. She paused, taking in the sight of Julia leaning over the sink and the uneaten food piled high in the water. "Has someone died? You could cut the atmosphere with a wooden spoon."

"No," Julia said, wiping her eyes with the back of her hand.

"Good! Then you're needed. All three of you." Dot planted her hands on her hips, surveying the room like a general preparing for battle. "It's the square... Katie's having a nuclear meltdown about everything that must be done before tomorrow, so we need all hands on deck."

Julia glanced back at the sink, at the congealing food floating in the murky water. She turned to Barker and Jessie, whose faces mirrored her own exhaustion. The thought of facing Wendy tomorrow still churned in her stomach, but Katie's panic was immediate and real.

"The community square needs its community," Dot declared, already heading back to the door with Lady and Bruce in tow. "Wrap up warm; it's fierce out there! People are saying snow is on the way."

Pushing aside her troubles, Julia managed a small smile. "She's right. We can't let Katie down, not after everything she's done to make this happen."

As Barker wrapped himself and Olivia in hats and scarves in the hallway, Jessie lingered in the kitchen, her voice soft as she spoke. "Are you that freaked out about facing Wendy again?"

Julia tightened the dripping tap and dried her hands on a dish towel. "I don't think she recognised me," she admitted, but the knot in her stomach refused to loosen. "But it's only a matter of time before she does, and when she does, I'm... I'm not sure I can face her."

3

*D*awn crept through the gap in Jessie's curtains, dragging her from a restless sleep. Her muscles ached from throwing rubble into skips and scrubbing slate floors until the early hours. The new square hummed with activity through her bedroom window as stallholders arranged their wares beneath strings of twinkling lights—the same ones she'd helped hang mere hours ago.

The aroma of fresh sourdough wafted from the artisan bakery stall, mingling with the earthy scent of fresh flowers arranged in metal buckets. Excited voices carried across the cobbles, punctuated by the scrape of tables being positioned and the clatter of display stands being assembled.

Jessie stumbled over a pile of discarded clothes. Her room was the usual chaos of scattered newspapers and coffee cups. Tidying would have to wait—again. Running her fingers through her tangled hair, she wrestled it into a messy ponytail while hopping into a clean pair of black jeans.

She hurried down the narrow staircase, tripping over her untied laces before she emerged from the side door of the post office into the cobbled alley. A battered red camper van occupied the corner, retro music she didn't recognise blasting from its open windows. A thick cable ran across the alley and into the yard behind the cafe, trailing into Barker's office. That man never could say no.

Jessie slipped through the café's back door. The kitchen was alive with the sweet scent of butter and vanilla.

"Sorry I'm late," she called out, but the rhythmic whirr of the mixer drowned out her words. Julia and her sister, Sue, worked in perfect sync, creating spiralled cruffins covering every available surface.

"Part croissant," Julia announced, tearing the pastry apart with a satisfying crackle. Steam curled from the layers as she held out half to Jessie. "Part muffin, and all delicious."

Jessie bit into the warm cruffin. Butter melted on her tongue as she worked through the flaky, rich layers. Her eyes closed in appreciation—trust her mum to perfect these on her first attempt at making such a gigantic batch.

"And you're not late; you're just in time for the filling," Julia said, practically bouncing on her toes as she reached for the piping bags. Her energy seemed almost manic after the late night. Jessie exchanged a glance with Sue, who was unusually subdued as she dragged the next batch from the oven.

"Has *she* shown her face yet?" Jessie asked.

"Wendy?" Julia's voice lifted with forced lightness. "Nope."

Jessie sighed, wishing she could wrap her arms around her mum and shield her from whatever had happened all those years ago. Julia only got this way when avoiding something that bothered her. Sue offered a helpless shrug behind Julia's back.

"If I can just avoid her today, everything will be fine," Julia said, arranging piping bags filled with the fresh raspberry jam Jessie made weeks ago, along with thick, yellow custard still a little warm from the pan. "Shouldn't be too difficult in a crowd."

Jessie's jaw tightened. She could either corner Wendy herself or get the story from Sue, but for now, she picked up a piping bag. The three of them worked in a comfortable quiet, only the gentle murmur of the kitchen radio filling the space between them.

The moment Julia disappeared down the basement steps with a tray of coffee and a cruffin for Barker, Jessie rounded on her aunt.

"What happened between Mum and Wendy?"

Sue's shoulders tensed as she concentrated on piping custard into a cruffin with unnecessary precision. "It was ages ago, love. I was only about thirteen. I don't remember much."

"But Mum's always talked about college like it was the best time of her life. All those stories about Mr

Jackson and being the star baker..." Jessie set down her piping bag. "What changed?"

Sue's attempt at a cheerful face clouded. "It was just the final few months. Like I said, I was only a kid. All I know is, Wendy was trying to cheat on her exam bakes and your mum, being your mum, noticed, and she didn't think it was fair."

"And?"

"Somehow, Wendy flipped everything around and made it look like Julia was the one who'd been cheating." Sue's hands trembled as she reached for another cruffin. "I'm not sure how it got sorted out, but it was until..." She glanced towards the door to ensure they were alone and said, "... Wendy tried to get her own back."

"What did she do?"

"Horrible things." Sue's voice dropped to a whisper. "She made Julia's life—"

Footsteps on the stairs made them both jump. Julia appeared in the doorway with Olivia toddling in at her side.

"Look what someone made!" Julia held up a piece of bunting covered in wobbly purple hearts. "Think we can hang it outside?"

Sue busied herself with the pastries, avoiding Jessie's questioning gaze. Jessie picked up her piping bag again, mind churning. Whatever Wendy had done, she wouldn't let history repeat itself. She'd find out the truth before Veronica let her get her feet under the table.

Barker hefted the box of upside-down books and dropped it into the recycling bin with a thud that echoed his mood. The morning sun struggled over the wall of the café yard as he stood there, hands on his hips. His own carelessness had cost him the launch—a simple tick box left unchecked in the printing specifications. The joys of self-publishing, and he couldn't get a penny of a refund.

A shrill voice cut through his self-pity. He recognised Prudence's distinctive tone, now pitched higher in what sounded like an argument. Following the sound, he stepped out to find her setting up a rickety wallpaper-pasting table at the edge of the market square in front of her camper. Reused glass jars filled with thick sauces clinked as she arranged them in messy rows, stuffing scraps of paper with handwritten recipes underneath them.

Katie stood before her, clipboard clutched to her chest. "You're not listening! You cannot set up here without proper registration. The council has strict regulations—"

"Regulations, is it? Nobody mentioned those, dear." Prudence's face crumpled in exaggerated confusion as she continued unpacking jars. "I'm just a simple cook trying to share my creations with the community, is all. I'm doing no one no harm."

"But the community square has designated selling areas for *approved* stallholders." Katie's nails tapped against her clipboard, but Prudence paid no attention. "It says it right here in the sign-up form you didn't fill in. This could cause serious problems for our opening day."

"Problems? Why would anyone have a problem with my homemade sauces?" Prudence's voice wavered with forced innocence, but her hands moved with purpose as she arranged her makeshift display. "They're delicious and healthy for you."

"And they're not allowed!" Katie's composure cracked. "You need proper documentation, food safety certificates—"

"Everything alright?" Barker approached the pair, hands tucked into his pockets.

"No, it's not." Katie's shoulders slumped. Her gaze caught on something behind him, and she pointed. "Is that wire running into your yard? Do you know this lady?"

"Not really," he admitted. "We met for the first time yesterday."

He surveyed the market square, taking in the transformation. Ten stalls dotted the space, their canvas tops rippling in the morning breeze. Food vans lined one edge, their windows already open and wafting enticing aromas. Wooden benches and raised planters filled with shrubs created a central walkway. To the left, a children's playground waited for its first visitors, while on the right, a public garden showcased neat rows of shared vegetable plots.

And set between the cobbles, right where they'd found the decades-hidden body, a memorial stone to Sebastian. The perfect location for Barker's third book launch. Or it would be, but not today.

"Listen," Barker said, resting a hand on Katie's

shoulder, "I've got a stall I won't be using anymore, and I'd be more than happy for Prudence to take it."

Katie clutched her clipboard tighter. "I suppose... but I'll have to adjust all the paperwork, and I've got so much going on already." Her voice rose to a squeak. "I didn't realise how difficult this would be. The land just fell into my lap, and I wanted to let everyone have a say in what we did with it. They voted, and I tried to give them everything they asked for, but—"

"Breathe, Katie." Barker clenched her shoulder. "Look around. You've made it happen. It's here. You've done good."

Prudence pursed her lips, scowling at them both as she continued unloading her sauces as though none of it affected her.

Brian South, Julia's father and Katie's husband, strode across the square, two takeaway cups in his hands from Vicky's Van, moved from the bottom of Mulberry Lane. His open-collared shirt revealed his usual flash of chest hair as he passed the cup to Katie, who accepted it with trembling fingers.

"You're not getting worked up again, love?"

"No," Barker answered for her, catching the gratitude in Katie's eyes. "My fault."

"Good, because you've done amazing." Brian's voice boomed across the square. "The best comeback story Peridale has ever seen. From losing Wellington Manor to starting your salon to this!" He squared his shoulders. "I won't take anything less than pride today, Katie."

A weak smile tugged at Katie's plump lips. "I just hope people turn up." She turned back to Prudence with a sigh. "Fine, you can have Barker's stall, but no trouble?"

"Trouble?" Prudence rolled her eyes. "Who do you think I am?" Before Barker could confirm his suspicions about her TV career, she disappeared into her van, slamming the door.

"I thought today was supposed to be a celebration?" Brian jerked his thumb at the van as though to say, 'Who's this woman?'. "And a reunion, of sorts. I was speaking with someone Julia went to college with—"

"Who?" The hairs on Barker's neck prickled.

He shrugged. "Some woman? I didn't ask her name."

"Where is she now?"

"Don't worry, Barker," he laughed, patting him on the back before setting off. "I've already pointed her in the café's direction."

Before Barker could return to the yard, a flash of grey curls hurried at him down the alley, and he turned to see Dot.

"We need some muscle to carry Ethel's gnomes across!" she declared, grabbing his arm. "The woman has made enough for everyone in the village to have three each." She scoffed at the idea as she dragged him towards her cottage on the other side of the village green. "Just wait till you see them—she'll be lucky to sell a single one."

But Barker could only crane his neck, staring back at the café. Was he imagining it, or was Julia laughing over a cup of tea with her old college nemesis?

Julia cupped her hands around the warm mug of tea. Across the table, Melissa Hargrove's face bore the same gentle smile Julia remembered from their college days, though fine lines now creased the corners of her eyes. She still wore the same bohemian style in flowing, colourful layers that brightened up the dull morning.

"I still can't believe you're here," Julia said. "How many years has it been?"

"We must have been eighteen?" Melissa traced the rim of her cup. "Fresh-faced and ready to take on the world with our baking dreams."

"And now you're a florist?"

"Life takes unexpected turns. But when I saw 'Julia's Café' above the door, I *knew* it had to be you. Always the determined one." Melissa's eyes sparkled. "I'm proud of you, Julia. You've done what you set out to do." She paused, tilting her head. "Do you have any children? A husband?"

"I didn't get there the first time. I'm on my second husband. Two daughters—Jessie's twenty-two, and Olivia's three."

"You have a daughter in her twenties?" Melissa blinked. "I suppose we are of that age to have adult kids, though you haven't changed a bit."

Julia laughed. "I feel like I've changed so much since then. Though I suppose some things stay the same—still baking, still drinking peppermint tea." She took another sip before adding, "Jessie came to us when she was sixteen. We adopted her. It's been quite the rollercoaster, but I couldn't be happier with my family." She studied Melissa's face. "What about you?"

"No husband," Melissa said, her smile faltering. "No kids. Never panned out after Conrad, and it's not too late, but..." She shrugged, her gaze drifting to the window. "Maybe that's for other people."

Julia's stomach clenched as memories of their college days surfaced. Conrad Michaels had swaggered through their classes, dark hair falling over his eyes as he charmed his way through the ladies. He'd lasted the longest with Melissa—six months.

Her mouth went dry. "Have you seen Conrad?"

"After he left me for Wicked Wendy, you mean?" Melissa's smile tightened at the corners.

Julia nodded. She remembered holding Melissa's hand over countless cups of tea in the college canteen, listening to her sob about how her life was over, how she'd find no one else. Julia had assured her, as anyone would, that the right person was just around the corner. Clearly, she'd been wrong.

"I reconnected with Conrad last year." Melissa's fingers slid around her cup. "Stroke of luck—he came into the garden centre where I work part-time, and just like you and me now, it was like no time had passed." She lifted her gaze to meet Julia's. "We're just friends, mind you. But we've been talking more lately. He's... different now. Nicer. Getting out from under Wendy's spell changed him."

Julia's chest tightened at the mention of Wendy. She wanted to shift the subject, steer clear of that wound. But Melissa had suffered at Wendy's hands, and curiosity won out.

"Were they married long?" Julia probed. "I heard she worked on television for a while?"

"She ruined that too," Melissa said, her fingers whitening around her cup. "She ruins everything she touches. Conrad left her a few years ago after she convinced him to invest all his money in a cooking school venture."

Julia's frown deepened. The words from the café rushed back—Wendy's sharp voice on the phone, demanding payment for a failed school. Had she been speaking to Conrad?

"Conrad's here." Melissa brightened, tossing a finger in the market's direction. "Selling his handmade clocks —he turned to woodworking during the divorce. And he's rather good at it. Better than he ever was at baking." She let out a sweet chuckle. "I had to push him to get a stall, but he never was that ambitious—it's his first market." She leaned forward. "You should buy one. I'm sure he'd give you a discount for old time's sake."

"I will," Julia said, her mind whirling. All these old faces appearing at once—it felt like the universe had organised some cosmic college reunion. "I suppose we're at that age now where everyone circles back to their old villages."

She lifted her cup, taking a long sip of tea to steady herself. The liquid had cooled, leaving a bittersweet taste on her tongue.

Through the café window, two figures caught Julia's eye. Her heart stuttered as she recognised Wendy's sleek brunette hair and designer coat, walking alongside Veronica, who was pointing out landmarks like Wendy was a tourist. They disappeared down the alley beside the café, heads bent close in conversation.

"What's wrong?" Melissa asked.

"Is it that obvious?"

"You've turned pale."

Julia set down her cup, the china clinking against the saucer. "You know she's here, don't you?"

The warmth drained from Melissa's face. "Where?"

"Here, in Peridale," Julia whispered, her throat tightening. "Wendy is the new food critic for the newspaper."

The sharp clatter of china made Julia jump as the cup slipped from Melissa's grip. Tea pooled across the wooden table as Melissa scrambled to right her cup.

"Oh—I'm so sorry." Melissa dabbed at the spill with a handful of napkins, her hands trembling. "I need to go —my stall. The flowers need arranging before opening. It was nice to see you again—"

Before Julia could respond, Melissa grabbed her bag and darted for the door, leaving a mess of sodden napkins behind.

"Wendy Michaels..." Julia sighed at the empty chair. She gathered the wet napkins, her mind spinning with everything left to prepare for her stall.

The bell above the door chimed, and Katie burst in, vibrating with excitement. "Julia! Are you ready to set up? The ribbon cutting is in less than an hour."

"Almost. Just need to box up these cruffins and—"

"Excellent, excellent." Katie beamed, producing a pair of large silver scissors from her jacket pocket. "And guess what? We've got a real local celebrity doing the honours."

Julia's stomach clenched. "Who?"

Katie winked and pressed the scissors into Julia's hands. "There's no one else but you, silly! If it weren't for you, that field would have two hundred gigantic houses on it. You're the heart of this village."

The metal felt cool and weighty in Julia's grip. She drew in a deep breath, steadying herself. She wouldn't let Wendy's presence poison this moment—not when they'd worked so hard to transform this neglected corner of Peridale into something special.

But where Wendy went, it seemed trouble still followed.

4

*J*ulia adjusted the last cruffin on the wooden crate, stepping back to admire their cascading display. The morning sun caught the sugar crystals, making them sparkle like frost. Sue bent over their small chalkboard as she wrote the prices in her neatest handwriting.

Around them, the other stallholders bustled about with their final preparations. To their left, a woman with auburn hair and tired eyes arranged pies on chequered cloth.

"Polly Greene," she said, offering a small wave. "Love what you've done with the crates. Swap a cruffin for a pie at lunchtime?"

"Julia. And I'd love to," she replied. "They smell delicious."

Sharp as glass, that distant laugh drifted through the crowd, tensing Julia's shoulders. She scanned the market square, past the flower boxes and benches, but couldn't spot Wendy. Her gaze caught Melissa's over at her flower stall. Her former classmate's face mirrored Julia's unease.

Next to Melissa's impressive display of blooms stood Ethel's gnome stall on one side and, on the other, the wooden clock stall. Conrad worked methodically, arranging his creations in neat rows. The years had weathered his boyish looks into something more rugged, but Julia could still see traces of the charming student who'd once turned every girl's head in college.

To Julia's right, Prudence fussed with bottles of homemade sauce. Julia squinted at her, trying to place the familiar face. Could she be the same chef whose cooking show she'd watched with her mother as a little girl? Prudence glanced at her, and Julia couldn't meet her stern gaze.

Their only actual competition seemed to be the pastry van—Ethan's Bakes—parked at the square's edge. Julia scanned his menu board—no cruffins, at least.

"I think you're ready." Sue straightened up, dusting chalk from her hands. "Are you sure you'll be alright if I handle the café?"

"It's just taking payments," Julia said, forcing a lightness into her voice. "Easy."

Sue's worried frown deepened. "That's not what I meant."

"I know." Julia smoothed her apron. "But let's not go there."

Katie's heels clicked against the cobblestones as she bounded over, her face flushed with excitement. "Julia! It's time!"

Julia's stomach lurched as Katie beckoned her

towards the red ribbon stretching across the alley entrance. The satin gleamed in the morning light, a splash of colour against the weathered stone walls of the café and post office.

Beyond the barrier, a modest gathering of locals huddled together, their eager faces familiar and comforting. Julia caught snippets of conversation as she approached.

"Those pastries smell divine," Shilpa said, inhaling.

"Everything looks so lovely," Amy agreed.

"Speech!" Evelyn called out, her turquoise kaftan billowing in the breeze. "I sense you know just what to say, Julia."

Julia's fingers tightened around the scissors Katie had pressed into her hand. The crowd wasn't as large as they'd hoped—nothing like the crowds filling the village green Katie had envisioned during their planning sessions. But Katie held herself tall, her professional mask in place as she gestured for Julia to step forward.

The metal felt cold against Julia's palm as she raised the scissors. Her gaze swept across the familiar faces but then froze.

There, at the edge of the group, stood Veronica and Wendy. Their eyes met, and recognition flickered across Wendy's features. The corner of her mouth curled upward in a slow, calculated smile that sent ice through Julia's veins.

She wrenched her gaze away, her heart hammering against her ribs.

Julia turned to the transformed space on the edge of the field behind her, remembering the empty pasture that had stood here just months ago. The new market square stretched like a canvas painted with vibrant stalls and eager faces. Her throat tightened—not just from Wendy's unsettling presence but from the weight of everything they'd overcome to reach this moment—the protests, the planning, the delays, the bodies... and now, something to celebrate.

"It has been an honour to be a part of this," Julia called out, her voice growing more assertive, "and it's about time!"

"Here, here!" Dot's enthusiastic cry rang out across the crowd.

Applause erupted as Julia sliced through the red ribbon. The satin parted with a satisfying swish, and Brian popped a champagne cork with perfect timing, drawing appreciative cheers from the onlookers. Vinnie, Katie and Brian's five-year-old son—and Julia and Sue's younger brother—stepped forward in a tiny suit clutching an enormous bouquet. He presented them to his mother, and Katie erupted into tears as she clenched them close.

"Well done, Mummy," he said in his shyest voice.

"Thank you, darling," Katie beamed as she smelled the roses, squeezing Julia's arm as people began streaming past them into the market. "We did it."

"Yeah, we did," Julia managed, trying to focus on this triumph rather than her churning stomach.

Julia was rooted in place as the crowd streamed past, their chatter fading to white noise. Veronica's hand landed on her arm, yanking her from her daze.

"I must introduce you to our new food critic,"

Veronica said. "Julia is our resident baker, so I'm sure you two will have much to discuss."

Wendy stepped forward, her silk blouse catching the morning light. Her perfume—something expensive and floral—wafted between them.

"Oh, we know each other," Wendy's voice dripped with honey. "Don't we, Julia? College days. Feels like another lifetime."

Before Julia could step back, Wendy leaned in. Her lips brushed Julia's cheek, soft and deliberate. The contact sent a jolt through Julia's spine, but her muscles refused to move.

Veronica beamed. "I didn't know that! Small world, isn't it?"

Julia's throat constricted. The Wendy before her bore little resemblance to the sharp-tongued girl who'd made her life hell. This woman's smile reached her eyes, her laugh melodic rather than cruel. Had time softened the edges of those memories? Had she built up that period of her life into something worse than it was?

"We must catch up later," Wendy squeezed Julia's arm, fingernails digging through her jumper. "I want to hear all about your charming little café."

Julia couldn't bring herself to say anything, the scissors still clasped in her hands. Wendy followed Veronica into the market, and Julia could breathe again.

Katie appeared at Julia's side, frowning. "You alright?"

Julia forced her lips into a smile, shaking off the fog of doubt. "Never better." She handed the scissors back, stiffening her spine. "Now, let's get selling these cruffins. Today is going to be a great day."

~

Jessie shifted her weight from one foot to the other, her stomach churning as she watched Veronica fawn over Wendy. She captured Wendy's practised poses and artificial smiles through her camera lens as she interviewed market-goers.

Seeking refuge from the fakery, Jessie wandered over to Ethel's stall. The gnomes weren't the traditional red-hatted garden variety—these were real works of art. One sported a mohawk and leather jacket, while another balanced on a skateboard. A punk rock gnome caught her eye, complete with tiny safety pins in its ears. She didn't seem to have sold many, but Jessie made a mental note to come back with some cash later—she had her eye on the one on the motorbike.

"What's up with you?" Dot's voice cut through her thoughts. "You've got a face like a slapped trout."

Jessie sighed, nodding towards where Wendy stood chatting with Mary Porter. "What happened with Mum in her final college days?"

"What do you mean?" Dot's brow furrowed.

"She was being bullied."

"Was she?" Dot's confusion deepened. "Are you sure? She mentioned nothing to me..."

"Never mind," Jessie muttered. "I must have got it wrong."

As she turned to leave, Dot's hand shot out to grab

her arm. "And why are you not interviewing me for the paper?" Before Jessie could respond, Dot cleared her throat. "The success of this market square is down to my quick thinking. That camp-in protest I arranged led to Greg Morgan's arrest. Without *my* determination to expose the truth..."

Jessie extracted herself from her great-grandmother's monologue. "Thanks, Dot. I'll include that bit about the protest."

She meandered through the market, her notebook clutched to her chest until she reached the flower stall. The sweet perfume of fresh roses mingled with food-scented air from the neighbouring displays. Behind mountains of seasonal blooms, Melissa—the woman who'd been in the café earlier with her mum—stood in a heated discussion with a broad-shouldered man. His weathered hands gripped a wooden clock as though it might shield him from their conversation.

"I can help," Melissa insisted, her voice carrying across the flowers. "Let me, Conrad."

"I've told you, Melissa, it's not your problem." Conrad's shoulders tensed. "Wendy wants money from me she isn't entitled to. I should never have let her talk me into investing. That's not on you. We weren't even speaking then."

"But I *want* to help." Melissa's fingers twisted around a stem, crushing petals. "She ruined my life back then, and she's ruining yours now."

"She ruined me a long time ago." Conrad's voice softened. "I'm starting to feel happy again. Finally found my peace, my centre, my craft..." He cleared his throat as he caught sight of Jessie hovering nearby. "How can I help you?"

Jessie pulled out her notebook, pen poised. "Are you talking about Wendy Michaels?"

The silence stretched between Melissa and Conrad, heavy with unspoken words. Their exchanged glances spoke volumes, and Jessie's journalistic instincts tingled. Here was the story—the proper story.

"Will you go on record about her?" Jessie pressed, her heart racing. "I need my editor to see through her."

"Absolutely not." Conrad's response came sharp and firm, his fingers tightening around the clock.

Melissa shook her head, lips pressed into a thin line as she rearranged a perfect display of chrysanthemums.

Conrad set the clock down with careful precision. "Wendy never changes. If she's working on the paper now, it's only a matter of time before she ruins it." His voice dropped to a harsh whisper. "And she has a habit of dragging everyone else down with her."

Jessie's gaze drifted across the market to where Wendy stood with Veronica at the bread stall. As Wendy theatrically sampled a slice of sourdough, her editor beamed. Wendy's words would soon fill her notebook, capable of making or breaking the market vendors' livelihoods.

Jessie's stomach churned. How could she get through to Veronica before Wendy ruined everything? Her editor was wholly taken in by Wendy's polished charm and promises of increased readership. But the whispers and sideways glances from the stallholders told a different story—a story Jessie was determined to uncover.

~

Barker leaned against the market stall, watching the steady stream of customers drawn to Julia's latest creation. The cruffins vanished faster than they could restock them, leaving only crumbs and satisfied smiles. His gaze drifted to Wendy as she meandered between the stalls, reaching for samples while Veronica scribbled notes beside her.

He shifted his weight, positioning himself to keep Wendy and Julia in view. Julia's shoulders remained tense despite her cheerful demeanour as she handed the change to Mary from The Comfy Corner.

At the stall to their right, Prudence hunched over her sauce display, her eyes narrowing each time another customer bypassed her in favour of the cruffins. Despite her scrawling 'Prudence White's Homemade Sauces' on a sheet of A4, the pen and paper borrowed from Barker's office, no one seemed to recognise her.

Curious, Barker pulled out his phone and typed 'Prudence White TV chef' into the search bar. The results loaded, revealing a striking photograph from what must have been forty years ago. The woman in the image stood tall and elegant in a pristine chef's jacket, her silver-blonde hair swept into an elaborate updo. She beamed at the camera from behind a gleaming kitchen counter, every inch the 1980s polished television personality.

Barker glanced back at the present-day Prudence, bundled in mismatched layers that concealed her figure. Though time had weathered her appearance, the same sharp eyes and proud tilt of her chin remained. What events had led her from television stardom to selling homemade sauces from a camper van in Peridale?

Barker plucked a cruffin from the display and stepped towards Prudence's stall. "Try one? They're still warm."

Prudence eyed the pastry with suspicion, her fingers hovering before accepting it. She took a delicate bite, crumbs falling into her layered clothing.

"Did you make this?" she asked, eyeing him suspiciously.

"No, but my wife did."

"Hmm, they're good." She dabbed at her mouth with a paper napkin. "Strange, but good. Perhaps too much jam." She licked her lips and went back for a second bite. "Very good."

Barker seized the opening. "Julia used to watch your cooking programme. Must have been during the early nineties."

Prudence's face darkened. "Past life. All ruined now." Her gaze fixed on something behind him, and Barker turned to see Wendy approaching their section of the market. Prudence's fingers gripped the edge of her table.

"Did she have anything to do with it?" Barker asked. "I heard she worked on a show with the same name."

"*My* show," Prudence grumbled, straightening up as a customer approached. "I don't know what you're talking about." She busied herself selling a jar of tomato, chilli and basil sauce, ending the conversation.

Barker watched as Wendy stopped at Polly's pie stall. The food critic swept past without acknowledgement, nose in the air. Polly shook her head, letting out a derisive snort of laughter at Wendy's back.

How many people at this market had crossed paths with Wendy before?

And now she was walking their way, all bright smiles and measured steps.

Barker moved behind the cruffin stall, positioning himself at Julia's side as Wendy approached. If he couldn't stop this unwanted reunion, he could at least be there for his wife.

~

Julia's stomach tightened as Wendy glided towards her stall, her perfect white teeth gleaming beneath crimson lips.

"Julia! How wonderful to properly catch up." Wendy's voice dripped with artificial sweetness. "It's been absolutely ages."

The warmth of Barker's hand slipped into hers, steadying her racing heart. Julia couldn't muster the energy to match Wendy's enthusiastic mask. The memory of their last encounter at college—Wendy's cruel smirk as Julia packed her belongings on the final day—remained sharp even after all these years.

"What have you been up to all this time?" Wendy asked, glancing at the cruffins. "You're a pastry chef?"

"I run the café you visited yesterday." Julia kept her voice level. "When you were shouting down your phone about a cooking school venture?"

The colour drained from Wendy's face, her polished

smile dipping for a fraction of a second, and Veronica glanced between them, her pen hovering above her notepad as the tension crackled. The editor's shrewd eyes narrowed, picking up on the undercurrent of hostility.

Julia straightened her spine, drawing strength from Jessie's sudden appearance at her other side. Her daughter's presence completed the protective circle around her, giving her the courage to meet Wendy's gaze head-on.

"Oh, I do apologise for yesterday." Wendy waved her hand. "First-day jitters, you know how it is. Starting a new job can be so stressful."

The sickly-sweet tone transported Julia straight back to that cramped office over two decades ago. She could smell Mr Jackson's coffee breath, see the disappointment in his eyes as Wendy dabbed theatrical tears from her cheeks. The evidence had been so perfectly planted— empty cake mix boxes stuffed into Julia's bag, discovered after a tip-off that she was cheating. Even now, the injustice of it burned.

Julia's jaw clenched. She wouldn't play this game, and she wouldn't give Wendy the satisfaction of a response. The market bustle faded to white noise as she stared at her old tormentor, seeing past the designer clothes and perfectly gleaming hair to the darkness beneath.

Wendy's smile tightened at the edges as Julia's silence stretched between them. The same flicker of calculation crossed her face that Julia had witnessed in Mr Jackson's office—when Wendy had realised her tears alone weren't enough. She'd launched into that devastating story about Julia's jealousy of her baking talents and how she'd tried to blackmail Wendy into keeping Julia's deceptive exam piece a secret.

The truth... flipped.

Julia had discovered those cake mix boxes in Wendy's bin, and she'd been the one to raise her suspicions to the other students before she took them to Mr Jackson, but by the time Julia had returned to gather the evidence, they'd gone.

"I *want* to believe you, Julia," Mr Jackson had said, and the disappointment in his voice still rang out after all these years. "You're the best baker on this course, but if what you're saying is true, *why* didn't you bring them to me first?"

Julia had been crying too much to admit Wendy had always scared her. She used to hover over Julia's shoulder while she baked, adding her comments to put her off, her snide remarks about Julia using her late mother's handwritten recipe book for reference, always pretending like she never liked a thing Julia baked when it came for everyone to sample...

The weight of two decades lifted as Veronica cleared her throat. "Perhaps we should try one of these famous cruffins?" She gestured to the display. "That is why you're here, after all."

"Of course!" Wendy's face lit up. "I'd be delighted. They all look *so* perfect."

Julia's hands trembled as she handed over one of her perfectly crafted pastries. The sugar sparkled in the morning light as Wendy assessed it closer than she had any of the offerings at the other stalls. After a moment, she lifted it to her crimson lips, biting right into the oozing jam and custard middle.

At first, Wendy's expression suggested approval—her eyebrows lifted, her eyelids fluttered, and she nodded as she chewed. Then, her face contorted. She dropped her head forward, coughing violently, her hair falling over her face.

Veronica patted her back. "Are you alright?"

Wendy straightened up, her fingers moving to her mouth. When she withdrew them, something small and curved lay in her palm—an acrylic fingernail covered in thick, sticky jam.

Julia's heart stopped. She stared at the artificial nail, immediately looking at Wendy's hands for a match, but she wore a simple French manicure.

Gasps rippled through the gathered crowd. The sound of cruffins being dumped in bins echoed across the square. Julia's stomach lurched as she watched her morning's work and reputation thrown away.

"A *fingernail*?" Wendy's voice carried across the market. "In *Julia's* cruffins!" Her face arranged itself into an expression of regret that didn't match the amusement in her eyes. She handed the frosty-mint nail to Julia and said, "I'm so sorry, Julia. I was hoping to give you a glowing review... I *honestly* was..."

Julia's hand tightened around the sharp nail as she caught the familiar gleam in Wendy's eye—the same look she'd worn in Mr Jackson's office all those years ago.

Some things, it seemed, never changed.

～

Jessie huddled beneath the market stall's awning as the rain hammered against the canvas. Soggy cruffins littered the ground, their sugar coating dissolving into sad puddles. The crowd had scattered, leaving only a few determined stallholders packing away their goods.

Her mother's vacant expression haunted her. Since Wendy's dramatic performance with the acrylic nail, Julia hadn't uttered a word. Even Barker's gentle coaxing had failed to draw her out of her shell as he guided her back to the café.

Veronica darted between the stalls, her polka-dot umbrella bobbing as she searched for her newly appointed food critic. "Has anyone seen Wendy?"

Polly stacked her remaining pies into boxes at the neighbouring stall while chatting with Ethan from the pastry van. Their heads were close together, sharing whispered words that carried on the wind.

"Wicked Wendy strikes again," Polly muttered, shaking her head. "Still up to her old tricks after all these years."

Ethan's jaw clenched as he helped Polly load a box into her car. "Mark my words, she'll get what's coming to her. People like that always do."

The venom in his voice made Jessie's skin prickle. As she watched them, their familiar intimacy suggested they were more than market neighbours.

"I hope you're right," Jessie muttered, gathering up the last of their unsold cruffins.

Veronica approached, her glasses speckled with raindrops. "Have you seen Wendy? She's disappeared."

"Good." Jessie kicked a ruined cruffin into the gutter. "Hope she never shows her face around here again."

Veronica's mouth tightened. "That's not fair. Wendy didn't choose to have the one with a fingernail in it."

"There were no fingernails in any of them!" The words burst from Jessie's chest, hot and frustrated. "She so clearly did that herself. It must have been up her sleeve. Only three people were in that kitchen when we made them—Mum, Sue, and me. None of us wear fake nails."

"Katie does." Veronica crossed her arms. "All the time, and she's in and out of that kitchen."

Jessie spun around, spotting Katie huddled under an umbrella nearby. "Katie, could you come here a moment?"

Katie hurried over, mascara trailing dark rivers down her cheeks. "This is a disaster. Everyone's leaving. The adverts in the paper didn't work, and—"

"It's still a cold, wet January," Jessie assured her. "Things will pick up, but first—can I see your nails?"

Katie held up her hands, displaying perfectly manicured tips matching her pink suit.

Jessie fished the incriminating nail from her pocket. "Recognise this?"

"Yes, as it happens." Katie dabbed at her tears with a tissue. "It's Dewy Mint, satin finish, with a high gloss topper. We use it at the salon."

Jessie clutched the acrylic nail tighter, her patience wearing thin.

"Well, it got in there somehow," Veronica said, her usual sharp perception oddly dulled.

"Wendy put it there!" The words burst out again. She stepped closer to her mentor, rain pelting her leather jacket. "Are you so desperate for a celeb food critic that you're ignoring what's right in front of your eyes?" Her voice cracked with disappointment. "Where's the Veronica who pushed me through my exams and fought tooth and nail to expose the corruption that almost took this land from the community?" Jessie gestured wildly at their surroundings. "Think about it, Veronica. Where is our office? Above Katie's salon. Katie stocks this polish."

"You're biased," Veronica countered, adjusting her rain-spattered glasses. "You took a dislike to her the moment you met her."

"Because I've been around enough fake people to sniff them out." Jessie's shoulders tensed as she remembered the calculating look in Wendy's eyes when she'd first walked into the newspaper office.

"I'll co-sign," Prudence called out as she packed away the last of her sauce bottles. "Good for nothing liar," she muttered under her breath before shuffling off towards her van.

"Yeah, us too," Polly said from beneath the market canopy. Ethan stood beside her, nodding in agreement as they huddled together against the cold, his arms wrapped protectively around her shoulders. "She's a nasty piece of work."

Veronica sighed. "Fine, but we need evidence."

Jessie's resolve hardened. "Katie, watch the stall," she instructed, tossing the cruffin tray aside. Katie nodded, visibly relieved to have a task to distract her from the chaos.

Jessie's boots splashed through puddles as she and Veronica raced down Mulberry Lane, the rain plastering her dark hair to her face. The familiar glow of Katie's salon emerged through the downpour, its neon sign casting a pink hue onto the wet pavement.

A bell tinkled as they burst through the door, bringing with them a gust of cold air. The salon's warmth enveloped them, thick with the scent of nail varnish and the hum of the radio playing bouncy pop music. Behind the nail desk, Clarice, Katie's fifty-something skittish apprentice, looked up from Mrs Coggles' manicure, her weathered hands steady despite her client's constant fidgeting.

"Do you mind waiting your turn?" Mrs Coggles barked as Jessie approached the desk, fishing the acrylic nail from her pocket.

"It's an emergency," Jessie said, holding the nail to Clarice. "Can you tell me where this came from?"

Clarice squinted through her glasses, setting down her file. She pulled out a carousel of nail samples, each wheel displaying different shades painted onto fake nails. She located a gap between two similar green shades and placed the nail. It fit perfectly, and Jessie could almost hear the crack as the nail was snapped off.

"Did Wendy come through here earlier?" Jessie asked, her heart racing. "Flashy brunette woman in fancy clothes?"

"Oh, her," Clarice nodded, her cheeks flushing. "I gave her a touch-up this morning."

"And was she alone at any moment?" Veronica pressed.

"Well…" Clarice shifted uncomfortably. "I had to run to the bathroom. Last night's prawn madras hasn't agreed with me all morning."

"Do you *mind*?" Mrs Coggles interrupted. "What kind of establishment is this?"

Clarice bowed, returning the nail to Jessie before resuming her work on Mrs Coggles' hands. "She came back about half an hour ago."

"She's upstairs?" Jessie's fingers curled into fists. "About time I give her a piece of my mind."

Jessie stormed up the narrow staircase, her boots thundering against each step. Veronica's protests echoed behind her, but rage coursed through her veins, drowning out everything except the need to confront Wendy.

"No good will come from rushing into something," Veronica called after her.

Jessie whirled around on the tiny patch of a landing, her dark hair hanging over her eyes from the rain. "How dare she try to ruin Mum's reputation over something that happened twenty years ago? Mum is an absolute angel, and Wendy is a waste of space…"

Her words trailed off as she flung open the office door. The familiar scent of coffee and newsprint hit her first, followed by the sight that made her blood run cold. In the corner of the leather sofa lay Wendy, her outfit pristine but her face contorted. White foam bubbled at the corners of her red lips, and her glassy eyes stared unseeing at the spray-painted countryside mural above.

Veronica pushed past, her usual composure cracking as she pressed two fingers against Wendy's neck. The silence stretched, broken only by the distant patter of rain against the windows.

"She won't be taking up any more space," Veronica gulped. "Our new food critic is dead."

5

*W*iping down the counter for the tenth time, Julia's movements were mechanical as whispers swirled around the packed café. Every time the bell above the door chimed, fresh speculation about Wendy's death filtered in with the newcomers. The constant scrutiny made her skin crawl—she caught all the glances in her direction, saw heads bowed together in hushed conversation.

"Did you hear about the nail in her cruffin?"

"First the sabotage, then she turns up dead..."

The words pricked at her like tiny needles. Julia gripped the cloth tighter, wringing it between her hands. The morning's humiliation still burned fresh—Wendy's theatrical gagging, the horrified gasps from onlookers, the nail that had somehow found its way into her carefully crafted pastry.

Jessie touched her arm. "You should sit down."

"I can't. If I stop moving, I'll—"

"But you haven't done anything wrong." Jessie huffed before turning to the packed café. "Alright, listen up, everyone!" Jessie's voice cut through the murmurs. She held up what she'd found earlier. "We found this nail wheel at Katie's Salon. And this—" She raised the nail from the cruffin. "Perfect match. Wendy was there earlier, alone in the salon. She planted it in the cruffin to make my mum look bad."

The café fell silent. Julia's hands trembled as she stared at the evidence of Wendy's final act of malice.

"So, make sure you spread the word," Jessie continued, her voice fierce. "Tell everyone you know. My mum was set up. The nail was planted. *End* of discussion."

A wave of sympathetic murmurs rippled through the café. Mary reached across the counter to squeeze Julia's hand. "We never believed you'd do such a thing, dear."

"Absolutely not!" Evelyn confirmed as the mystic B&B owner settled into her usual spot near the counter. "You've never so much as burnt a scone, let alone let a nail fall into a bake."

A ghost of a smile touched Julia's lips at the vote of confidence. The crushing weight that had settled on her chest since the market incident began to lift, if only slightly.

"I had a feeling that Wendy wasn't to be trusted," Evelyn added.

"Surprised you didn't see her death in the tea leaves," Dot mumbled from her perch by the window.

"I didn't," Evelyn replied, adjusting her flowing

sleeves, "but I did see that there'd be an army of gnomes; I wasn't sure how it would come to fruition."

Julia watched as Ethel counted her earnings at a nearby table. "Well, I had a lovely afternoon," she announced. "You said I'd sell none, Dorothy, but I made fifty quid!"

The normality of their usual banter felt surreal against the backdrop of the day's events.

"But why would Wendy want to make you look bad, Julia?" Shilpa asked calmly. "She's only just turned up."

The question hung in the air, echoing Julia's own thoughts. Why indeed? After all these years, what could Wendy possibly have gained by trying to destroy her reputation once again?

"Because that's what she does to people who see the real Wendy." Polly's voice carried across the café from her corner spot. "I worked for her for years."

Julia lifted her gaze, studying the pie vendor's drawn features. She'd been cheerful for most of the day, but her pale face had hardened into sharp angles.

"I wrote a book about her." Polly paused to sip her tea. "I couldn't name her directly—legal reasons. But now?" A hollow laugh escaped her. "Now it doesn't matter. Look it up. *My Decade Working Under the Wicked Witch*."

"Ding dong, the witch is dead, I suppose," Dot muttered.

Polly drained her cup and swept out of the café, leaving a wake of whispers behind her.

"Bit odd to use this opportunity to promote her book," Jessie whispered, nudging Julia's arm.

But Julia barely heard her daughter's words. Her mind kept circling back to Wendy—the sharp-tongued girl from college, the polished food critic, the body on the office sofa. She'd despised Wendy, yes. Feared her, even. But this ending felt... wrong. Final in a way that twisted Julia's stomach into knots.

Her heart sank as Detective Inspector Laura Moyes strode into the café, blowing her vape smoke behind her before the door shut. Her presence silenced the chatter, and a wave of customers surged forward, voices overlapping with theories and accusations.

"I'm here to ask the questions," Moyes said as she held up her hands, "not answer them."

Two uniformed officers positioned themselves by the door. The familiar sight of their uniforms brought bile to Julia's throat—this was becoming serious. Very serious.

"If anyone saw anything suspicious," Moyes declared, scanning the full café, "now's the time to speak up."

Half the café leapt to their feet, arms raised like eager schoolchildren. Julia caught Moyes' eye and tilted her head towards the kitchen. Understanding flickered across the detective's face, and she followed Julia through the beads.

Away from the clamour, Julia sighed. "I know what people are saying."

"They're pointing fingers at you, Julia." Moyes' voice was gentle but firm. "The timing of the nail incident, followed by—"

"I was in here the whole time. From the moment she found that planted nail until—" Julia's voice cracked. "I never left the café. Sue was here. So was Barker. Amy Clark, Mary, and—"

"We believe she was poisoned."

The words hit Julia sideways. "You're not suggesting it was one of my cruffins?"

Moyes sighed, her expression heavy. "I wish I wasn't, but—"

Movement behind Julia made her turn. Her stomach dropped at the sight of forensic officers in white suits hovering in the back doorway, evidence bags at the ready.

Julia wanted to scream, to refuse entry to her pristine kitchen. This was exactly what Wendy would have wanted—to leave chaos in her wake. But protesting would only make her look guilty.

She stepped aside, watching as the officers filed in, their presence turning her sanctuary into a crime scene. The familiar clink of measuring cups and whisks—usually a comfort—now felt like nails on a chalkboard as evidence bags rustled.

"Leave no cruffin unturned," Julia called out, her voice carrying across the hushed café. "Search the entire café if you have to. I have nothing to hide—I certainly didn't like Wendy, but I didn't kill her."

The words tasted bitter, like burned sugar at the bottom of a pan. Her regulars shifted in their seats, tea cups frozen halfway to lips, cakes abandoned on plates. The silence pressed in, broken only by the stiff movements of the forensics team and the steady drumming of rain against the windows.

Julia watched the empty market stalls through the

back door, their covers thrashing in the wind. Puddles formed around boxes and cups—remnants of the ruined celebration. Her morning's cruffin display lay scattered, each pastry now a potential murder weapon.

Her stomach turned. Wendy was destroying her again, even in death. Like in college, Julia could only watch her dreams collapse under Wendy's lies. But now, rather than Mr Jackson's disappointment, she risked losing her hard-earned reputation.

Even now, in death, Wendy made her feel powerless.

∼

Barker's golf umbrella did little to shield him from the rain as he watched Prudence hoist boxes onto her camper van's shelves. Her movements were frantic, jars clinking together as she shoved them in place.

"Need a hand with those?"

"No, thank you." Prudence snapped. She reached for the extension cord trailing from her van, giving it a sharp tug. "I'll be on my way."

"That's still plugged in!" Barker lurched forward as the wire went taut.

Prudence dropped the cord. "I was only planning to stay for one day. There are busier markets not far from here. Better opportunities."

"It won't look good if you leave now."

Prudence snorted a laugh. "What do you know?"

"I'm a retired detective, for one," he said, arching a sympathetic brow at her. "And I'm a PI now. If you're in trouble, I can help you."

"Why do you people keep calling me *trouble*?" Prudence spun to face him, rain streaming down her weathered face. "Because a woman is dead, and I *used* to know her?" Her laugh was hollow. "Half the market knew her."

The yard door creaked open, and DI Moyes stepped out, her boots splashing in the puddles. She nodded to Barker, joining him under his umbrella.

"Did I hear that right, Barker?" she asked, tugging her vape device from her jacket pocket. "This woman knew Wendy?"

Barker glanced between Moyes and Prudence. The former TV chef's eyes pleaded with him to stay quiet from within her camper van. For a moment, he wavered —but Julia's stunned face over the past few hours flashed through his mind, like the whole morning had been an out-of-body experience.

"I'm sorry, Prudence, but my loyalty is to my wife. And if you leave knowing something..." He turned to Moyes. "Prudence used to work with Wendy on a TV show."

"Is this true?" Moyes fixed her gaze on Prudence, blowing out the smoke before she pocketed the device. "Silence won't help you now."

Prudence muttered something unintelligible under her breath, her shoulders hunching as though trying to disappear into the van's messy furnishings, as layered and eclectic as her wardrobe.

"I'll take that as a yes." Moyes stepped closer, extending a finger into the van. "You're not to leave the village until you've been questioned and your

65

whereabouts have been accounted for, understand?"

Prudence grumbled her agreement before Moyes darted back inside, leaving Barker alone with Prudence as the changing winds drove sheets of rain against his face. Prudence's glare could have melted steel. She yanked the door shut, slamming it with enough force to rattle the whole vehicle.

"Sorry," Barker called through the downpour. "I had to—"

The opening notes of *Rainy Days and Mondays* blasted through the van's tinny speakers, drowning out the world.

"I suppose you'll want to keep using my electricity?" he muttered, turning away from the van. The extension cord still snaked across the muddy ground towards his basement office.

Inside, he found Brian sprawled on the floor with Olivia and Vinnie, helping them build a tower from wooden blocks. The children's laughter stung against the grim atmosphere outside.

"All sorted?" Brian asked hopefully.

"No," Barker replied. "Not quite."

Barker sank into his leather chair, his gaze drifting to the cord trailing under his door. The thought settled in his stomach like lead—was he powering a murderer's hideout?

～

Jessie paced the length of the basement office as the camper van woman's music blasted down from above, its cheerful tune at odds with her churning thoughts. She paused mid-stride, running her fingers through her dark hair in frustration.

"We need to do something, Dad," she said. "We can't let this stick."

Barker glanced up from his laptop, the screen's glow hollowing out his face. "I already am trying to do something. I've been searching into what might have happened between Prudence and Wendy, but there's not much connecting them online. Not together, at least."

His fingers tapped across the keyboard. "Prudence hosted *Culinary Delights* from 1984 to 2002. Articles say it ended due to low ratings."

"And Wendy?"

"The show came back for a single series in 2003 on a satellite channel with Wendy hosting. Never got renewed, and it barely made a ripple in the press."

Jessie crossed her arms, leaning against the old filing cabinet. "I wouldn't be surprised if Wendy was behind the change. That must be why Prudence hates her." She shook her head, leather jacket creaking. "But it's not enough to go on here and now."

"I might have just lost my way in with Prudence."

"She can't expect you to cover for her," Jessie said, shrugging. "And how long are you going to let her keep plugged in down here?"

"I can't just unplug her, can I? In this weather?"

Jessie sighed. "No, you're right. Living outside this time of year is rough." She shuddered at the memories of her younger days on the streets before the warmth of Peridale. She kicked away from the filing cabinet. "There has to be more to this. That flower seller, Melissa, and the guy who makes them fancy wooden clocks, Conrad —they both knew Wendy from before. I overheard them talking about her, and when I tried to get them on record, they shut down."

"What did they say?" Barker asked, staring over his laptop.

She yanked her notebook from her jacket pocket, flipping through the pages. "Conrad mentioned something about Wendy convincing him to invest money and Melissa wanted to help him, but he wasn't having any of it. And then there's Polly with her tell-all book. We should try to get a copy." Her pen tapped against the paper. "And that pastry truck owner, Ethan— did you see how he was whispering with Polly? They both had it in for Wendy."

Barker's typing slowed as he absorbed her words. "Why are so many of them here in Peridale right now? The timing is odd."

"Wendy had enemies everywhere she went," Jessie said. "And she was from round here once upon a time. Fern Moore, she said. But maybe she's got enemies in every town she goes to?" She laughed at the thought, but she couldn't feel the humour. "All we know is, it wasn't Mum, which means it had to be someone else who crossed paths with her before."

He nodded, running his hands down his stubbly cheeks. "Then I suppose we already have five suspects."

She slumped into the chair opposite his desk. "We need to figure this out. For Mum's sake." Her fingers traced the edge of her notebook, remembering how excited they'd all been about the market opening. "This isn't how this was supposed to go."

Jessie's head snapped up at the sound of footsteps on the basement stairs. Veronica burst in, her spiky grey hair dampened by the rain, her enormous blue-framed glasses steaming up.

"The police found something." Veronica fumbled with her phone, her hands trembling. "At the newspaper office. It seems to have rolled under your desk."

She thrust the phone towards them. On the screen was a picture of a small glass vial sealed in an evidence bag.

"Poison?" Jessie's stomach lurched. "So it wasn't the cruffin after all."

"They found tea things in the sink, partially washed." Veronica pushed her glasses up her nose. "We only drink coffee—but someone had tea with Wendy up there. They killed her in *our* office."

Barker leaned forward, his reading glasses catching the lamplight. "That narrows it down. We need to work out who wasn't at their market stall between Wendy's performance with the nail and when you found her."

"We found her just before noon," Veronica remembered before pulling out her notepad. She flipped back a page. "Clarice said Wendy had been there for half an hour. And we got to Julia's stall to sample the cruffins at about half-past ten."

"Not the smallest window," Barker muttered. "But it could be worse."

"An hour," Jessie stated. "We find out who wasn't where they should have been during that hour." She paused, remembering Barker's stall. "What about your book launch?"

"On hold." Barker waved his hand dismissively. "New copies will take seven to ten days to arrive. Until then, I'm all in on this case."

"Me too." Jessie's fingers curled around her notebook. The story that had fallen into her lap was bigger than she'd imagined, but she couldn't shake the knot of worry about where it might lead.

Veronica sighed, pocketing her phone. "Well, you've finally got your exciting story." She fixed Jessie with a stern look. "But be careful. And everything comes to me first. *The Peridale Post* needs these details."

A sharp laugh escaped Jessie. "Funny, isn't it? Wendy will boost our circulation after all, just not in the way you were expecting."

"Ironic," Veronica said, her smile sad. "I'm sorry, Jessie, it seems, once again, you were right. You sniffed out that she was a bad seed within minutes."

"Seconds." Jessie winked. "And at least she didn't spread her roots at our paper." She nudged Veronica's arm. "Think of the positives—it's going to make quite the front-page story for the next issue."

～

The squeak of the swing chains pierced the evening silence as Julia pushed Olivia higher. Droplets from the earlier rain caught the street lamp's glow, making the new equipment glitter in the dark.

Katie perched on the edge of a nearby bench, her

fingers twisting in her lap as she stared at the market square. Crime scene tape fluttered in the breeze, enclosing the market stalls. Her usual bubbly demeanour had vanished, replaced by a haunted expression that made her look older than her years.

"Higher!" Olivia squealed, kicking out her legs.

Julia's hands moved automatically, her mind elsewhere. The image of forensics officers in her kitchen wouldn't fade. Sue's twin daughters, Pearl and Dottie, chased each other around the climbing frame while Vinnie hung upside down from the monkey bars, his face reddening. Sue hovered beneath him, arms outstretched.

"Vinnie, careful!" Katie called out, but her voice lacked its usual energy.

Sue's jaw clenched and unclenched as she helped Vinnie down. She'd barely spoken all evening. Her eyes kept darting between Julia and Katie, as though trying to decide who needed her support more.

Julia inhaled deeply, trying to ground herself in the present moment rather than dwelling on the day's events. But even the chilly evening air seemed to carry whispers of scandal and death as dog walkers passed, checking out the new square and the crime scene.

"That's *her*," she heard a woman whisper, nodding in Julia's direction. "*That* woman."

Julia's hands paused mid-push, causing Olivia to protest. She resumed the motion, unable to find words to defend herself. It seemed it would take longer for the truth about the stolen nail to spread, but of course it would when the lie was so mouth-watering.

Julia watched Olivia slide off the swing and run over to where Vinnie and the twins were building an imaginary house beneath the climbing frame. Their high-pitched voices carried across the playground as they debated whether their pretend home needed a swimming pool or a treehouse.

The empty swing beside her creaked as Sue lowered herself onto the rubber seat. The chains felt cool against Julia's palms as she gripped them, her feet scuffing patterns in the wood chips below.

"Remember the old park?" Sue's voice was soft, nostalgic. "Up by the police station before they demolished it?"

Julia's lips curved into a smile. "We'd hide out there whenever Dad was in one of his moods."

"Or when Gran was being... *Gran*."

A laugh bubbled up from Julia's chest, the first genuine one she'd managed since that morning. It felt foreign, almost wrong given the circumstances, but somehow necessary.

"I remember."

"You were always the one picking me back up when I was down," Sue said, twisting slightly in her seat to face her.

"That's what big sisters do." Julia paused, her expression growing serious.

"Which is exactly what I'm going to do now, but we need to talk about it first."

Julia's fingers tightened around the chains—talking was the last thing she wanted to do tonight. The chains of the swing bit into her palms as she gripped them tighter, anchoring herself to the present.

"Gran's been asking questions," Sue continued. "She wants to know why you never told her about Wendy back then—about what happened."

Julia stared at her feet, watching as they carved deeper grooves into the wood chips. "I only ever told you," she said quietly. "All the horrible things she did... I didn't want anyone else to get upset."

"Like when Wendy defaced our mother's grave, or was spreading rumours that you had somehow caused her death..." Sue's voice trailed off.

The old pain crashed over Julia like a wave. She squeezed her eyes shut, but the image blazed behind her eyelids—flour thrown on the headstone, flowers scattered and trampled. She'd never been able to prove it had been Wendy, but it had happened the day after Julia insisted that Mr Jackson look further into the cake box incident because she would never admit to something she hadn't done, no matter how things looked.

"She put a rat in my locker," Julia said, the words tumbling out before she could stop them. "Where do you even find a live rat?"

"Seriously?" Sue's swing creaked to a halt.

Julia nodded, and suddenly, they were both laughing —a strange, desperate sound that carried across the playground. The absurdity of it all hit her at once: the rat, the grave, the awful rumours. It felt good to laugh about Wendy's cruelty now, even if the hurt still lingered.

"What *was* her problem?" Sue asked, wiping tears from her eyes.

Julia kicked at the wood chips beneath her feet. "I don't know, I never tried to find out..."

The laughter faded as quickly as it had come. She watched Olivia chasing the twins around the climbing frame, the three of them squealing in delight while Vinnie piled up the wood chips into a mound.

"The last thing I want is to get dragged into another of Wendy's messes," Julia said, her voice barely above a whisper. "But maybe it's time I figured out what was going on with her."

Sue's swing creaked as she nodded. "What are you going to do?"

"Clear my name, for starters. Get things back on track—for me, for Katie, for everyone who's put their heart into this market." Julia's gaze swept across the abandoned stalls. "Maybe I'll finally learn who the real Wendy was."

"The type of woman who'd plant a nail in a cruffin twenty years after you caught her cheating?" Sue shook her head. "I'd say count your blessings that she's dead and can't do worse."

"But there's someone else out there just as bad as Wendy," Julia continued, lowering her voice.

"Someone who went as far as poisoning her," Sue finished for her, and Julia nodded. "Be careful, Julia."

"In a weird way," Julia said, considering her words carefully, "I might be on the same page as the poisoner. We both clearly know what it's like to be wronged by her."

Julia scooped Olivia into her arms as she ran past, the toddler's warm weight grounding against her chest. She turned to Katie, who still sat hunched on the bench, shoulders curved inward.

"It'll be fine once the rain clears," Julia said, mustering conviction she didn't quite feel. "We'll sort everything. I promise."

Katie managed a weak smile, smoothing her pink trousers with trembling fingers.

Leaving Sue to round up the twins, Julia strapped Olivia into the car seat in her vintage aqua blue Ford Anglia. The drive home up the winding lane was accompanied by Olivia's soft chattering and the rhythmic swish of windscreen wipers clearing the last drops of rain.

Their cottage emerged from the dark on the edge of the village, warm light spilling from the windows onto the wet garden path. Inside, Barker knelt by the fireplace, carefully arranging kindling. The scent of woodsmoke filled the room as flames caught and grew.

Mowgli, their Maine Coon, bounded over, tail wagging, circling their legs as Julia wrapped her arms around Barker's waist. He turned into her embrace, holding her close, his familiar spicy aftershave wrapping around her like a blanket.

"We'll fix this," he murmured into her hair.

Julia pressed her face against his chest, letting out a long breath. "I know," she whispered. "But tomorrow."

6

*W*armth cocooned Julia as she drifted awake, burrowing deeper into the duvet. For one blissful moment, her mind was empty of yesterday's troubles. She rolled towards Barker's side of the bed but found only cool sheets.

A flash of grey fur darted past as Mowgli leapt from the bed, batting at the curtains as he ran. Bright white light flooded in through the gap, making Julia squint. She sat up, reaching for her powder blue dressing gown —a Christmas present from Barker—and sliding her feet into her worn sheepskin slippers.

Padding to the window, she drew back the heavy curtains and gasped at the sight. The countryside stretched out before her, transformed overnight into a winter wonderland. A thick blanket of pristine snow covered everything in sight, smoothing the rolling hills into gentle white waves.

Following the sound of slurping, Julia wandered

into the kitchen. Jessie sat at the breakfast bar with her cornflakes while Barker and Olivia enjoyed the snow in the back garden. They were bundled up against the cold—Barker in his navy wool coat, Olivia in her pink snowsuit. Together, they rolled a snowball almost as tall as Olivia, leaving a dark trail in the untouched snow.

"Morning," Jessie muttered around a mouthful of mushy cornflakes. "It's Sue's day to open the café, so don't freak out, but I snuck in and turned your alarm off—assumed you'd be up tossing and turning all night."

Despite the yawn fluttering her lips, Julia said, "I wasn't."

"I'm glad one of us slept." Jessie caught the yawn before spooning in more cornflakes. "Those market stalls don't half rustle in the wind. It was a relief when the snow started."

Julia's gaze landed on a peculiar ceramic figure perched on the corner of the breakfast bar. The gnome wore a miniature apron splattered with what appeared to be flour, but its face—if you could call it that—was a jumbled collection of features that seemed to float off. One eye sat higher than the other, and its nose curved at an impossible angle.

"What's that?" Julia stifled another yawn as she poured coffee from Barker's still-warm French press. "Or should I say, who is that?"

"You, I think. Or Ethel's interpretation of you." Jessie grinned. "Bought it from the market while she was setting up. Cool, isn't it?"

"That's one word for it." Julia tilted her head,

studying the gnome's abstract features. The longer she looked, the less sense it made.

"You people don't appreciate art," Jessie shot back, tipping her bowl to drink the last of her cornflake milk. A dribble escaped down her chin. "I think she's a genius."

Through the kitchen window, condensation had formed a misty veil over the garden view. Julia watched as Olivia trundled around with a tiny snowball while Barker worked on constructing what looked to be the snowman's body.

"The market is going ahead today?"

"Everyone was setting up when I left," Jessie said. "The clock guy was there, and the pie woman, and the pastry dude. Didn't see the flower woman."

Julia wrapped her hands around the warm coffee mug, absorbing its heat as she watched Jessie push her breakfast bowl aside. The ceramic scraped against the wooden counter, making way for her phone.

"So, I've been thinking about the plan of attack for today," Jessie said, opening her notes app. "Step one, interview the suspects. We catch one out, and then we clear your name and get on with our lives without Wendy's vicious shadow hanging over us."

"Good plan." Julia sipped the coffee. "Easier said than done."

"That's not the entire plan." Jessie's fingers tapped against her phone screen. "I was thinking about who'd be best to interview who. I'll take Polly and Ethan since they seem to be a couple, and Melissa and Conrad already shut me down once. Dad has messed up his chances with Prudence by not covering for her, so I thought you could talk to her—you're both into baking. And Melissa is yours, what with the college connection." She narrowed her eyes. "Bit weird you've never mentioned her before."

"You don't speak to Dolly and Dom anymore," Julia pointed out. "You were friends with them on the same patisserie and baking course when you first joined the café."

"You've got me there," Jessie said, tilting her head side to side. "I seemed to grow up, and they were stuck like overgrown kids. They did my head in, to be honest. Point taken." She returned to her phone and said. "Which leaves Dad to talk to Conrad, and he's meeting him in half an hour." She craned her neck towards the back door. "*Dad*, it's half past!"

Through the window, Julia saw Barker give a thumbs up as Olivia burst through the door, her cheeks pink from the cold. "Can I have a carrot, please?"

Julia retrieved one from the fridge and handed it to her daughter, who clutched it before dashing outside. A wave of tenderness washed over Julia as she watched Olivia's excitement. It had snowed before in her lifetime, but this was the first time she'd been old enough to appreciate it.

Julia drained the last of her coffee, the warmth spreading through her chest as she set the mug in the sink. "What's this about Barker meeting Conrad?"

"Oh, yeah." Jessie looked up from her phone. "Conrad found him online since Dad's the only PI in the area. He called first thing this morning."

"Seems I'm not the only one eager to clear my name." Julia rinsed her mug, watching the coffee dregs swirl down the drain. "He's not waiting around."

"Bit dodgy, if you ask me." Jessie tucked her phone away. "So, what do you think about the plan?"

"Perfect plan." Julia planted a kiss on top of Jessie's head. "Veronica's lucky to have you."

"And doesn't she know it." Jessie gathered her things. "Speaking of, I need to go see what whacky headline she's come up with for tomorrow's issue." Pausing at the edge of the breakfast bar, Jessie squeezed Julia's shoulder. "Don't let Wendy's games get you down, okay? Even dead, she's—"

"I appreciate it, love, but I don't think I need a pep talk," Julia interrupted, setting her mug on the draining board. "I'm ready to face this."

As Jessie left, Barker and Olivia rushed in, bringing in a gust of fresh snow. Mowgli darted out, skidded, and darted right back inside.

"Sleep well?" Barker asked, helping Olivia out of her snowsuit.

"Like a log." Julia kissed him before heading off to the bathroom. "Come on, let's get down to the village. We have work to do."

"Good idea," Barker called after her, "just one question... what on earth is this goblin thing staring at me from the breakfast bar?"

~

After dropping Olivia off at her nursery, Julia's knees ached as she pushed aside another heavy box in Dot and Percy's attic. Shafts of winter light pierced through gaps in the roof tiles, illuminating the dancing dust. Her fingers brushed against something soft—an old red jumper from St Peter's Primary. The musty fabric felt thin and worn beneath her touch, bringing back memories of playground games and chalk dust. Olivia would wear the same red jumper when she started school next year.

"Found what you're looking for?" Percy's voice drifted up from below.

"Not yet," Julia called back, pushing the jumper aside. A stack of her old exercise books tempted her, but she forced herself to stay focused.

"If you wait until your gran returns from walking the dogs, she might know where those old cookbooks are."

But Julia struck gold. A box labelled 'Julia's Bedroom' in her own younger—and much neater—handwriting made her heart skip. She remembered packing it, fresh-faced and hopeful, ready to start her new life in London with Jerrad a few years after finishing college. The thought of her first husband felt like peering through a clouded glass at someone else's life.

Inside lay treasures from her teenage years. She smiled at an old photo that caught her eye—Sue with gangly teenage limbs, Dot looking the same with fewer grey hairs, still in her usual navy skirt and white blouse uniform. Behind them stood the café building, back when it was an old-fashioned toy shop.

At the bottom of the box lay what she sought—three heavy *Culinary Delights* cookbooks. The covers were sun-bleached, but the pages still held that unmistakable scent of baking.

Prudence White beamed from each cover in frilly aprons, her hair teased into impressive heights. Julia opened the first book, her fingers brushing the crinkled water stains left by her thirteen-year-old tears. Dot had found it in a charity shop after Julia's mother passed, knowing how much she loved watching the show with her mum. The other two books came as Christmas gifts in the following years.

Voices drifted up—Dot was back. Julia tucked the cookbooks under her arm and climbed down the rickety ladders before folding them back into the attic.

"That you, Julia?" Dot called from the sitting room. "I want a word with you. What's this I've been hearing about you being bullied in college?"

Julia headed straight for the door. "Later, Gran!"

Slipping out before Dot could corner her, she stepped into the crisp snow and headed across the village green, clutching her lost treasures. She snuck down the alley between the café and the post office towards the market, reaching the red camper van.

She rapped her knuckles against Prudence's door, but Karen Carpenter's voice drowned out any chance of being heard. Through the window, steam rose from what looked like several pots bubbling away on the tiny stove. The rich aroma of garlic and herbs mingled with the winter air.

"Prudence?" Julia called out. "It's Julia? From the café?"

Nothing.

Perhaps later would be better.

With a sigh, she turned away from the van. The market square buzzed with mid-morning activity despite the lingering snow. Her gaze landed on Melissa's flower stall, where bright splashes of colour defied the white blanket covering the cobbles. Julia raised her hand in greeting, but Melissa's head disappeared behind a display of white tulips.

Before Julia could ponder Melissa's odd behaviour, Evelyn hurried down the alley, her turquoise kaftan billowing around her as she rushed forward. Her face was ashen, silver hair escaping from beneath her turban.

"Julia, dear! There you are. Something awful has happened." Evelyn's hands trembled as she approached. "The police finished searching my B&B. Wendy was staying there, and they went through everything."

Julia gulped. "It's alright, Evelyn. They went through my kitchen, not that they found anything. Take a second." She rested a hand on the B&B owner's shoulder. "What did they find?"

"Nothing." She inhaled, her crystal pendant swinging as her breathing slowed. "But when they left, I started sorting through the post that's built up over the week, and I found *this*." She extended her arm, keeping the fabric of her kaftan between her fingers and the paper she held. "I didn't want to contaminate it with fingerprints. I'll take it to the station, but you must see it first." She paused before asking, "You are investigating, aren't you?"

Julia offered a tight smile. "You know me too well."

Her stomach lurched as she read the crude message assembled from magazine clippings: 'YOUR REIGN OF TERROR IS OVER. WATCH YOUR BACK.'

"It's not subtle," Evelyn pointed out, clutching the crystal with her free hand. "And I don't think someone sent it to me."

"No, I don't think so." Julia read over the words again. She took a picture on her phone without touching the paper. "Seems like someone wanted Wendy to be scared before they killed her."

"But I don't think she ever saw it," Evelyn said, folding the paper back into its envelope. "I don't like to speak ill of the dead, but she wasn't the most pleasant guest I've ever had." She glanced around. "Quite rude, to be honest. Nothing was good enough for her. The pillows were too lumpy, the radiators not hot enough, the food inedible." Moving closer, she asked, "Is it true someone *poisoned* her?"

"It's looking that way," Julia said. "Thank you, Evelyn. I appreciate you showing me this. Take it to DI Moyes—hopefully, she'll be able to find the sender."

Evelyn nodded, her expression thoughtful. "The universe has a way of setting itself right, and when it doesn't, we always have you."

As Evelyn fluttered off to the police station, Julia sighed. As touched as she was that Evelyn seemed to think she had everything under control, she wished the universe would set itself right for once.

She crossed the market square towards Melissa's flower stall, hoping to talk to someone connected to Wendy. But the stall stood empty, a 'Back Soon!' sign propped against a bucket of sunflowers.

"Julia," Conrad said, nodding at her. "You haven't changed. How's things?"

"They've been better," she admitted, unable to return the compliment. The years had been tough on him and she would have passed him in the street without recognising him. "I'm sorry for your loss."

He suppressed a laugh. "Please, don't be. Are you looking for Melissa?"

"I am. Know where she went?"

He shook his head. "Sorry, no clue."

Julia resisted the urge to muddy the water between Barker and his potential new client, so she hung back on the questions. Leaving Conrad to his clocks, she turned back to the market. While some shoppers browsed the remaining stalls, many stood empty today—including her own. She hadn't been able to face another day of scrutiny, another chance for something to go wrong.

Frustration simmered as Julia reflected on her unproductive morning. With no one else to turn to, she glanced back at the café and caught movement by the red camper van. Prudence peeked out, scanning the square. Their eyes locked, and Prudence froze before retreating inside and slamming the door.

Julia hesitated, tempted to try again with the former TV chef, but she stopped herself. Repeating the same mistake wouldn't get her anywhere. Prudence wasn't ready to talk, and if Julia wanted answers from her childhood idol, she'd need a different strategy. Deep down, she hoped Prudence was innocent—for the little girl who once idolised her—but Prudence seemed desperate to hide, and Julia needed to know why.

7

$\mathscr{B}$arker balanced the stack of blankets against his hip as he approached Prudence's red camper van behind the post office. The door creaked open at his knock, revealing Prudence's weathered face.

"These should help keep you warm," he offered, extending the pile towards her.

"Excuse me?"

"Blankets."

"Hmm." Prudence's eyes narrowed as she leaned out, plucking at each blanket with critical fingers. "Too thin," she muttered, tossing one aside. "Too scratchy." Another joined the first. "Too small." She snatched the remaining blanket before slamming the door with enough force to rattle the van's windows. "That'll be all."

"I have some questions, Mrs White," Barker called through the metal. "If you have a moment?"

"*Miss* White," she barked in reply. "And I do not have time."

Barker sighed and wished this wasn't unfolding how he'd pictured the situation while digging the blankets from the airing cupboard at the cottage. But here they were.

"It is rather important," he continued regardless. "How long do you plan to stay plugged into my office?"

"I'm only trapped in this village because of you!" she shot back. "Now, if you don't mind, I am very busy!"

Barker sighed and gathered the rejected blankets. As he turned, he found Conrad Michaels waiting nearby, shoulders hunched, hands deep in his overcoat pockets. Once considered the most handsome man in college—at least, according to Julia—Conrad's face now sagged with a deep, weary worry. It was a burden that seemed older than the recent events weighing on him.

"Don't take it to heart," Conrad said, attempting an unconvincing lightness. "Prudence has always been a stubborn old ox. You should have seen how she used to talk to directors—I've seen her make grown men cry."

Despite Conrad's attempt at casual conversation, tension radiated from him. He glanced around the market, where stallholders finished their morning setup. In the distance, Katie wielded a shovel against the snow, scattering grit in her wake.

"Were you one of them?" Barker asked.

Conrad blinked. "I'm sorry?"

"The men she made cry."

He laughed. "Oh, no. That was always my ex-wife's department." He paused, his brows creasing at his words. "Working on television, I mean. Although now that I've said it, I can't deny the tears Wendy caused me." He rocked back on his heels and said, "I don't have long. Given the pitch fees, I was hoping for more customers."

Barker offered him the gate into the yard. "Wendy's little trick with the planted nail in my wife's cruffin might have spoiled that."

"Yes, I suppose you're right." Conrad sighed as he followed. "But I've long since stopped feeling guilty for the sins of my ex-wife, of which there were many."

Barker led him down to the basement office, where the warmth from Julia's busy kitchen seeped through the floorboards. Fresh baking and coffee wafted down as Conrad sank into a chair.

Though Barker had already pieced together parts of the puzzle, he kept his expression neutral. Best to start fresh.

"What prompted you to seek a private investigator, Mr Michaels?" His voice remained steady and professional.

"Conrad is fine." He took a deep breath, his pale face stark against the darkness of the office. "I need to clear my name. With Wendy's unexpected death, I fear people might suspect me." His voice tightened. "Our divorce wasn't pleasant. She took everything she could, and she didn't stop trying to bleed me dry until the day she died."

Barker nodded, pulling forward his notepad. "And when did you last talk to her?"

"In person?" Conrad scratched at the grey stubble across his jowls. "It must have been a few weeks ago. But she's been calling me nonstop. I don't know how she got my new number, but she always had a way of tracking me down."

Barker jotted this down, noting Conrad's nervous energy. Something felt off about this timeline. Given Wendy's confrontational nature, it seemed unlikely she'd pass up a chance to torment her ex-husband at the market launch if she was that keen to talk to him. She must have walked right past his stall on her rounds while chaperoned by Veronica. Yet Conrad claimed they hadn't crossed paths. Barker shifted in his leather chair.

"My wife mentioned you met Wendy at college?" Barker kept his tone casual, watching for Conrad's reaction. "What was Wendy like back then?"

A shadow darkened Conrad's features as his gaze drifted to the filing cabinets. "She was ambitious, driven... charming. We clicked right away. I thought she was going to make it big." His voice carried the sound of regret. "She always got close to the big time but could never quite cross the finish line. I think that always frustrated her."

"And the marriage?" Barker leaned forward, pen poised over his notepad. "Why did it end?"

"Is that important?"

"If you think people are going to suspect you might have killed her, it's a good place to start to clear your name."

"Yes, I suppose it is." Conrad's shoulders sagged, his posture crumbling under the weight of the questions. "It wasn't one thing, you see. It was the little things, but they all boiled down to one root cause—her career. Or rather, her ambitious plans for her career."

Barker nodded, leaning forward. "Ambition can be destructive if it overshadows everything else. Was that the case with Wendy?"

Conrad huffed a bitter laugh. "You could say that. At first, I didn't mind. It was exciting—being Mr Wendy Michaels, standing on the sidelines of the studio while she called the shots. The crew treated me like royalty just because I was with her. I could ask for coffee—the good stuff, with froth on top—and it would appear in my hand within minutes. No questions asked."

"You liked the perks," Barker observed with a small smile. "But it didn't stay that way?"

"No, it didn't," Conrad admitted, his voice softening. "It didn't take long for me to realise I wasn't a partner to her. I was just... there. A prop, someone to witness her success. Wendy thrived on attention—she needed an audience, always."

"And when the cameras weren't rolling?" Barker pressed, sensing this was where the cracks began.

Conrad scrunched his eyes closed, shaking his head to block out the memories. "That's when the strategising started. She was always planning the next move, thinking ten steps ahead. She wanted to write a book, open a restaurant, open a café, start an academy... our life was an exhausting game of chess—and it took me too long to realise I wasn't even a piece on the board."

Barker reached for the box of tissues and slid it across the desk, but Conrad waved it off with a stiff hand, sniffling as he straightened up.

"When did things change?" Barker pushed. "Was there a tipping point?"

Conrad opened his eyes, red-rimmed and glassy. "The cooking academy," he said flatly.

Barker tilted his head, intrigued. "What happened there?"

"She had this *brilliant* idea," Conrad said, his voice dripping with sarcasm. "Five years ago, just before our marriage fell apart, Wendy decided her path to glory was opening a 'cooking academy.' She sold it to me like a golden ticket to success."

"And you supported her?"

"More like funded her," Conrad shot back, bitterness creeping into his tone. "Every penny I had. I wish I'd seen through her sooner. Wendy wasn't a good teacher —she wasn't even a decent cook—but she thought her name alone would draw people in."

"What went wrong?" Barker asked.

"What didn't?" Conrad leaned back, his hand rubbing his temple. "People demanded refunds when they realised what a scam it was. Most of them got their money back through small claims courts. And despite her name being attached to the school, all the paperwork was in my name. She made it clear that the failure was my fault. It was supposed to be her big break, but I went down with the ship."

Barker scribbled a note but kept his attention on Conrad. "That must have been devastating—for both of you."

"For me, yes," Conrad said, his mouth turning down in a snarl. "Wendy didn't care. Even after everything, she had the cheek to demand I pay her back for what she'd invested. I never saw a penny of my investment again, but that didn't matter to her. I never mattered to her."

Conrad gripped the arms of the chair, his fingers turning white as his temper prickled beneath the surface. Barker didn't want to upset Conrad further—especially if he was innocent—so he seized the opportunity to steer the conversation.

"Thank you for being so candid," Barker said as he finished making notes. "Your honesty makes my job easier." He cleared his throat, setting down his pen. He leaned back in his chair and asked, "Why do you think others will point fingers at you now?"

Conrad's face crumpled. "Because we were so connected. When she wronged Prudence with that TV show, I was there. She fired Polly, and I was there. Ruining Ethan's bakery, yet again, I was there." His voice cracked. "When she crushed Melissa... I... that was half my fault." He exhaled, his voice growing small. "I didn't mean to fall in love with Wendy, but she was so... hypnotic. And now, for whatever reason, they're all here, and I know what they'll think."

Barker nodded his understanding, wondering which thread to pull on. He knew a little about Prudence and Melissa's pasts, and Polly had shouted about her book, but he knew nothing about the pastry chef.

"Tell me about Ethan," he asked, flipping to a fresh page in his notepad. "You said Wendy ruined his bakery?"

"Ethan confessed to me that Wendy made a move on him, and he rejected her. They met through Polly. He's Polly's fella, and Polly used to be Wendy's assistant."

Conrad shook his head again. "That's what she did to Melissa—Melissa was her friend, and I was Melissa's boyfriend..." He sighed, his head sinking further. "I'm not proud of what I did. My life has been one mistake after another since the day I met Wendy... I should have rejected her when I had the chance, like Ethan did."

Barker nodded, eager to know more. "And what did Wendy do to Ethan?"

"I need to get back to my stall," Conrad said as he stood.

"Then we'll walk and talk."

Conrad frowned as they stepped out of the office's warm shadow and into the lively market square. "Why do you care about Ethan?" His words came out more defensive than curious.

Barker adjusted his scarf against the cold. "Because if you want to clear your name, we need to find the poisoner. Given how many people here have a history with Wendy, it seems like a good place to start."

The market was quiet. Stallholders called out to passing customers, the smell of fresh bread and sizzling bacon mingling with the crisp winter air. Barker stayed close as Conrad wove between the benches, and he seemed eager to get away.

"Ethan had a little bakery in Riverswick," Conrad began. "It wasn't flashy, but it was his. He inherited it from his dad and poured everything he had into it. Then Wendy came along." His tone darkened, and his hands clenched into fists. "She bombed it with negative reviews —every website, every social media platform she could find. And people believed her. His customers stopped going, and before long, the bakery closed. It broke him."

"How did Ethan and Wendy meet?" Barker asked, watching the emotions flicker across Conrad's face.

"Polly introduced them, you see, back when she was still Wendy's assistant. He was just a nice guy trying to keep his business afloat. Wendy destroyed him."

They reached Conrad's stall, a quaint setup featuring handmade wooden clocks of various shapes and sizes. The craftsmanship was meticulous, each clock polished to a warm glow that stood out against the dull winter light.

"You made these?" Barker asked, impressed.

Conrad gave a slight, almost shy nod. "It was something I started during the divorce. After years of standing by, I needed to use my hands to feel like I was building something again instead of watching everything fall apart." He sighed. "I'd wasted so much time."

Barker traced a finger over the smooth wood of a pendulum clock. "They're beautiful. A far cry from how chaotic things sounded with Wendy."

Conrad chuckled, the sound bitter. "Chaos was her currency. It wasn't just Ethan. After his bakery closed, he had to take care of his dying father. Wendy knew he was ill but didn't care." He pressed his lips into a thin line. "She never cared about anyone but herself."

Barker's gaze lingered on the intricate clock face of a cherrywood timepiece, its brass pendulum swinging gently. The craftsmanship was impeccable, each detail painstakingly carved. He could almost hear the quiet pride humming in the air around Conrad.

"How much for this one?" Barker asked, nodding toward the cherrywood clock.

Conrad blinked, clearly startled by the shift in conversation. "You want to buy it?"

"I do," Barker said, running his fingers along the smooth edges again. "It would look good in my office."

A faint flicker of warmth crossed Conrad's face—barely perceptible, but it was there. "Two hundred," he said, his voice softening. "But for you, let's say one-seventy-five. Call it a thank-you for not turning me away yet."

Barker reached into his pocket for his wallet, handing over the cash without a second thought. "I'll take it," he said with a small smile. "And I'll consider it a down payment on your good faith, Conrad."

Conrad gave a slight, grudging nod as he carefully lifted the clock off the display and began wrapping it in thick brown paper.

Barker waited until Conrad handed him the neatly bundled clock before his tone shifted back to business. "And one last question," he asked. "Where were you between half-past ten and noon yesterday?"

"Here, at my stall."

"And you didn't leave at any moment?"

Conrad shook his head. Barker didn't quite believe him. Before he could press further, a customer approached the stall, a middle-aged woman admiring a delicate mantel clock. Conrad gave Barker an apologetic look, then turned on the charm, engaging the woman in soft conversation.

Barker stepped back, watching as Conrad worked. The man seemed genuine, but something about his story didn't sit right with Barker. Was Conrad a broken man desperate to clear his name—or a master manipulator who had learned to shift blame, just like his ex-wife?

He pulled his coat tighter against the wind and returned to his office with his new clock, setting it on the desk next to his framed wedding picture. There was more to Conrad's story—Barker was sure of it.

8

*J*essie leaned against the doorway of Barker's office, arms crossed as she listened to him recount his conversation with Conrad Michaels. The vestibule door let out an enticing warmth while the café's courtyard froze her behind off.

"So, Conrad thinks Wendy ruined Ethan's bakery because he wasn't interested in her?" she clarified, raising an eyebrow. "Bit weird."

Barker nodded, closing his notepad. "That's what he claims. But given Wendy's reputation, it doesn't sound far-fetched. She seemed to make enemies for fun."

Jessie frowned. "And Conrad's alibi was that he didn't leave his stall?"

"That's what he said," Barker admitted, sighing. "But I know there's something he's not telling me.

"You need to figure out if your new client is a liar." Jessie pushed off the doorframe, already zipping up her jacket. "I'll see what Ethan has to say for himself."

"Careful," Barker warned, his tone mild but firm. "If Conrad's telling the truth about the reviews, Ethan might still hold on to a lot of anger."

"Anger can be useful." Jessie winked, pulling her press badge from her pocket. "It makes people careless."

Leaving Barker to the comfort of his snug office, she slipped out through the back gate, cringing at the blaring music from Prudence's camper van. Jessie spotted Ethan's pastry van parked at the far end of the market—the only food van to show up for the second day. It was a battered old thing, with peeling paint and a scruffy chalkboard menu where he'd rubbed out prices and raised them more than once. A small queue had formed, but what caught Jessie's eye was Polly, sitting a few metres away at a folding table. Her tell-all book about Wendy was fanned out like a winning poker hand —and people were buying copies.

"Didn't take her long," Jessie muttered, weaving through the crowd.

She joined the back of the queue as Ethan worked quickly, his hands steady as he wrapped pastries in brown paper. Up close, Jessie noticed he looked like he was holding back the heaviest sigh of his life, as though he wanted to be anywhere but at the market.

"Who's next?" he grunted when it was Jessie's turn.

Jessie stepped forward and smiled. "A croissant, please."

"Anything else?"

Jessie held up the newspaper badge. "As it happens, yes. I'm with *The Peridale Post*, and I'd like to confirm something I heard—about your bakery closing because of bad reviews?"

Ethan stopped holding in that sigh, letting it out like a hot wind. His face flushed red as he folded his arms tight against his chest. She'd rattled him from her introduction alone and had him exactly where she wanted him—on the back foot.

"Lies," he spat, knocking over a display of Danish pastries as he batted his hand to swat away the accusations. "Now, if you don't mind, I—"

"Lies from who?" Jessie kept her tone naïve. "If you feel someone has stitched you up, this could be the perfect avenue to reply."

"Do you think I came down with the last shower, darling?" He let out a harsh laugh, running a hand through his dishevelled hair. "The person who left those reviews died yesterday, and you're here asking questions about my old bakery? Pull the other one."

Not so on the back foot, after all. He grabbed a croissant from the display, bagged it in a brown paper bag, swung it around twice to seal it, and tossed it onto the counter.

"So, it was Wendy who left them?" Jessie pressed, straightening her back. "What sort of things did she claim?"

Ethan's laugh turned bitter. "You didn't even bother to do your research?" He shook his head in disbelief. "Wendy was sick in the head because her life didn't turn out how she thought it would, and when I didn't give her what she wanted, she took it out on me—just like she did with everyone else who 'wronged' her." He leaned over the counter, looming over Jessie as his voice dropped to a harsh whisper. "It doesn't matter what she said. It was all made up. Another of her messed up fantasies."

"It sounds like you hated Wendy."

"You would have too if you'd known her." His hands trembled as he rearranged the Danish pastries he'd knocked over. "I had enough going on when she decided it was my time to be knocked down a peg. She deserved everything she got, in the end."

Jessie couldn't stop her brow arching. "You're glad someone murdered Wendy?"

Ethan glared at her, hearing the trap he'd walked himself into. Jessie wondered if he'd try to take back his comments, to play things a little more coyly, but he leaned in closer, a smirk pricking up the corners of his lips.

"For the first time in months," he whispered darkly, "I slept like a baby."

His eyes darted past her to the growing queue. Two women whispered among themselves, pretending to study the menu board while they eavesdropped on every word. Jessie knew her window was closing.

"One last question," she pressed. "Did you see Wendy pull a nail out of her mouth?"

He nodded. "Her best performance yet."

"And where were you when word spread about her death?"

"Where else?" He gestured around the van. "I can't

afford not to be here every waking hour because of her. Do you know how many markets I've travelled to this year already to make ends meet?"

"I can't imagine that's easy," Jessie said, though she couldn't push herself to sound sympathetic after his outburst. "And you're sure you didn't leave this van?"

Ethan sniffed, shaking his head. "No," he said, his tone sharpening. "Now, if you don't mind, you haven't paid, and I have other customers to serve."

Jessie grabbed the brown paper bag and tapped her phone against the card machine before leaving the van. She walked over to the benches buried under the snow and looked over her shoulder. Ethan watched her like a hawk for a lingering moment before he darted away. She peeled back the brown paper and took a bite, wishing she hadn't. The pastry was stale—it must have been left over from yesterday's batch. She spat it into a nearby bin and tossed the rest after it.

Jessie's fingers danced across her phone screen, writing bullet points of Ethan's suspicious comments. He hadn't tried to mask how much he had detested Wendy, and like Barker with Conrad, she didn't believe his quick answer of claiming to have been at the market. Jessie had been at Julia's stall then. If only she'd have known a murder was coming, she could have scoped out the other stallholders.

"*Jessie!*" Dot's voice cut through her concentration. Her great-grandmother hurried over from Ethel's stall, her navy skirt swishing around her knees, beige wool socks pulled up to meet them. "I'm glad I caught you.

What's all this business with your mother and that Wendy woman? I've been hearing strange things."

"I'm a little busy here, Dot." Jessie kept typing, pretending not to hear as she added details about Ethan's trembling hands and defensive posture. "I'm at work."

"Hmm." Dot's finger jabbed at the screen. "Well, that's not true."

"What's not?" Jessie looked up, startled.

"That bit about the pastry man being in his van *all* afternoon." Dot joined Jessie in looking over at the van, but Ethan wasn't risking looking away from his customers. "I saw him leave in a huff yesterday. He had quite the row with that pie woman who's moved on to hawking her books, slammed down his shutter, and marched off."

Jessie's heart quickened. "Which direction did he go?"

Dot waved vaguely behind the post office. "That way, and we both know, if you follow the path down, loop around the police station, go past the B&B, down one more street, and turn right..."

"The newspaper office on Mulberry Lane," Jessie said. "Not exactly conclusive, but it's something."

"You're welcome," Dot replied, adjusting her brooch. "So, what is going on with your mum? Sue mentioned something about Wendy bullying Julia once upon a time, but that doesn't sound right. She would have told me, for one, and—"

"You should probably ask Mum yourself," Jessie said, already planning her next move.

"I will when I can get away from the stall," Dot grumbled, glancing back as Ethel chose who to serve next from the three people waiting. "Somehow, those hideous gnomes are selling like hotcakes! I bet even Evelyn couldn't see that one coming."

"The people have spoken," Jessie said, patting Dot's arm. "Thanks again for the tip."

She glanced at the van again, glad to know Ethan had lied. But why? And where had he gone? Both things would be difficult to prove, but it was proof that he'd lied to her. She'd expected as much, press badge and all, but as she copied and pasted her notes into a text message to Veronica, she knew his quotes would at least spice up the next issue of *The Post*.

At Polly's stall, a crowd gathered around her books, and she seemed to revel in holding court with all her admirers. Jessie wanted to get her hands on a copy of the book, but she'd rather wait to catch Polly alone than confront her with questions in front of a crowd. If how she'd stood up and announced that she'd written a tell-all book about Wendy in the café was anything to go by, she didn't mind creating a scene.

"Strange couple," Jessie muttered as she sent the text message.

Jessie tucked her phone away and headed to the post office. She pushed open the door, setting off the familiar bell chime. Shilpa looked up from sorting parcels, her reading glasses perched on the end of her nose.

"Ethan? The pastry van man?" Shilpa shook her head after Jessie asked the question. "Didn't see him, love. But that woman in the camper van was acting peculiar. I saw her skulking off around that time."

"Which way did she go?"

Shilpa shrugged. "Couldn't tell you. Was busy with the afternoon post."

Another dead end. Jessie stepped back into the cold, spotting Richie stacking empty barrels outside his bar.

"Lost yesterday to a hangover," he admitted when she asked, wiping his hands on his jeans. "I'd say I had fun, but my two-day headache says otherwise."

Further up the street outside the police station, PC Puglisi's eyes lit up as she approached. "You still single—"

"Not now," Jessie cut him off, quickening her pace.

In the B&B's garden, Evelyn meditated cross-legged on a bamboo mat, unaffected by the snow. Her eyes remained closed as Jessie approached.

"I stayed at the market," she said before Jessie could ask, peering through one eye. "Mostly in the new gardens. I didn't see anything. Sorry, dear, but I sense you're on the right path."

Already feeling defeated, she carried on to Mulberry Lane. The nail salon buzzed with activity despite the police presence upstairs. Clarice focused on waxing a man's eyebrows, making him flinch as she ripped off the tiny strips.

"Ethan?" Clarice studied the photo on Jessie's phone. "No, I didn't see him. But..." She lowered her voice. "I heard footsteps running down the stairs about five minutes before you and Veronica found her."

Jessie tried not to purse her lips, but she didn't manage it. "Why didn't you say anything yesterday?"

"Because I didn't know there was a body upstairs."

The client frowned at Clarice and then looked up at the ceiling with a worried look. It disappeared when she yanked off another strip, and Jessie turned to leave.

"Great," Jessie muttered to herself. "Five minutes earlier, and we'd have caught them in the act."

9

*W*hile fresh snow fluttered past the café's kitchen window, steam curled from the mixing bowl as Julia poured hot pineapple juice into the batter. The familiar scent transported her back to childhood Sunday afternoons in her mother's kitchen with messy hands and wide smiles.

"Dad thinks Conrad's hiding something." Jessie perched on a stool at the stainless steel island, watching Julia work. "He didn't seem too jazzed to be asked about his past with Wendy."

Julia lined the cake tin with pineapple rings, positioning cherries in their centres. "And what about Ethan?"

"He practically spat when I mentioned Wendy. Said she review-bombed his business when he was already struggling. Called her a failed nobody who ruined everything she touched."

The words struck a chord. Julia drizzled golden syrup over the fruit. "That sounds about right."

"Oh, and Dot is on the warpath. She cornered me, demanding to know why you never told her about the bullying." Jessie's boots scuffed against the stool legs. "Why didn't you?"

"Because you know what my gran is like," Julia said, sighing. "She would have barged in, shouting the odds, and made things worse."

"Yeah, you're right." Jessie paused. "I just can't believe you let Wendy get away with it..."

Julia's hands stilled over the cake tin. "What do you mean?"

"Well, all she did to you, you could have got your own back on her and nobody would have blamed you, but you didn't."

Julia smoothed the batter over the fruit. "No, I didn't. I tried to be the bigger person, no matter how small I felt." The words settled in her chest, and she didn't regret that choice. "And now I'm trying to solve her murder," she said, glancing through the beaded curtain to the quiet café, suspiciously quiet even for a snow day. "Cleaning up her last mess."

"Someone got their own back," Jessie muttered as Julia slid the tin into the oven. "I'm going to keep trying to find out if anyone saw Ethan." She paused at the door. "What are you making, anyway?"

"Pineapple upside-down cake."

"Retro," Jessie laughed, heading out.

Julia checked the recipe next to the yellowed page of the old *Culinary Delights* cookbook, making sure she hadn't forgotten anything. "Retro indeed." When Jessie left, Julia said to herself, "And hopefully, just the ticket into Prudence's good books."

The café door burst open with such force that Julia instinctively reached for a teapot, expecting her gran's dramatic entrance. Instead, Shilpa from the post office stormed in with a face full of thunder.

"Latte, extra strong," Shilpa huffed, glaring at the display cabinet. "And whatever's sweetest. To go."

"Careful." Julia kept her tone light as she reached for a takeaway cup. "The last woman who came here demanding an extra strong coffee didn't meet such a delightful end."

Shilpa's scowl deepened. "Well, someone else will not meet a delightful end soon if she doesn't move her camper van."

"Prudence trouble?" Julia levelled off the coffee grounds with a few bangs against the counter.

"Trouble isn't the word for it." Shilpa glared through the wall in the direction of the van. "That constant music is driving me up the wall, and she's blocking the back exit. Three deliveries today—*three!*—couldn't get the stock in because of her." Steam hissed from the milk frother as Julia worked, but Shilpa wasn't finished. "Is she plugged in here? The wire looks like it goes through—"

"She's plugged into Barker's office," Julia admitted, sliding the latte across the counter and selecting a chocolate-centred cruffin. "I think she blindsided him."

"Pull the plug!" Shilpa snatched up her order. "If someone doesn't do something, I'll call the police. You can't park on double yellow lines for a few hours, let alone days!"

The bell above the door had barely stopped jingling from Shilpa's exit when a loud bang echoed from the back door. She wiped her hands on her apron, passed through the beads and across the kitchen, and pulled open the door to find Prudence huddled in the snow, her silver hair dusted with white flakes.

"Brown sugar," Prudence announced, peering past Julia into the kitchen. "For my sauce. I'd get some, but it's..." Her words trailed off as her gaze landed on the stack of cookbooks on the island. Her face hardened. "Where did you get those?"

"My gran's attic," Julia said, brushing flour from the cover of the topmost book. "They're mine. Prudence, I..." A hot flush crept up Julia's neck, and she couldn't look at the dishevelled woman on the back doorstep as she said, "... I was a huge fan of yours when I was a little girl."

Prudence's shoulders tensed. "Past life," she muttered, shifting her weight from foot to foot, clearly uncomfortable with the praise. She sniffed. "What's that smell?"

"Pineapple upside-down cake."

"Really?" Her eyes narrowed. "Can't stand the stuff."

"Oh." Despite spending the past hour following Prudence's recipe to the letter, Julia couldn't help but smile at her abrupt manner. "I have some brown sugar to spare. Would you like to come in? It's quiet and warm here—might be nice to get out of that van for a while?"

Prudence's eyes darted around the kitchen, taking in every detail with the precision of someone who'd spent decades in professional kitchens. Her gaze landed on Julia's pristine work surface, lingering on the stack of well-loved cookbooks.

"Are you the lady who made the cruffins?" Prudence's tone carried an edge of accusation.

"That's me."

"Very good," Prudence muttered, then spun on her heel. "Too much jam, but very good."

Julia's heart sank. She'd thought they'd made a connection, however brief. But before she could close the door, a tremendous rattling announced Prudence's return. She burst back in, arms laden with a box of glass jars, a pan that still bubbled away, and fresh ingredients.

"I hope you have a real gas hob," Prudence declared, dumping her box directly on the cookbooks. "I can't stand the electric ones." Her eyes flicked to the books beneath her supplies. "And I'm not signing these, either, so don't ask me to."

Now that Julia had Prudence exactly where she wanted her, with an unwanted pineapple upside-down cake baking away in the oven, she had to choose her next move carefully. The cuddly bear version of Prudence White that Julia had known through the TV had grizzled with time, and one wrong poke would be all it took to scare her off.

So, Julia did what her instincts told her—she made Prudence a pot of tea, set it next to her, and left her to cook in peace.

There'd be time for questions, but first, Julia had to gain her old idol's trust before she could discern if she was a murderer.

10

The Beatles' melodies drifted through Barker's basement office as footsteps and clanking pans echoed from above. Olivia scribbled on her colouring book beside him, humming along to *Here Comes the Sun* while he typed. The familiar sounds of Julia's baking had taken on an aggressive edge this afternoon as she stomped about and rattled pans—a physical manifestation of her inner turmoil, and he wouldn't hold it against her.

His fingers flew across the keyboard as he dug deeper into Conrad's claims about the cooking school. A small article in the *Riverswick Chronicle* caught his eye—dated two years ago. It detailed a group of disgruntled students planning legal action against what they termed a 'fraudulent cooking school.' He clicked through several archived pages but found no follow-up story.

The Wendy Michaels Culinary Delights school's old website loaded at a snail's pace, broken images littering the pages like digital confetti. Conrad and Wendy beamed at the camera in the few remaining photographs; they stood in what looked like a renovated working men's club. Despite Wendy's name emblazoned across the header, Conrad appeared in every shot, posing as an instructor partaking in staged demonstrations.

The website's copy promised 'excellence from two skilled chefs with television experience, both in front of and behind the camera.' Yet, as Barker scrolled through page after page, he found no mention of formal qualifications or real-world kitchen experience.

Conrad had admitted Wendy was the face of the operation, but these photos painted a different picture—one where Conrad played a more significant role than he'd let on.

Barker clicked through to the review section, scanning dozens of one-star ratings. The complaints painted a damning picture—unprofessional teaching, unsafe conditions, missing equipment. One review made him sit up straighter: 'DO NOT WASTE YOUR MONEY! I witnessed nothing but chaos after paying £2000 upfront for this course. The final straw came when Conrad lost control, screaming at another student for being ungrateful before hurling a mixing bowl across the kitchen. It bounced off the counter and struck someone! This man is dangerous and shouldn't be teaching anyone.'

His stomach churned. The mild-mannered clockmaker who'd sat across from him, confessing about Wendy's manipulations, seemed worlds apart from this violent instructor. A five-star review stood out among the sea of complaints: 'Don't listen to the negativity... see the quality for yourself!'

Clicking the reviewer's profile, Barker found a generic username and cloudy sky avatar. But the account's other reviews told a different story. Recent posts gave lukewarm praise to local restaurants, while earlier ones savaged the Lang Bakery in Riverswick with claims of contaminated food—hair, fingernails, even glass.

Barker's breath caught. This had to be Wendy's revenge account targeting Ethan's business. But as he scrolled further, he found positive reviews for woodworking equipment shops and speciality clock parts dealers. The realisation hit him like ice water—this was Conrad's account. He'd helped Wendy destroy Ethan's reputation even after their marriage ended.

The timestamps on the reviews were a year old. Conrad hadn't just been Wendy's victim—he'd been her willing accomplice.

"Let's stretch our legs, Liv," Barker said, pulling on his gloves. "Daddy has to have a few words with his new client."

The crisp winter air bit at Barker's nose as he helped Olivia button her coat. Fresh snow blanketed the courtyard, undoing Katie's earlier efforts with the shovel. She persisted anyway, clearing paths between the market stalls where only two customers lingered, their hands deep in their pockets and not coming out to buy anything.

Several vendors had already started dismantling

their displays. Ethel, stubborn as ever, stood shivering by her gnome collection, her nose and ears bright red against her pale face. The planned late summer opening would have painted a different picture.

"Granny Katie!" Olivia's excited squeal pierced the quiet as she bounded through the snow.

Barker caught Katie's eye. "Mind watching her for a moment?"

Katie's thumbs-up preceded her theatrical spin with Olivia, their shared laughter echoing across the square.

Now alone, Barker made his way towards Conrad's stall. He loaded boxes into his car frantically without noticing Barker's approach. Once the boot slammed shut, Conrad jumped into the driver's seat and pulled away.

Barker matched his pace to Conrad's vehicle, maintaining what he hoped was an inconspicuous distance.

"Fancy a gnome?" Ethel's voice caught him as he passed. "I have a detective one, a PI one, and an author one—take your pick."

Barker glanced at the trio of figurines, each bearing an uncanny and unsettling resemblance to himself. "Maybe later."

Barker pressed himself against the rough brick wall of the alley, his breath misting in the frigid air as Conrad pulled up and ducked into the phone box on the corner outside the post office. The glass panels fogged from Conrad's exhaled breaths while he jabbed at the buttons.

Through the warped glass, Conrad's shoulders tensed as he waited. His words carried on the still winter afternoon. "I *know* how much money I owe you. I'm working on it, but it will not be that simple! My biggest stress might be gone, but I need more time." His voice rose. "I'm not *asking* for more time. I'm *telling* you, it'll take longer. I can't just pull money from thin air!"

The receiver slammed down with enough force to rattle the entire phone box. Conrad stood motionless, his chest heaving.

Barker's plan to confront him about the reviews dissolved. Better to watch and learn. He melted deeper into the alley's shadows as Conrad emerged.

He tilted his head back and released a primal scream into the snowy sky. The sound echoed across the village square, startling a flock of pigeons into flight. Without a backward glance, he jumped into his car and sped away, slipping and sliding across the ice without slowing down.

The café door chimed as Julia poked her head out into the cold air as Shilpa emerged from the post office at the same time.

"What was that?" they asked in unison, their breaths visible in the frosty afternoon.

Barker brushed snow from his coat sleeves. "My new client showing his true colours."

The phone box stood empty now, its glass panels still clouded from Conrad's heated conversation. Barker turned to Shilpa. "Is there a way to figure out the most recent dialled number?"

"1471 should do it." Shilpa hugged herself against the cold.

Inside the phone box, Barker pressed the numbers,

listening as the automated voice recited the digits. He typed them into his phone's search bar, his gloved fingers clumsy on the screen. The results loaded. Quick Cash Solutions LTD—a payday loan company. The website revealed astronomical interest rates and reviews that rivalled the cooking school's testimonials in their vitriol.

Snow crunched under his boots as he joined Julia on the café doorstep. The warmth from inside carried the scent of vanilla and cinnamon, and a rich tomato sauce he'd never smelled before. Someone was making a racket in the kitchen.

"Something smells good," he said.

But Julia didn't accept the compliment. "What's going on?"

"It seems Conrad is in big financial trouble." Barker kept his voice low. "And given that roar, he's in over his head." He glanced back at the phone box, wondering if he should have approached. "Desperate men make poor decisions." The weight of realisation settled in his stomach. "Have I taken on a murderer trying to clear his name?"

∾

Jessie pulled her jacket tighter against the biting cold as she trudged through the pristine snow towards the market square. The grey sky hung low, stealing what little daylight remained.

Her breath caught at the sight of Veronica crouched by Sebastian's memorial stone at the market's opening.

She arranged sunflowers against the granite, and Jessie hung back, giving her editor space with her memories.

"Sorry." Veronica dabbed beneath her polka dot frames with a gloved finger when she spotted Jessie. "I was just—"

"You don't have to apologise." Jessie stepped closer, the snow squeaking beneath her boots. "Just wanted to check you hadn't fallen or something."

"On account of me being so old?" Veronica teased, laughing away the tears. But one hand remained on the memorial stone. "I can't believe it's been over a year since we closed my brother's cold case." Her voice wavered. "All those years not knowing what happened to him, and now..." She traced the engraved letters of Sebastian's name. "Here we are again with another murder to solve."

Jessie squeezed Veronica's shoulder, feeling the tremor beneath the wool coat. She hated seeing Veronica like this—she was always so strong and knew what to do, but she could still crumble when it came to her brother.

"You were right about her." Veronica pulled a folded newspaper from her jacket. "Your gut instinct is killer, for want of a better word."

Jessie's stomach dropped as she read the bold headline: 'Vilified Former TV Chef Murdered.' The words floated above a glossy professional picture of Wendy, the sort that only seemed to exist on LinkedIn.

Jessie's fingers traced the newspaper print, her breath catching at the flood of comments beneath the article. "People really hated her, didn't they?"

"They're still coming forward." Veronica adjusted her giant frames. "Former colleagues, old schoolmates—all with stories about her cruel streak. Makes me feel rather foolish for falling for her charm."

"It's alright to be wrong about people." Jessie handed back the paper. "That first email from her was pretty convincing. She had the gift of the gab—people like her usually do."

"We needed something." Veronica's smile faded, her eyes dropping to Sebastian's memorial.

Jessie studied her mentor's face, noting the shadows beneath her eyes and the tight set of her jaw. Something wasn't right. "What aren't you telling me?"

"Physical circulation for the paper is down." Veronica's voice cracked. "Nobody seems to want to buy the paper copies anymore, and people just read the headlines on the Peridale Chat group now, commenting there instead of clicking through to our articles. Revenue is down, and advertisers are pulling out."

"But we've already made cuts." Jessie's boots crunched in the snow as she shifted closer. "We downsized the office—it's just us two left and—"

"They're threatening to go online only if numbers don't improve soon." Veronica wrapped her arms around herself. "The world is changing, Jessie."

"Then we'll give people something worth reading about." Jessie squeezed Veronica's shoulder, her gaze snagging on Polly across the market. Wendy's former personal assistant counted notes with a satisfied smirk. "Get yourself into the warm. Go home and stop worrying—I've got work to do."

Jessie strolled over to Polly's stall, the smirk still playing on her lips. Ethan's van was already gone, leaving a vacant space in the market square. Polly, arms crossed tight, glared at Jessie's approach—Ethan must have given her the heads-up.

"What do you want?" Polly demanded, her voice clipped.

"To buy a copy of your book." Jessie feigned innocence, pulling a tenner from her pocket. "I've heard it's *riveting*."

"Too late," Polly snapped, gesturing to the empty crates beneath her stall. "Sold out. I'll need to get some more."

"Might be too late by then." Jessie shrugged, feigning indifference. "Wendy's the flavour of the week, but it'll be someone else soon. People move on fast these days."

Polly's glare intensified, but she remained silent. She tucked her auburn hair behind her ears before crossing her arms tightly against herself.

"You must have worked for Wendy for a long time," Jessie continued, tilting her head, "to have so many things to say about her in a book."

Polly hesitated, her eyes darting around the market square as if checking for eavesdroppers. "We met after she left college. She was schmoozing around a network party she'd snuck into, and I was an underpaid production assistant on *Culinary Delights*." Her voice softened, a hint of wistful nostalgia creeping in. "I noticed how she was doing *everything* wrong. Laughing too loud, fawning too much, eating too much from the buffet. She was so wet behind the ears—and when I found out we'd grown up in the same area, I could smell the Fern Moore on her the moment she told me."

"So, you created her?"

"I helped her clean up her image," Polly said, glaring at Jessie. "I pointed her to the people she should talk to if she wanted to get ahead."

"And that's how she ended up working with Prudence?" Jessie asked. "On her show?"

"Prudence's show was dying, and she needed something new. The network liked Wendy's no-nonsense approach. It was the early 00s, and she was going to be to cooking shows what Simon Cowell was to talent shows."

"But it didn't work," Jessie pointed out. "Not really. She might have taken over the show, but it didn't last."

Polly shrugged. "No, it didn't."

"But you stayed her assistant?"

"She always had another venture," Polly said. "A book to write, a convention to attend—it didn't matter, as long as I got my slice of the pie."

"And how did you get into making pies?"

Polly shifted on the spot. "I need to make a living somehow. You need something to sell if you want to attend markets, and I was always coming to these things with Ethan, so it made sense."

Jessie narrowed her eyes. "Do you actually make your pies?"

"Are you here to ask about pies or Wendy?" Polly's voice rose.

"So, you *want* to talk about Wendy?" Jessie said, tapping the table where the books had been. She wished she'd bought one earlier. "You saw it all, didn't you? Every shady dealing, every rude comment."

"I did."

"And you wrote it all down."

"That's showbiz," Polly said, looking irritated.

"That must have annoyed Wendy."

Polly scowled. "It did," she said. "She filed an injunction against me, so I couldn't name her in the book, but it doesn't matter now, does it?"

"No, it doesn't. But it's great timing for you. For you to have as many books as you had ready to make all that money today."

Polly tucked the wad of notes into her jacket's inside pocket. She must have made several hundred—more than she would have made selling pies.

"Isn't this a little beyond the remit of a local paper?" Polly said, planting her hands on the table before leaning across to Jessie. "You're talking like a detective."

"I have some personal stakes in solving this." Jessie shifted her weight, glancing back at the soft glow of the back of the café. "Wendy put on that show with the cruffin that made my mum look guilty, and you know how people like to talk in these little villages." She thought of the questions she'd been brewing all day, and the most intriguing one sprang forward. "Why did you stop working with Wendy?"

"She over-invested in that cooking school and convinced Conrad to do the same. Tried to get me to throw my coins in, but I was wiser than that. She even crawled out of the woodwork to beg her brother and sister for money, but they refused." Polly scoffed at the idea, and Jessie wondered what had happened with Wendy and her siblings—would they know or care that she was dead? "I knew it was a sinking ship."

"Rats are the first to flee," Jessie said before she could consider if she should. "So, these siblings of—"

"Look, I know you harassed Ethan earlier, and he might be weak, but I won't stand for it." Polly's jaw tightened. "If you want to know what's happening, talk to Conrad. He was her right-hand man for years, and nobody hated her more than him. It didn't take him long to move on."

Jessie squinted. "What do you mean?"

"I saw him and Melissa getting all cosy by the fire in The Plough last night." Polly's lip curled into a smug smile. "He didn't even wait a day for his ex-wife to go cold."

"Interesting," Jessie muttered, wondering if Polly was too quick to deflect. "Two more questions," she said, louder. "Where were you at the time of Wendy's poisoning?"

"Right here."

"Can you prove it?"

"Can you?" Polly fired back.

Good point.

"Your final question?"

"How many copies of your book did you sell before today?"

Polly's glare could have melted the surrounding snow. She zipped up her coat with a sharp yank and stalked away without answering. Her silence told Jessie everything she needed to know—it couldn't have been many. If Polly had a bestseller on her hands, she would have bragged about it.

Jessie watched Polly's retreating figure with a mix of frustration and intrigue. Polly's evasive answers and sudden departure spoke volumes about her character. Forthright, ambitious, and quick to put Ethan down—no wonder she'd stuck with Wendy for so many years, only to exploit her after the fact. She typed a fresh message of her Polly notes to Veronica and sent a copy to Barker and Julia.

"Birds of a feather flock together," she said as she left the market.

～

"Prudence, do you need..." Julia called out as she checked the message from Jessie, and her voice trailed off as she stepped through the beads, "... *anything*?"

Prudence and her sauce jars had gone, and she'd left the mess behind. Saucepans swayed in a mountain in the sink; splashes covered the counters; knives and chopping boards were abandoned. And from the looks of it, she'd taken the cookbooks with her. Perhaps Julia had given her too much space to get on with her cooking.

"Unbelievable," Julia said, shaking her head. "That woman..."

The bell above the café door tinkled, and Julia glanced up from wiping down the island. She ditched the cloth and entered the café as DI Laura Moyes and her girlfriend, Roxy Carter, stepped inside. Julia's heart lifted at the sight of her oldest friend, Roxy, whose fierce red hair was as untamed as ever. Roxy beamed, throwing her arms open wide.

"Why didn't you call me?" Roxy demanded, enveloping Julia in a tight hug before pulling back to hold her at arm's length. "Why didn't you text? Do you know how I found out? The staffroom! I've been at some teacher training course in London, and when I got back, *everyone* had your name in their mouths. Someone poisoned a woman, and it's something to do with a cruffin?"

Julia sighed, shaking her head. "I've just been getting on with it."

"We do that, don't we?" Roxy said, narrowing her eyes in mock exasperation. "Well, don't worry. I set them straight."

"Everything they said was probably true."

"So, you poisoned the new food critic?" Roxy asked, arching a brow.

"No, not quite."

"But you did used to know her?" She leaned in, her voice dropping to a scandalised whisper. "And what even is a cruffin?"

Julia laughed, pulling her friend in for another hug. "I'll explain everything. But first, it's better if you try one. It's easier than explaining."

Roxy slid into a chair, brushing snow from her coat, while Moyes sat beside her. Her sharp gaze roamed the café, though the radio on her hip was silent for once. This visit was unofficial, Julia realised, but that didn't mean Moyes didn't have something to say—she seemed to be itching to reveal something.

Julia carried over a fresh cruffin and two lattes, setting them on the table. Roxy grabbed the pastry with both hands, biting in with gusto. "Oh my god," she mumbled through a mouthful. "You've been hiding these from me?"

"I spent months perfecting the recipe," Julia said, folding her arms and trying not to sound too bitter. "All for nothing. The café's takings today are the lowest I've had in years."

Moyes spoke up. "It'll turn around, Julia. People have short memories. The café will be buzzing again soon."

"So, what happened?" Roxy asked.

"Where do I start?"

"The beginning, mate."

So, that was what Julia did. She talked Roxy through those horrible last months at college and everything she knew about how Wendy had been navigating life since then. Roxy listened, but she didn't hide her disappointment.

"I wish you'd told me back then," Roxy said, wiping her fingers on a napkin. "I'd have thumped this Wendy straight in the nose."

"I know." Julia grinned. "That's why I didn't tell you."

Moyes cleared her throat. "Any updates? I know the ex-husband hired Barker."

Julia nodded, her mood shifting. "Barker followed Conrad earlier. He was in a phone box, arguing with a loan company. He seems to be in a desperate position."

Moyes raised an eyebrow. "That fits. We found

transactions from Conrad to Wendy—two hundred quid every fortnight for six months. But he missed the last payment."

"Maybe he'd had enough?" Roxy chimed in. "Nothing worse than an ex who won't move on—Violet still calls every few months, asking for another chance, usually after too much vodka." She checked her watch and jumped to her feet. "Oh, bugger. Is that the time? I promised to cover the second shift at after-school football. You'd think they'd cancel it with the snow, but no—they just moved it indoors." She leaned down, kissing Moyes' cheek and squeezing Julia's shoulder. "Don't let anyone get you down, alright? That cruffin is a work of art."

With that, she swept out, the bell jingling behind her, leaving Julia's spirits lifted—it was always lovely to see her old pal.

Moyes watched her go, then turned back to Julia. "Are you alright?"

Julia hesitated before answering. "I will be once all of this is behind me. For years, Wendy wasn't a part of my present. Just a bad memory. And now..." She trailed off.

"She won't be part of your future," Moyes said firmly. "Not for much longer. We're close to a breakthrough—I can feel it."

Julia straightened in her seat. "What do you mean?"

"The official cause of death came back as a heart attack brought on by convallatoxin." Moyes paused to check if Julia knew, but she shook her head, and Moyes continued, "It's a cardiac glycoside toxin found in flowers. Melissa—the florist at the market—reported some of her plants stolen. Lily of the valley. She said she thought little of it until she heard Wendy's cause of death."

Julia frowned. "Melissa? That might explain why she ran off earlier."

Moyes' eyes narrowed. "How well did you know her?"

"We used to be friends, but we drifted. You know how it is. Life takes you in different directions."

Moyes nodded, a flicker of understanding softening her gaze. "I hate bumping into people I used to know. They look at you like you're still the person you were when they knew you. And you never are. Not really."

Julia smiled faintly. "No, you're not."

Moyes stood, draining her latte. "Look after yourself, Julia. This will all blow over soon. You'll see. Your café will be full again before you know it."

Julia watched her leave, her words lingering like the faint scent of flowers. Almost immediately, the bell chimed again, and Katie trudged in, huddled in a pink puffer jacket. Dark circles shadowed her eyes, and she fussed over a broken nail.

"The stallholders are complaining." Katie sat in Roxy's chair. "They're not making money and threatening to get refunds. They're saying this market was..." Her bottom lip wobbled, and she said, "... they're saying it's all a *con*!"

Julia made another latte and set it in front of Katie. "The weather's not helping."

"It's not just the weather, though, is it?" Katie picked at her chipped nail varnish. "A murder isn't helping things. It's not like she died at the market, but she might as well have."

"We can't let her ruin everything we've worked for." Julia suppressed a yawn, glancing back at the clock— she'd never been more relieved to see that it was time to close. "Why don't we hand out some more flyers? We never visited Fern Moore last time we went out."

Katie wrinkled her nose. "What's the point?"

"You've put too much into this to give up now." Julia pulled a stack of bright paper from beneath the counter. "We just need to put some stickers over the 'Opening Soon' part to 'Now Open!' and they're as good as new. Some masking tape and marker pens will do it."

Katie stirred her latte with little enthusiasm. "I suppose it's better than sitting here watching the snow fall." She glanced through the window at the dark village green. "Maybe people just don't realise we're open in this weather."

"Exactly." Julia grabbed some markers from the pot on the counter. "There's still hope yet."

If Wendy came from Fern Moore, maybe answers were waiting there.

11

*G*rey tower blocks loomed over Fern Moore's courtyard, their utilitarian design stark against the white snow. Julia stamped her feet, trying to restore feeling to her frozen toes. Her Oxfords, utterly inappropriate for this weather, had long since given up any pretence of keeping her feet dry.

"This is hopeless." Katie's usually bubbly enthusiasm had deflated even further after an hour of handing out market flyers to uninterested residents. "No one wants to talk to us."

"That's just Fern Moore. I've had an idea." Julia pointed towards the warm glow spilling from Daphne's Café on the corner. "Let's grab a hot chocolate, warm up, and then we can post these through letterboxes until we've run out. We could cover half the flats with what we have left."

Katie's shoulders relaxed. "That sounds much better than standing here freezing while people ignore us."

"Nothing worth having comes easy," Julia said, squeezing Katie's arm. "The market will get there."

A flash of colour caught Julia's attention. Through the bright windows of the corner shop, bunches of flowers bobbed past. Melissa emerged, her arms laden with blooms.

"Katie, go ahead and order the hot chocolates," Julia said. "I'll catch up."

Julia followed Melissa to the ground-floor flats. Even in the gloom, one flat stood out—its window boxes overflowed with greenery despite the winter chill.

"Melissa!" Julia called out.

Keys clattered to the concrete as Melissa spun around. "Julia!" An awkward laugh escaped her. "I didn't see you there."

"I was just in the area handing out flyers for the market." Julia held up the stack of papers before scooping up Melissa's keys. "It's not going so well."

"No." Melissa lingered on her doorstep, accepting the keys with an unsure smile. "I didn't sell much today. I'm starting to think it might have been a waste of the pitch fee."

The silence stretched between them, punctuated by the distant thud of rap music from one of the flats above. Melissa shifted her weight, then gestured to the locked door. "Would you like to come in for a cup of tea?"

Julia glanced back at the café, where Katie was waiting in the queue. "I can't stay long, but a quick one would be lovely."

She followed Melissa into the flat, the scent of flowers wrapping around her like a welcoming floral blanket—she'd never been readier for spring after the long and bitter winter they'd had. Every surface hosted flowering plants: orchids, peace lilies, and countless others Julia couldn't name. Tendrils of ivy cascaded down bookshelves, and windowsills overflowed with succulents.

"I've never been able to keep houseplants alive," Julia admitted with a laugh. "I killed my daughter's monstera while she was away travelling."

"A little water twice a week, replace the topsoil when it looks dull, and give them enough sunlight," Melissa said, smiling as she fluffed at some ivy hanging from the fireplace. "You can't go wrong."

"When you put it like that, it sounds easy."

Julia settled at a small dining table while Melissa busied herself with the kettle. As the tea steeped, Melissa arranged her flowers from the corner shop into various vases and jugs.

"I can't bear to see the discounted flowers wilting away because nobody wanted them," she explained, trimming a stem. "A little nurturing, and they've still got life in them yet."

Julia glanced at the framed pictures on a shelf by the dining table and spotted one of Melissa in her college days. She sat under a tree in her apron between lessons, all smiles as she grinned at the camera—Julia couldn't be sure, but she might have been the one to take that picture. They'd had their whole lives ahead of them, both with the same dream of opening their own cafés one day.

"Do you have a shop when you're not at the market?"

Julia asked, eager to know more about Melissa's life in the years since.

"Oh, no." Melissa misted a drooping fern with a spray bottle. "I mostly sell on social media. Birthdays, weddings, that sort of thing." She paused, lowering the bottle. "I did think about opening somewhere after that flower shop closed down on Mulberry Lane years ago, but overheads are so expensive these days, and I barely keep this roof over my head since I moved back. I only got this place from the council because I moved in before my mother passed." Her eyes flicked to Julia. "I never turned into a big success like you."

Julia felt her cheeks warm as she blew on her tea. "I remember that flower shop. The woman who owned it, Harriet... she was murdered. It was a shame what happened to her." She sipped the strong tea. "Wendy, too."

"Is it?" Melissa's voice turned flat, emotionless. She caught herself, shoulders tensing. Finally, she sat down, her hands clasped together on the table. "Look, I'm not going to pretend to mourn for a woman I never liked in life. That's where I draw the line. I've done my bit, and now it's time to move on."

"Your bit?"

"Reporting to the police about my lily of the valley flowers going missing." Melissa pointed at those very flowers in a vase by the back window. "I noticed my inventory was missing when I was setting up in the morning, right after I had tea with you in the café, but I thought I might have left them here, so I didn't think much of it." She sighed, parting her hands. "But they weren't here when I got back, and after I heard Wendy was poisoned, I thought I'd better report it." She glanced at the flowers on the windowsill, tilting her head as though admiring them. "There are quite a few poisonous flowers, and lily of the valley, while beautiful in any bouquet, is poisonous from stem to petal in the wrong hands."

Julia shifted in her chair, cradling the warm cup. "Do you know who might have taken the flowers?"

Melissa shook her head. "Someone who knew they were poisonous, I suppose. It's not exactly common knowledge, but it's not a secret either."

Julia nodded. "And did you notice anything suspicious at the market?"

"What do you mean?"

"Well, there were quite a few people who seemed to have something against Wendy. Conrad, Polly and Ethan, Prudence..."

"I don't really know Prudence," Melissa said, straightening a vase. "But I know Polly and Ethan. Suspicious how?"

"Ethan was seen storming off around the time Wendy was killed."

"Oh yes!" Melissa's eyes lit up. "I did see him rush past my stall."

"How do you know each other?"

Tea sloshed over the rim as Melissa picked up her cup. "Oh, just through the craft scene," she said, grabbing a cloth to mop up the spill. "We all post online selling our wares, trying to make ends meet. Social media is the town square of the future, or so they say."

"I've never wrapped my head around it," Julia admitted. "I've always preferred the face-to-face stuff."

"You're lucky to have your café. I bet you bought it before all this inflation made everything impossible?"

Julia nodded, somehow feeling guilty for the fact. "What about Conrad?" she pressed, remembering what Jessie had shared about Polly's revelation of seeing them together in the pub. "He seems to think people will assume he's guilty. My husband is a PI and—"

"A PI husband too?" Melissa's lips twisted into a tight smile. "Nice house, lovely café, perfect family—I envy you, you know. It's funny, isn't it, how we can all start in the same place and end up so different?" She sighed, staring into her untouched tea. "But that's life."

Julia studied Melissa's tense posture, noting how she'd changed the subject when Conrad's name came up. The old wound from their college romance clearly hadn't healed, but something else lurked beneath the surface. Were they rekindling their relationship now that Wendy was out of the picture?

Julia took another sip of tea. "I heard you were getting quite cosy with Conrad at The Plough last night."

"I would hardly call it cosying up," Melissa said, rolling her eyes and lifting her tea without drinking. "I was hugging him, as a friend would. You said yourself he's worried about the attention this will bring him."

"He never used to mind attention."

"Yes, but that was before Wendy crushed his spirit," Melissa spat with unexpected venom. "I could... well, for want of a better word, kill her for what she did to him. But it seems someone beat me to it." Melissa's shoulders dropped as she met Julia's gaze. "Look, Wendy was a viper. She grew up here, in the flat above. We weren't exactly friends at school, but both of us coming from Fern Moore and going to St Peter's Primary in Peridale, we stuck together. We were a year or two above you, I think."

Julia watched Melissa's face harden as she spoke about her past with Wendy. The bitterness in her voice seemed to seep into the cosy flat's atmosphere, dulling even the vibrant flowers surrounding them.

"We were totally different as teenagers," Melissa continued, absently stroking a nearby leaf. "She became so obsessed with what people thought about her, trying to change her reputation even back then—I wasn't 'cool' enough for her, so she ditched me."

She moved to the window, gazing out at the surrounding flats. "Then, after high school, we were both on this estate, just two more Fern Moore kids with no direction or anywhere to go in life. I did nothing for a year, claiming benefits, and I didn't want it to turn into two years." She glanced back at Julia. "Wendy heard from someone that I was thinking of going to college to learn to bake, to try something new, and she latched onto me and that idea. Made it seem like we could go together, make something of ourselves, open our own bakery..." Her voice cracked. "And how did she repay me? She stole my boyfriend."

A loud thump from above made Julia jump, followed by the scraping of something across the floorboards.

"That'll be Shelly," Melissa explained, glancing up at the ceiling. "Wendy's aunt—she still lives there. You might find out more about Wendy from her, but I don't think they've been on speaking terms for years." She turned back to Julia, forcing a smile. "Now, do you want to stay for dinner? I don't have much in—I've been having guests stay, and they've eaten me out of house and home—but I have some tins of soup."

"Thanks for the offer, but I should get back," Julia said, gesturing towards Daphne's. "I left Katie there, and I've been gone longer than I meant to be. Before I go—" She paused at the door. "What do you think happened to Wendy?"

Melissa shrugged, wrapping her arms around herself. "If you think it's Conrad, you're barking up the wrong tree." She moved closer, lowering her voice. "You said that Ethan was seen leaving the market then. Maybe there's something in that? He hated her more than anyone." Her eyes darkened. "You know she ruined his bakery when his father was on his deathbed?"

Julia nodded, wondering where this was going.

"Polly said it almost destroyed him," Melissa whispered. "He's never been the same since—always held onto that resentment. But you'll want to talk to them about that. Before you go, I have something for you." She disappeared into a jungle of plants, returning with a small pot of trailing ivy. "Nobody leaves empty-handed. It's Hedera helix—English ivy. Almost impossible to kill, even for a plant murderer." A ghost of a smile crossed her face. "Twice a week."

"Twice a week," Julia repeated, cradling the pot carefully. "Thanks, Melissa. I'll try my best."

Outside, the snow had stopped. Through the café

window, Katie sat scribbling names on a notepad. Julia stepped back, her gaze drawn to the flat above. Maybe Auntie Shelly had something to say that Melissa wouldn't. She decided to make one more visit before that hot chocolate.

～

Julia climbed the concrete steps to the floor above, her footsteps echoing in the stairwell. A worn welcome mat lay before Shelly's door, its edges frayed and colours long since faded. She knocked, shifting the ivy plant Melissa had given her to her other arm.

"I'm coming! Hang on..." a voice called from inside. The sound of slow shuffling approached, followed by several locks being undone.

The door creaked open to reveal a frail woman gripping a walker, her silver hair pulled back in a loose bun. She peered at Julia through thick glasses, her expression guarded.

"What do you want? Money for charity, is it?" She adjusted her grip on the walker. "Because I can only spare a few quid, what with the price of gas lately."

"No, nothing like that," Julia said, shaking her head. "I'm here to ask about Wendy... you are Shelly, aren't you?"

Shelly's eyes narrowed as she studied Julia more closely. "You police? Press?"

"No, I'm not. I'm... someone who used to know Wendy."

"One of them, are you?" Shelly sighed, shuffling aside. "You'd better come in."

Inside, Shelly gestured towards a worn armchair positioned by an electric fire, and Julia accepted the seat. She placed the plant by her feet, noticing there was no other chair—Shelly had given her the only comfortable spot by the fire.

"I take it you heard?" Julia asked.

"That she finally crossed the wrong person?" Shelly pursed her lips, her chin disappearing into her neck. "Yes, I heard. People around here still remember her. I had eight people knock on my door to check on me yesterday, and I'll tell them what I told you... don't expect tears from me because you won't get them." She still lingered with the walker, her hands gripping it tightly. "Tea? Cake?"

"No, thank you." Julia shifted to the edge of the chair. "Do you want to—"

"You're my guest." Shelly held up her hands. "If I can't feed you, a seat is the least I can do. So, what is it you want? Because if Wendy owes you money, I'm afraid I can't help you there."

"No, it's nothing like that," Julia said. "I'm here because I wanted to find out more about Wendy. We went to college together, and we didn't exactly... get on."

"Wendy didn't get on with *most* people. If anyone, for that matter." Shelly's mouth twisted. "I can't believe she was married for as long as she was, not that I was invited to the wedding or anything. After everything I did for her..."

Julia let the silence sit for a moment, sensing there was more on the tip of Shelly's tongue.

"She'd have gone into care if it wasn't for me," Shelly muttered, almost under her breath. "Even by the age of seven, her father was ready to wash his hands of her. I felt sorry for her, as anyone would, but I quickly learned what he'd meant." She met Julia's eyes, her narrowed stare boring into her. "Do you think a child can be born evil?"

The question caught Julia off-guard, but she shook her head. "I wouldn't like to think so."

"No," Shelly said, sighing. "Nobody would, but she was a cruel child. Always terribly jealous of her siblings. She was the middle child. Her sister was a talented violinist—she plays for the national orchestra now. And her brother was close to being a professional footballer, if not for his ankle. He became an accountant in the end, but the point is, she was the child who didn't present any 'talent,' shall we say." She frowned. "Perhaps my brother cared too much about that stuff. He always was an overachiever, but the way Wendy took it out on them was beyond wicked." She glanced at Julia, but she didn't seem able to hold the stare as she whispered, "Terrible, awful things. She flushed her sister's fish down the toilet... alive. And her brother wouldn't have broken his ankle if she hadn't snipped the laces on his football boots."

"That's awful," Julia said, gulping. "It sounds like she wanted attention."

"You have children?"

Julia nodded. "Two."

"And do they ever act out like that?"

"Jessie was a handful when she was a teenager," Julia admitted, though nothing as terrible surfaced. "Nothing like that."

"No, I didn't think so." Shelly's fingers tightened around the walker, her knuckles turning white. "I thought I could change her, but... she only got worse. She had to move high school four times because of the bullying—she was *always* bullying someone about something. I think it made her feel powerful... in control." She sniffed, shaking her head. "And when she wasn't, she was stealing. I had this pet rat—oh, how I adored that rat—and she swore on my life that she didn't take it." Her eyes met Julia's with a steely glare. "I can't believe I didn't drop down dead at that very moment because I *know* she did."

Julia gulped, unable to hold Shelly's stare. "I'm sorry to tell you this, but a rat appeared in my locker at college one day."

Shelly gasped, a shaky hand going up to her mouth. "A little brown thing with white spots?"

"I didn't get the best look at it." But Julia nodded. "I think so."

"I knew it." Shelly clenched her eyes. "I *knew* it, and she promised and twisted and... did what Wendy did. My poor baby Frank. I know they don't live long, but he was such a good boy." She unclenched her eyes and a tear tumbled down her cheek. "I should have kicked her out then, but I gave her another chance. I always did. She always knew I did, and a part of me worried I'd never get rid of her, until one day..."

Shelly's voice trailed off as she turned with her walker, shuffling towards the sideboard. The elderly woman's movements were slow and deliberate, but she knocked a stack of magazines off the side table on her way.

"Oh, dear," Shelly said, making a half-hearted turn. "Never mind those. I've always been clumsy."

Julia rushed to help, gathering the scattered magazines. As she collected them, a loose page caught her attention—something was off about it. Her fingers trembled as she opened the magazine, revealing jagged edges where letters had been cut out. Her stomach dropped as she noticed more gaps, enough missing letters to spell 'TERROR.'

"These magazines..." Julia's mouth went dry as she looked up at Shelly, seeing her in a new light. "There are letters missing..."

"Are there, love?" Shelly's voice remained unconcerned as she retrieved an old letter from the drawer.

She handed it to Julia, the paper creased and covered in hasty scrawl.

I'm off to be famous and make something of my life. Thanks for nothing, you old bag.

"That's the last I heard from my *dear* niece," Shelly said through pursed lips. "And to tell you the truth, I breathed the biggest sigh of relief."

Julia swallowed hard, her grip tightening on the

magazines. "Someone sent Wendy a threatening letter. It said her reign of terror would be over."

"You don't think it was me, do you?" Shelly laughed. "I picked those magazines up in the café. I always do. They're so expensive these days, and people leave them lying around when they're done with them. There's no harm in it. Recycling, isn't it?" She brightened. "Now, how about that cup of tea?"

"No, thank you." Julia picked up the potted ivy. "Would it be alright if I took these magazines?"

"If you must, though I haven't had a chance to read those ones yet."

"I'll drop some more off," Julia promised, her heart hammering as she gathered her things and headed for the door. "Thank you."

～

The industrial ceiling pipes snaked overhead as Julia pushed open the door to Fern Moore's only café. The orange walls cast a sickly glow across the metal tables and chairs, creating an atmosphere that couldn't have been more different from her own cosy establishment. Yet the familiar hum of local chatter filled the space, proving that some things remained constant.

Katie's blonde head bobbed as she scribbled in her notepad with a fluffy pink pen, her half-empty hot chocolate growing cold beside her. Two empty sugar packets lay crumpled next to the cup. She hadn't noticed Julia's arrival, too absorbed in whatever scheme occupied her thoughts.

She approached the counter where Daphne stood, rearranging the sandwiches in the display case. "You only ever come in here when there's trouble," Daphne snapped, glancing up. "What do you want?"

"These magazines." Julia placed them on the counter, cutting to the chase. "Do you know who left them in here?"

"What sort of question is that?" Daphne's eyebrows shot up as she continued her rearranging. "How many magazines and newspapers get left in your café?"

"Good point," Julia conceded.

As Julia scanned the café, a flash of auburn caught her attention. Polly and Ethan were huddled in the corner near the toilets, their heated discussion punctuated by sharp hand gestures.

"They come in here most days lately," Daphne said, following Julia's gaze. "I think they're renting a room from someone."

"Who?" Julia asked.

"Do I look like a magic eight-ball to you?" Daphne pulled out a cigarette. "Look, are you going to order something? Because if not, I'm going on my break."

Julia gestured at Katie. "My stepmother ordered me a hot chocolate."

"Oh, *her*." Daphne rolled her eyes. "Miss Dolly Parton. I should have known she'd be one of yours."

As Daphne stepped outside for her smoke break, Julia glanced at Katie, still absorbed in her notepad. Julia approached the bathroom door as casually as possible, trying to avoid drawing attention.

"I *told* you we should have packed up and left," Polly's voice carried across the space.

"You sold most of your books today," Ethan countered.

"But the police are asking too many questions!"

"And how will it look if we leave? I need to make the pitch fee back. We *can't* leave."

"But I don't want to stay here anymore."

"We've got a free room, at least." Ethan rolled his eyes. "She's doing us a favour." His gaze suddenly locked onto Julia. "Can I help you?"

"I thought it was you." Julia attempted to smooth over the awkward moment. "I had the cruffin stall next to you?"

Polly's previously friendly demeanour had vanished, and Julia guessed the offer to swap a pie for a cruffin had long expired.

"Don't you think I noticed your husband is the PI who's taken on Conrad?" Polly bit back. "And your daughter is the journalist sniffing around. And what does that make you?"

"Someone who wants to know the truth."

With that, Polly stormed out, Ethan close behind before shooting Julia one final glare.

Strange, Julia thought to herself.

Julia settled into her chair across from Katie, the cold hot chocolate doing little to warm her spirits. The bitter tang of the drink lingered on her tongue as she placed the magazines on the table.

Katie's face glowed with enthusiasm, her pen poised over her notepad covered in looping handwriting.

"You were right, Julia," Katie said as she scribbled. "Nothing worth having comes easy. I started writing down my thoughts to get them on paper. It's something my Auntie Mary showed me." Her voice softened. "I don't know how I managed without her, you know. She's full of little bits of wisdom, just like you, and when I was writing, I realised how far I'd come."

Julia was glad to hear it, though her attention lingered on the snippet of the conversation she'd overheard between Polly and Ethan. Why was Polly in such a rush to leave, and why did Ethan want to stay?

Turning back to Katie, she asked, "What did you figure out?"

She tapped her pen against the paper. "The market is there; we just need to make sure people know about it. I need to rethink the social media strategy and get a wider distribution of the flyers, and we need some kind of stunt..." Her eyes lit up. "Do you think Barker would make a bigger song and dance about his book launch when the new ones arrive? I know he wanted a quieter launch this time, but his first book was a bestseller, and his second book did well."

"I can ask," Julia said, her attention drawn through the window to Melissa's flat, then drifting up to Shelly's above.

"Did you find what you were looking for?" Katie asked.

Julia's fingers traced the edges of the magazines. "I found something," she said, uncertainty creeping into her voice. "I'm just not sure what."

"Remember," Katie said with a wink, "nothing worth having comes easy."

∼

Through the drizzle, Julia hurried across the village, keys jangling in her cold fingers. The café's darkened windows reflected her exhausted expression as she reached for the lock.

"Just wait there, young lady!"

Her grandmother's commanding voice cut through the evening air. Dot marched towards her across the snow-covered village green, a determined finger outstretched in Julia's direction.

"I don't know why you're avoiding me, but I don't like it one bit."

"I'm a little busy, Gran, that's all."

"Yes, I can see that." Dot's lips pursed into a thin line. "Family meeting at The Comfy Corner tonight in one hour. The table is booked. No excuses. No exceptions."

Julia nodded, knowing better than to reject a dinner summons from her gran. "I'll be there."

"Good." Dot gave her a curt nod, looking her up and down. "And get changed while you're at it. You look like you've been through the wars."

Julia glanced down at herself. Her jeans were soaked through, her jumper dusted with flour, and catching her reflection in the window, she noticed her usually curly hair had flattened against her head. It had been one of those days.

In the kitchen of her dark café, she looked for the

cookbooks again, hoping that Prudence hadn't taken them on her way out. But after checking every shelf, they were still nowhere to be found.

They'd spent years hiding in her gran's attic, but she wanted them close—they stirred memories of a simpler time.

A young girl grieving her mother, trying to look after her younger sister, making sense of why their dad was always running around the country hunting antiques and why they had to live with their gran.

Maybe not so simple after all, but the thought of the cookbooks still made her feel warm inside.

Even if Prudence, in reality these days, was anything but warm.

A commotion from outside drew her attention. Through the back door, she found police officers confronting Prudence about her van behind the post office, threatening arrest.

"I'm doing nobody any harm!" Prudence cried, clinging onto her van door while the officers tried to pull her out. "This isn't right!"

"You've been told you can't park here," one of the officers cried. "Resisting won't make this easier."

Julia stepped in beside DI Moyes. "If Prudence moves the van, will she be out of trouble?"

DI Moyes nodded, blowing her vape smoke into the air. "As long as she doesn't leave the village."

Julia sighed. "I have an idea, and Barker isn't going to like it."

12

Thick fog blanketed Peridale as Julia smoothed down the red vintage dress, its white trim catching the light of the bedside lamp. The fabric hugged her waist before flaring into a full skirt—exactly the sort of dress she'd planned to wear over Christmas, if only there'd been an occasion.

"Almost ready?" Barker adjusted his tie in the mirror while Olivia sat cross-legged on their bed, stroking Mowgli with exaggerated gentleness.

"Softly, softly," Olivia whispered to the cat, who purred contentedly under her careful touch.

Julia turned so Barker could zip up her dress. "What do you make of Conrad sending money to Wendy? The timing of him stopping seems suspicious."

"Having the loan people on his back wouldn't have helped," Barker said, his fingers tracing up her spine with the zip. "And I still think he's hiding something from me."

"And Melissa," Julia added, stepping away to help straighten his tie. "She knows more than she's letting on about those flowers. The way she rattled off details about how toxic they are—"

"Like someone who's studied their effects?"

"Exactly." Julia's hands stilled on his tie. "And she got a little defensive when I brought up Conrad. Almost like—"

"Like she's protecting him?" Barker caught her hands in his. "They're both hiding something. The question is, are they hiding it together or from each other?"

Olivia giggled as Mowgli rolled onto his back, paws batting at the air. The sound broke through Julia's racing thoughts, grounding her in the simple joy of getting dressed up with her family, even if only for dinner at The Comfy Corner.

"It's Polly and Ethan I want to find out more about," Barker said, staring off into the distance. "After what you overheard at Fern Moore, they're obviously up to something. They were far too defensive with Jessie, and—"

The melodic strains of *Close to You* drifted through their bedroom window, the soft music slicing through the evening fog. Julia froze, her hands still resting on Barker's tie.

Barker's brow furrowed. "Am I going mad, or can you hear that too?"

"Oh, you can hear it," Julia said, crossing to the window. "Do you want the good news or the bad news?"

"Julia..." His tone carried a warning.

"Prudence isn't plugged into your office anymore."

Julia tugged back the heavy curtain. Prudence's van glowed softly through the swirling fog at the bottom of their garden. "The bad news is..."

A sharp knock echoed from the back door. Before either of them could respond, the door creaked open.

"Need water," Prudence called. The tap squeaked, followed by the sound of bottles being filled.

Julia and Barker stood in their bedroom doorway, watching Prudence shuffle out and disappear back into the fog, but not before shooting a particularly sour look at Barker.

"Julia..." Barker groaned, rubbing his temples.

"What else was I supposed to do? The police were causing trouble."

"Maybe you should have let them?" he huffed. "We don't know what kind of trouble she'll bring us. Can we even trust her?"

"This is a good way to find out," Julia said, smoothing her dress. "It's not like either of us has got anything from her yet." She grabbed her handbag from the dresser and checked the time on her bedside clock. "Come on, we don't want to be late. My gran's already on the warpath—she's going to want to know everything."

❦

"A *rat*?" Dot exclaimed at their table in The Comfy Corner. "Wendy put a living rat in your locker?"

"And not just any rat," Julia said, pulling her chair in closer. "Her aunt's pet rat—Frank."

"Poor Frank," Jessie said, lifting her beer bottle in a toast. "What happened to him?"

Julia wished she knew. "He jumped out and ran off, and nobody was in a hurry to chase after him. If only I'd known he was a pet."

"What possessed her to do such a thing?" Brian, Julia's father, asked, as bewildered as Dot—and everyone else around the table. Mary had seated them in the snug, a small room off the main part of the restaurant, and Julia was glad of the privacy.

"Symbolic, isn't it?" Jessie said, as though it were obvious. "Julia ratted her out for trying to cheat in the exam."

Julia almost laughed. Even after all these years, she'd never made the connection—or even tried to—beyond the shock of the cruelty. Everyone else around the table, from Katie to Percy—Sue and Neil were at home, their twins down with a cold—looked suitably horrified.

"Well, at least it wasn't one of them wild rats," Dot said after a moment, waving her hand at the ground as though an army of 'wild rats' might march through at any second. "Imagine if it had bitten you. You might have died from The Black Death!"

"I think she was a few centuries too late for that," Barker corrected after sipping his pint. "And technically, it was the fleas that—"

"Well, rabies, then!" Dot cut in. "It's lunacy. It's—"

"Evil," Brian concluded.

A murmur of agreement rippled around the table.

"I still don't understand why you didn't tell us," Dot

urged, her pursed lips softening into a more sympathetic expression now that she'd heard most of the story. "We could have sorted it out."

Julia sighed, noticing her father hadn't said the same. He'd taken her mother's death hard and had still been avoiding what was left of his family life at the time.

"Because I didn't want to make things worse," Julia said finally. "And the less she knew about my life, the better. I made the mistake of taking Mum's old recipe book into college, and once she found out she'd died, it was more ammunition for her." She paused, holding back the detail she'd only ever told Sue. "She egged the grave. And poured flour on it, and salt all over the flowers we planted."

The table fell silent as everyone digested Julia's words. The fire crackled in the corner of the snug, its warmth doing little to melt the chill left by memories of Wendy's cruelty. Julia felt a wave of gratitude for her family's support, despite their shock and anger at Wendy's actions from years past. After so many years of locking those memories away, a weight lifted at letting the light in.

"Evil!" Brian said again quietly, his fist clenching. Katie rested her hand over his, squeezing tight. "Just pure evil."

Julia shifted in her seat. She wasn't sure if Wendy was evil—just maladjusted. Learning about her upbringing and how her parents had given her away twisted something in Julia's gut that she hadn't expected. The bullying hadn't stemmed from nowhere, and Shelly had admitted that Wendy's father put too much emphasis on his children being 'talented.' After years of wondering, Wendy finally made some sense to her.

"I think she was jealous I could bake so naturally," Julia admitted, shifting again. "Not to toot my own horn, but she wasn't very good, and you know it's always been like second nature to me. I started so young, and—"

"You're the best baker in Peridale!" Dot declared, thumping a finger on the table. "Nobody even comes close, and everybody knows it."

"Well, I think Wendy wanted to be the best in the country. I think she just wanted to win."

"And look where that got her," Jessie muttered.

They sat in contemplative silence once more.

Percy's eyes lit up. "Oh, Dorothy! Don't forget what we wanted to show them. It might be useful."

"Oh, yes." Dot fumbled with her phone, squinting at the screen as her fingers moved painfully slowly across it. "Ethel insisted I take a picture of her at her gnome stall to commemorate the occasion, and I didn't realise at the time, but it was after that performance from Wendy with the nail in the cruffin."

She turned the phone around, pushing it towards the middle of the table. "I took it from behind the stall, so it's looking out at the other side. And look who's there —and who isn't."

The group leaned in to study the image. Julia did the same, taking in the details—Jessie behind the cruffin stall while Julia had hidden away in the café, too mortified to face anyone after Wendy's theatrical display with the nail. Prudence's sauce jars stood unattended.

Ethan's van appeared empty, but Polly remained at her bookstall.

"Two of your suspects are missing," Dot declared with satisfaction. "It isn't looking good for them."

Barker cleared his throat. "It proves they weren't there at that moment. It's not conclusive. There's about an hour window before Wendy was found dead."

"Yes, but that can't have been the only picture taken at the market." Jessie's eyes widened. "Dot, you're a genius!"

"Thank you." Dot nodded in agreement. "I know."

"That you are, my love," Percy added. "Why, exactly?"

But Jessie turned to Katie. "Can you check the social media accounts for the market? People might have taken pictures and tagged or used hashtags or whatever... there might be more to see from other people's perspectives."

Katie exhaled, pulling out her pink phone. "I haven't been able to face what people have been saying."

"Now might be the time," Julia said, nodding at Jessie's suggestion. "It's a good idea."

"Well, it was my idea, really," Dot interjected, fluffing up her curls.

Mary Porter burst through the snug's door with a tray of steaming bowls balanced expertly in her hands and up her arms. "Soup before your mains," she announced, her cheeks rosy from the kitchen heat. "On the house, of course."

"Oh, Mary, you don't have to keep giving us free food," Katie protested, but Mary waved her off.

"Nonsense. You're family now." Mary distributed the

bowls with practised efficiency. "And this is how I treat my family." She paused to kiss Katie's cheek, then gave Barker's shoulder an affectionate pat. The gesture carried the weight of gratitude—if not for Barker's investigation into the Wellington Heights twisted tree cold case last year, Katie might never have discovered Mary was her aunt.

Olivia's plastic spoon had barely touched the soup when it splashed across her dress. Her bottom lip trembled before she burst into tears.

"I'll take her to clean up," Jessie offered, already half-rising from her chair.

"No, it's fine—I'll go." Julia lifted Olivia from her seat, cradling her against her hip to avoid spreading the soup stain.

As they made their way to the bathroom, movement in the corner of the room caught Julia's eye.

There, in what the regulars dubbed 'lovers' corner'—Mary's designated spot for watching over potential romance—sat Melissa and Conrad, heads bent close in conversation.

Mary appeared at Julia's elbow. "They've been coming in quite a bit these past few weeks," she whispered, nodding towards the pair. "Do you know them?"

"Sort of," Julia replied. "I used to."

Julia lingered by the bathroom door, her eyes fixed on Melissa and Conrad through the gap. The intimate way they leaned towards each other sent a chill down her spine. Melissa's fingers crept across the wooden table, inching closer to Conrad's hand.

Olivia's wails crescendoed, the sound bouncing off the bathroom tiles. Julia pressed her lips together, torn between maternal duty and investigative instinct. A few heads turned in the restaurant, and Julia caught Melissa's startled glance in their direction.

Before they could spot her watching, Julia ducked into the bathroom. Her hands trembled as she dampened paper towels and dabbed at Olivia's dress. The soup had left an orange stain across the white fabric.

Just friends, Melissa had claimed. Yet everything about their body language spoke of something deeper, something hidden. Julia's mind raced back to their conversation in Melissa's flat—how defensive she'd been about Conrad, how quick to deflect attention elsewhere.

"Messy," Olivia whimpered, squirming as Julia scrubbed at the stain.

"I know, sweetheart. Almost done." Julia's movements slowed, but her thoughts accelerated. If Melissa had lied about her relationship with Conrad, what else might she have lied about?

The bathroom door creaked, and Julia's heart jumped—but it was just another customer. Julia lifted Olivia onto the counter, focusing on the dress while her peripheral vision caught Melissa and Conrad's reflection through the door before it closed. Their hands had met in the middle of the table now, fingers intertwined.

The evening air nipped at Barker's ears as he stood outside The Comfy Corner, phone pressed to his cheek. Casper's gravelly voice brought a touch of warmth despite the cold, though his eldest brother had never sounded quite so old.

"Just wanted to check in, little brother," Casper said, already sounding ready to wrap up the brief call that had pulled Barker away from the table. "Sorry we couldn't make it up for Christmas."

"No worries, we had a full house as it was," Barker replied, peering through the window into the snug where Jessie and Katie were deep in their social media research. "How are you and Heather?"

"Can't complain. Thinking of taking the camper van down south when the weather improves. We might pass through your neck of the woods."

"You're welcome to park in our garden," Barker said, trying–and failing—to hide his annoyance about their new guest. "Seems everyone else is."

The familiar, comfortable silence settled between them. Casper, an army veteran, had never been one for lengthy conversations, preferring actions to words. Their calls had become less frequent, but the bond remained strong.

"Better go. Heather's made dinner," Casper said, clearing his throat. "Lamb chops." Barker heard Heather call something in the background. "She wants to know if Olivia liked the penguin?"

"Tell her it hasn't left Olivia's side since Christmas morning."

"Good, good. Take care, Barker."

"You too, Cas—"

A shadow moved in Barker's peripheral vision. He spun around to find Katie huddled on the doorstep, hugging herself against the cold. Startled, his foot hit a patch of ice, and he stumbled backwards.

Katie lunged forward, grabbing his arm. "Steady there."

Barker steadied himself on Katie's supportive grip. Her eyes held that familiar determined glint that always made his stomach tighten.

"I couldn't help but notice Casper's name on your phone before you slipped out," Katie said, her voice carrying a hint of rehearsal. "How is he?"

"Good," Barker replied, pocketing his phone. He knew exactly where this conversation was headed. "We should go back—"

"Look, I know this has nothing to do with what's going on right now, but did you..." Katie twisted her hands together and said, "... did you ask him if he knows anything about who your father might be?"

These conversations with Katie always left him wrong-footed. Every few weeks, she brought it up, and every few weeks, he gave her the same answer. "No, nothing yet. It was just a quick check-in."

"But remember our deal last year?" Katie's voice softened. "You help me find my mother, and I help you find your father. You found my mother, and she might have been dead, but it brought me my Auntie Mary. Let me help repay the favour."

"You don't owe me, Katie."

"But I promised." She stepped closer, her breath carrying a hint of wine. "We promised each other."

Barker glanced longingly at the restaurant's warm interior. "It's not going to be so simple for me. My mum didn't tell me. Or anyone, for that matter. And one of the last things she said to me was not to look for him. I promised I wouldn't—"

"Don't you want to know where you came from?" She ducked to meet his avoidant gaze. "Aren't you curious?"

"Katie, I—"

Her hand found his shoulder. "Ask your brother."

"I did. Years ago."

"Then ask him *again*."

"Please, Katie—"

A sharp rap on the window interrupted them. Through the frosted glass, Barker spotted Jessie's urgent wave beckoning them inside. He released a relieved breath—perhaps too obviously—and slipped past Katie into The Comfy Corner.

The scene that greeted him stopped him in his tracks. Every face around the table wore expressions of shock and scandal—even Mary, who'd emerged from the kitchen, stood frozen with a serving spoon suspended mid-air.

"You'll want to see this, Dad," Jessie said, her fingers flying across her phone screen. "We did find something in the tagged pictures, and we almost missed it, but—"

"My sharp eyes noticed," Dot cut in, adjusting her brooch with pride. "Go on, Jessie. Do that thing again."

Jessie pinched the screen and zoomed in on what appeared to be a typical market photo—a young woman posing with one of Julia's cruffins held aloft in that affected way social media demanded. But as the image expanded, Barker's attention locked onto Conrad's clock stall in the background. His stomach dropped.

Half-concealed behind Conrad's battered Volvo stood Conrad himself, locked in an intimate embrace with none other than Wendy. And their lips were pressed together in an unmistakable kiss.

～

Still in the bathroom, Julia finished dabbing at Olivia's soup-stained dress with a damp paper towel. The door creaked open, and Melissa's reflection appeared in the mirror. Her cheeks were flushed, perhaps from wine or something else entirely.

"Julia! Twice in one day." Melissa smiled, leaning in for a quick hug. "What brings you here? Oh, is this your youngest!" Her face lit up. "What an angel."

"An angel covered in soup." Julia laughed. "Say 'hello,' Liv."

"Hello," Olivia chirped as Julia let her down onto the floor. "Hungry, Mummy."

"We'll go back in a minute," Julia said, ruffling her hair. "We're just here for a family dinner." Pausing, she wondered if she should confront Melissa about the hand-holding she'd just seen—but decided to give her the benefit of the doubt. "And you?"

"Oh, I'm here with Conrad." Melissa leaned against

the sink, fiddling with her bracelet. "The poor man's been absolutely beside himself since... well, you know. The police seem convinced he had something to do with Wendy's death. They think he wanted to stop the payments he'd been making to her for that blasted cooking school." Julia watched Melissa's nervous movements in the mirror as she rambled on. "I'm just trying to be there for him, as any friend would. Take his mind off things with a nice meal out." Melissa's lips curved into a sympathetic smile that didn't quite reach her eyes. "I hate seeing him like this."

Julia's mind flashed to the image of their fingers intertwined at the corner table, the intimate way they'd been sitting. The word 'friend' hung in the air between them, its falseness as obvious as the blush staining Melissa's cheeks.

Melissa's shoulders slumped as she dabbed at her eyes with a tissue. Her carefully maintained composure cracked, tears welling up and spilling over.

"Are you alright?" Julia asked softly.

"No, I'm not," Melissa replied, her voice quivering. "Nothing's alright."

Julia reached across the sink for the blue paper towels. She passed a handful to Melissa, who accepted them with trembling fingers.

"I've tried to keep going like normal, but I barely slept last night." Melissa twisted the paper between her hands. "Wendy's already taken so much from me. I promised myself I'd never let her get to me again, but... someone's trying to frame me, I know it." She glanced around the empty bathroom before moving closer to

Julia. "They took those flowers from *my* stall for a reason. I know how it looks." She blew her nose, the sound echoing off the bathroom tiles. "Everyone knew about our history. I'm the perfect person to blame, aren't I? If I could afford to hire Barker like Conrad did..." She trailed off, fresh tears falling. "Mary mentioned you're something of a super sleuth?"

"I wouldn't say that exactly." Julia clasped her hands tight, her fingers wringing together. "But I have helped sort things out now and then."

"You were always like that." Melissa smiled through the tears. "Remember when my college bag was stolen on the bus? You tracked down where they must have got off and found it dumped in that bush."

The memory surfaced in Julia's mind—a younger Melissa crying over her lost coursework, Julia piecing together which stop the thief had taken. She smiled at the recollection.

"You were always good like that," Melissa said softly.

"I'll try to help you," Julia said. "But you need to be honest with me. Are you and Conrad together now?"

Melissa's brow furrowed as she shook her head. "No, why would you think that?"

"I saw you holding hands at your table."

"Oh." Melissa's gaze dropped to the floor. "We've just grown close lately. Too much has happened for anything more, but... I'll always care about him."

Melissa dabbed at her eyes one final time before disappearing into a cubicle. The lock clicked shut behind her.

Julia guided Olivia towards the bathroom door, her

mind churning over Melissa's words. The tears had seemed genuine, but something about the conversation nagged at her. Melissa's initial composure had crumbled. Her former classmate's behaviour reminded Julia of their college days when Melissa would seek Julia's help with coursework or personal problems.

Back then, Julia had always jumped in to assist, but now she wondered if she'd been too quick to offer her help this time.

As they stepped back into the restaurant's warmth, Julia's uncertainty wavered. Perhaps she was being unfair, viewing everything through a lens of suspicion after Wendy's death. But then again, the last time she'd ignored her instincts about someone's true nature, she'd ended up with a rat in her locker.

Julia stepped back into the dining room just as Barker confronted Conrad at his table. Their voices carried across the quiet restaurant.

"Don't deny it, Conrad," Barker's tone hardened. "It's right there on the screen."

"T-that's not me," Conrad stuttered.

"It is," Barker insisted. "You were kissing Wendy the morning of the market."

Conrad shrank into his chair. "Fine!," he cried. "Look, I thought if I showed some interest, she might back off about the money. I was desperate, alright? But that doesn't make me a murderer." He ran a hand through his dishevelled hair. "It only proves I haven't been entirely truthful."

Conrad's phone buzzed. The colour drained from his face as he read the message.

"What is it?" Barker asked.

"Unknown number." Conrad's hands shook. "'You'll pay for what you've done.' I keep getting these kinds of messages. It's been happening for weeks. I thought it was from Wendy, but—"

Julia stepped forward and asked, "What have you done?"

"I-I don't know," he said, searching her eyes as though for an escape. "I didn't kill her. I didn't. I swear, I *didn't.*"

Conrad bolted for the door, shoving Barker aside. Barker stumbled backwards into Mary, and she dropped her soup tray. Hot liquid splashed across Julia's vintage dress. Typical. Twice in one evening.

Melissa emerged from the bathroom, scanning the room. "Where's Conrad?"

"He ran off." Julia dabbed at her dress with a napkin. "He got a strange message on his phone."

"*Another* one?" Melissa muttered, snatching her coat off the back of her chair. "I've told him to go to the police time and time again, but he insists it's under control." She threw on her coat before tucking money for their meal under her plate. "I should find him. He needs a friend right now."

"Be careful," Julia called after her.

Back at their table in the snug, Dot had her arms folded and her lips back to being pursed. "Nice of you to rejoin us—everything's gone cold."

"Not everything," Julia said, her mind churning as she slipped into her seat behind her untouched Peridale

Pie and mash. "In fact, I'd say things are starting to heat up."

~

Jessie hunched over her phone at Richie's, her fingers cramping from endless scrolling through social media. Empty glasses lined the bar where other customers had sat hours ago. A half-drunk espresso martini sat beside her laptop.

"Still at it?" Richie wiped down the counter, nodding at the latest edition of *The Peridale Post* spread out next to her.

"Trying to save Mum's reputation," Jessie replied, rubbing her tired eyes. "Trying to save the paper... just trying my best, really."

"What have you found?" Richie leaned across with a twinkle in his eyes. "Anything juicy?"

"I've been combing through Peridale Chat for market photos." Jessie pulled up her timeline notes. "Dot's picture was taken around ten-thirty, and according to what Veronica remembers, we found Wendy at almost noon. Prudence and Ethan were definitely missing then. And Melissa? Nowhere to be seen in that photo of the girl with the cruffin at eleven."

"So between eleven and twelve—"

"Wendy left for the office, and someone went with her." Jessie slumped forward. "But I can't find a single photo from that time frame. It's like everyone stopped taking pictures right when we needed them most."

A yawn escaped before she could stifle it.

"I'm closing up soon," Richie said, stacking glasses, "but you're welcome to stay while I clean."

"It's alright." Jessie packed away her laptop. "Early start at the café tomorrow, and those long shifts drag when it's as quiet as this."

Outside, fog had settled thick and heavy over the village green. The warm glow from Dot's cottage windows barely penetrated the gloom on one side, while the post office and café had vanished completely into the white void on the other.

As she pushed through the dense fog, a dark silhouette materialised near the café's entrance. The figure, dressed entirely in black, hunched over the letterbox.

"Can I help you?" Jessie called out, her voice cutting through the silence.

The figure spun around, shoving past her with unexpected force. Jessie's feet slipped on a patch of black ice, sending her crashing onto her side. Pain shot through her body as she hit the frozen ground. Ahead, the mysterious person also lost their footing, stumbling on the treacherous surface.

Gritting her teeth against the stabbing pain, Jessie scrambled up and gave chase. But the figure had already melted into the fog, leaving only footprints that quickly disappeared in the murky whiteness. Something caught her eye—a mobile phone lay abandoned on the ground, an old model with physical buttons and a tiny green screen.

Using her café key, Jessie let herself inside, locking the door behind her. On the doormat lay what had been posted through the letterbox—an A4 sheet with words cut from magazine clippings spelling out 'BACK OFF!'

Jessie eased herself into a chair, wincing at the throbbing pain in her back. She snapped a photo of the threatening letter and sent it to her mum.

JESSIE

I think this means we're getting close…

13

Through the kitchen window, grey light filtered in as Julia finished packing Olivia's lunch. The snow from yesterday had turned to slush, making the garden path treacherous. Steam curled from the fresh cup of tea she'd made for Prudence as she navigated towards the camper van.

Before Julia could knock, the door swung open. Prudence stood there, wrapped in layers of mismatched clothing, already sipping from a chipped mug.

"I'm heading to market." Prudence set down the cup and thrust a cardboard box of sauce bottles at Julia. "Make yourself useful."

Julia caught the box, nearly dropping her extra cup of tea. The weight of the glass bottles surprised her. "I could drive you down if you'd like?"

Prudence's mouth tightened, but she gave a sharp nod. Julia was starting to understand Prudence—she needed help, but she could never ask for it. She either took it without asking or waited for the offer.

Setting the box of fresh sauces by the ashes in the firepit, Julia cleared her throat. "About my cookbooks..."

"*My* cookbooks."

"They were gifts from my gran," Julia kept her voice gentle but firm. "And they mean a lot to me. I used to watch your show with my mother before she passed away, so they have a lot of sentimental value."

Prudence's rigid posture softened slightly. "Your mother died?"

Julia nodded. "When I was twelve."

"I was fifteen." Prudence's voice grew quiet. "Cancer."

"Snap," Julia said.

The word hung between them in the cold morning air. For a moment, they stood in silence, connected by an old shared grief that transcended their current tensions.

Prudence disappeared into the van, and Julia's heart sank. Perhaps she'd pushed too far, too fast. The morning chill crept through her cardigan as she waited, listening to the muffled sounds of rummaging from within.

The door creaked open, and Prudence emerged, clutching the old cookbooks to her chest. Her weathered fingers traced the embossed letters of her name on the cover before extending them towards Julia.

"I never wanted to write these, you know." Prudence's voice carried a hint of her former warmth. "They seemed so silly when people could copy down the recipes from the show. But the money..." She chuckled to herself. "... the money was good, not that I saved it, mind you. But seeing them now has brought back a lot of memories."

Julia accepted the books, holding them close. "Thank you. Some good memories, I hope?"

Prudence's gaze grew distant, a small smile playing at the corners of her mouth. "Yes. Those were happy years. Before the ratings slide, before the world changed, and changed, and changed again." Her smile faded. "Before they started treating me like a has-been."

"Before Wendy turned up?" Julia ventured, and Prudence nodded. "What was she like?"

"Helpful, at first. A shot in the arm that I thought I needed—they *convinced* me I needed her." Prudence's lips twisted. "They kept calling her 'fresh,' which must have meant that I was 'stale.' I brought her on as an assistant during my cooking with the public segments."

"I remember those!" Julia grinned, nodding at the memories. "I think we might have applied."

"You and thousands." Prudence's laugh was genuine, a glimpse of the woman Julia remembered from her childhood television screen. "That was always my favourite part of the show—out of the stuffy studio and into real people's homes."

Julia caught herself staring, remembering DI Moyes' words about bumping into people from years ago—how we expect them to be the same person they were. She looked away, not wanting to burden Prudence with those expectations of the past. In that moment, the murder investigation faded away, and Julia was that little girl again, sat cross-legged in front of the screen, hanging on every word from a woman she didn't know, but adored.

AGATHA FROST

"I can show you," Prudence said, wafting Julia into the van.

Julia hesitated for a moment, unable to believe she'd been invited inside She climbed into the cramped space, but it was warmer and cosier than it looked from the outside. The scent of herbs and spices mingled with old leather. Stacks of boxes lined the sides, filled with what looked like memorabilia from another life. A small television balanced precariously on a fold-out table, its ancient dials worn smooth with use.

Prudence rifled through a cardboard box, muttering under her breath as she pulled out plastic cases. She found the one she wanted and slotted it into an old VHS player. The familiar sound of tape rewinding filled the space. Julia perched on the edge of the worn sofa, watching the static-filled screen flicker to life.

The image that appeared wasn't the cosy kitchen studio Julia remembered from the *Culinary Delights* of her childhood. Instead, harsh lighting illuminated a modern set with chrome fixtures and gleaming surfaces. It looked more like a spaceship than a kitchen.

"Wendy suggested new ways," Prudence said, her voice tight. "Fresh ideas—out with the old..."

On screen, Prudence and Wendy stood in someone's home kitchen. Prudence's bouffant hair from the book cover was gone, replaced with something sleek and straight that didn't suit her much. Julia's stomach clenched as she watched Wendy tear into the contestant's cooking technique, her cruel words bringing back memories of similar attacks in college.

The camera zoomed in on the contestant's trembling

hands as they presented a lopsided Victoria sponge. Wendy leaned forward, her lips curling into a smirk that didn't reach her cold eyes.

"Let me be *honest* with you," Wendy began, her tone dripping with faux sympathy. "If I served this to my worst enemy, I'd expect a lawsuit for emotional distress. It's not just bad—it's *offensive*. The texture? Like chewing on a brick. The flavour? I've had more excitement licking a postage stamp."

The contestant's face fell, but Wendy wasn't finished. She picked up a fork and poked at the cake, her nose wrinkling in exaggerated disgust.

"And what is this supposed to be? A sponge? It's so dense, I'm surprised it didn't collapse the table."

Prudence shifted uncomfortably beside her, clearly trying to interject, but Wendy steamrolled on.

"I'll give you one thing—it's memorable. Unfortunately, for all the wrong reasons." The contestant's eyes welled up, but Wendy's expression remained icy. "If this is your best, I'd hate to see your worst."

Prudence ejected the tape before they sat in the silence left behind by Wendy's harsh critiques.

"*Entertainment*, they called it." Prudence's fingers twisted together. "I didn't want to go along with it, but I didn't feel like I had a choice. This show was my life, and it needed to survive. But this made the ratings worse." She yanked the tape out. "And then Wendy got me fired."

Julia sighed. "How?"

"She knew I had a live microphone on and goaded

me into talking bad about the executive producer. I was so frustrated and *angry*... and I didn't hold back. Twenty years of grievances poured out of me as I walked right into her trap." She slotted the tape back into its case. "And I lost everything. My show, my endorsements... and after all those years of hard work, I didn't have the energy to try and get it back, so I let it all slide away."

Julia's heart broke for Prudence. "What happened to the show?"

"Wendy took over. They moved it to a digital channel." A bitter smile crossed Prudence's face. "It was cancelled the next year. That was my silver lining. I hoped I'd never see her again, but I did. She always seemed to pop up at markets and fairs, always trying to flog her latest project. I always stayed out of her way, but she always made sure to smirk at me whenever our eyes met. Like she was telling me she'd won, but I knew the truth—she might have taken everything from me to claim it as her own, but she *never* rose to *my* heights." She gave a satisfied nod. "And now she never will."

Julia's heart raced as she watched Prudence gather her things. The question burned in her throat—did you kill her?—but something held her back. Perhaps it was the shared moment they'd just experienced or the vulnerability Prudence had shown in sharing her past.

"Let's go," Prudence announced, stepping out of the van. "These sauces won't sell themselves, and I'm going to need to recoup my costs for the next batch."

They loaded the boxes into Julia's aqua blue Ford Anglia, the vintage car's boot creaking as they stacked the sauce bottles carefully. The drive down to the market was slow, the wheels crunching through yesterday's slushy snow. Prudence hummed quietly beside her, lost in her own world.

Julia found herself relaxing in the peaceful moment. Despite everything—the murder investigation, the threatening note, the chaos at the market—she couldn't deny that she was growing fond of this older version of Prudence. The gruff exterior masked someone who'd been deeply hurt, someone who understood loss.

"I have a question," Julia started, knowing she was stepping on safe territory. "How did you end up at this market? I know you said you were always bumping into Wendy, but far too many people connected to her were here for it to be a coincidence."

"Someone slipped a flyer under my wiper while I was at a market in Oxford," she revealed. "Didn't see who they were."

The car rolled to a stop in the new parking space behind her café. Julia pulled up the handbrake with a metallic clank.

"Prudence, I need to ask you something about Wendy..."

But Prudence had already grabbed her box and darted towards her stall, leaving Julia alone in the car. The window of opportunity had slammed shut once again.

Julia didn't regret letting the moment pass without pressing harder for answers, though she knew she should have. Understanding Prudence's story had changed things, even if it hadn't cleared up the mystery of Wendy's death.

Julia pushed through the café's front door, the bell's cheerful jingle at odds with her troubled thoughts. Sue and Jessie were already inside getting ready for the day ahead.

"Light bake today?" Julia hung her coat on the rack.

"Hardly worth firing up the ovens." Sue concentrated on piping delicate swirls onto a carrot cake. "Nobody's coming in anyway."

Julia's steps faltered as she spotted the note on the kitchen island. 'BACK OFF!' The magazine cut-out letters seemed to pulse against the white paper, making her stomach clench.

Sue's hands trembled slightly as she continued icing, her gaze avoiding the threatening message. "You need to stop getting involved in these cases. It's not safe."

"This one got involved with me." Julia gestured at the empty tables beyond the counter. "This is Wendy's doing. We need to set the story straight and solve this to get our customers back."

Jessie shifted in her chair, wincing. "I nearly had them last night. If it weren't for that hidden ice—"

"Thank goodness for the ice." Julia's voice sharpened. "They could have been armed."

Moving closer to examine the note, Julia noticed something caught beneath one of the letters. "Have you seen this?" She leaned in, squinting. "There's an auburn hair stuck here—between the 'B' and the paper. It's been glued in."

"Could be a coincidence," Sue said.

"Or it could be Polly's," Jessie replied.

Julia straightened, her jaw set. "I'm calling DI Moyes."

∼

PC Jake Puglisi rocked on his heels, his police radio crackling at his hip. Through the kitchen window, Julia and DI Moyes huddled over the threatening note. Barker maintained his position by his office vestibule door, resisting the urge to join them.

"Your newsletter said *The Man in the Field* would be out by now," Puglisi said, his eyes bright with enthusiasm. "Can't wait to read the finished thing... if you have a copy?"

"There've been some technical difficulties with the printing." Barker shifted his weight, glancing back at the kitchen window. "It'll be out soon, hopefully. Though this case has thrown a spanner in the works."

"Tell me about it. Boss hasn't stopped since that woman dropped dead in the newspaper office." Puglisi nodded towards Moyes. "She's barely slept."

Barker leaned closer, sensing an opening with the young and eager constable. In an almost gossipy tone, he revealed, "I've taken on one of the suspects as a client."

"Oh?" Puglisi's eyes widened. "Which one?"

"The ex-husband."

"I think he did it," Puglisi whispered, bouncing on the balls of his feet. "It's always the ex, isn't it?"

"Me too." The words slipped out before Barker could stop them.

While he wasn't entirely convinced of Conrad's guilt

yet, getting the young—and loose-lipped—PC on his side could prove useful. He let the silence sit until Puglisi looked fit to bursting.

"Found anything fishy?" Puglisi asked in a hushed tone, leaning closer.

"A few things."

"You know he's got previous?" Puglisi muttered, glancing at the window. Barker said nothing, sensing more was on the way. "Nasty business, that." He shook his head. "You can't go around hitting students with mixing bowls. And those threatening messages he sent when she tried to sue? Proper creepy."

Did he now? Barker thought to himself as he filed away this new information.

"*Puglisi!*" DI Moyes called from the kitchen door.

He rolled his eyes. "Duty calls. But save me a copy of that book when it's ready, yeah?"

"Oh, I will." Barker patted his shoulder, his mind already racing with this fresh revelation about Conrad's past.

Barker crossed the market, a mess of melted snow and grit. A decent number of stallholders braved the day, but customers were thin on the ground as the wind whipped up a frenzy. Puglisi's words echoed in his mind. It was all adding up to a damning picture. Helping Wendy ruin Ethan's business, the precarious money situation, the kiss, and now assault and threatening letters.

Barker found Conrad carefully buffing a clock, his actions deliberate and nearly robotic—his mind seemed to be somewhere else.

"We need to talk," Barker said.

Conrad's hand stilled. "There's nothing to talk about."

"You lied to me."

Conrad sighed, placing the cloth down. "I panicked. Look, I don't need your services anymore. Hiring you was a mistake."

"A mistake to hire a PI when your ex-wife turns up dead?"

Conrad's eyes flickered. "I'll pay you for the hours you've worked. It might take a while, but—"

"I know about the loan," Barker interrupted. "The payments to Wendy. The court case. The fake reviews of Ethan's business." He stepped closer. "You're not so innocent, Conrad."

"You don't know the first thing!" Conrad roared, his temper flaring up in a heartbeat.

He swept his arm across the stall, knocking over a crate filled with intricately crafted clocks. Barker lunged forward, catching a few, but several plummeted to the ground, cracking against the paving stones.

Barker watched as Melissa rushed over from her flower stall, her hands outstretched in a placating gesture.

"Conrad, please," she said, her voice soft but urgent. "Don't get yourself so worked up."

But Conrad was beyond reason. He whirled on her, his face contorted with rage. "Just leave me alone," he screamed, his voice cracking. "Everyone just leave me alone!"

He stormed off, leaving the trail of shattered clocks

in his wake. Melissa stood frozen, her hand pressed to her mouth as she struggled to hold back tears. Barker felt a pang of sympathy for her, caught in the middle of this tangled web.

Across the market, Barker noticed Ethan and Polly watching the scene with smug expressions. They seemed to take a perverse pleasure in Conrad's meltdown. But their satisfaction was short-lived as police officers emerged from the café and made a beeline for Polly.

Polly's face fell as the officers approached her pie stall, her smug arrogance crumbling before Barker's eyes. She began to protest loudly, her voice rising to a shrill pitch that drew curious stares from every corner of the market. The scene grew increasingly chaotic as she planted her feet and refused to budge, forcing the officers to take her by the elbows.

Ethan, on the other hand, kept his head down and focused on his work, not saying a word—almost like he'd expected his girlfriend would be arrested.

~

With a bag of frozen peas pressed against her lower back, Jessie perched on a stool in the café kitchen. The ancient mobile phone lay before her on the counter, its tiny screen and physical buttons a relic from another era. Her fingers fumbled over the keypad, desperately trying to navigate through the archaic menu system.

"Who designed this old brick?" Jessie said to herself. "It makes no sense."

"Here, let me try." Sue reached across with a dry smile. "These things were actually quite simple once you knew the shortcuts." Her smile grew. "Wow, it has *Snake* on it. I used to love that game." Her finger hovered, but she didn't click. "What are you looking for?"

"Messages?" Jessie asked.

"Sent or received?"

"They're separate?" Jessie couldn't hold her laugh in. "Barbaric. Let's try the sent messages."

The phone's screen flickered as Sue accessed the sent messages folder. "Here's the last one—sent just before midnight."

Jessie squinted at the dim display. That would have been moments before she caught the person who'd dropped the phone posting the note through the letterbox.

> Let's put an end to this tomorrow.
> Workshop. After the market closes.
> Come alone.

Through the beads, Julia's voice mingled with DI Moyes' as they discussed Polly's arrest in the café.

"Do you think Polly sent this?" Sue asked.

"Maybe?" Jessie shrugged. "If she did and the police keep her in overnight, Conrad might be waiting at his workshop for a while."

The back door creaked open, and Barker stepped in, shaking off the cold. Jessie thrust the phone towards him and explained where she'd found it.

"You've been withholding evidence?" Barker stated

flatly, his expression hardening. "Why did you keep it to yourself?"

"Whose side are you on?"

"The side of the truth," Barker replied. "Jessie—"

"I thought it might be useful." Jessie shifted the frozen peas, wincing. "And it's not even been twelve hours yet. Aren't you glad I did? I've found you a meeting between Conrad and whoever's been harassing him. If it's not the same person who killed Wendy, I'll turn myself in for withholding evidence and let them throw away the key."

Barker's jaw clenched, but after a long exhale, his expression shifted to one of concentration.

"Trying to figure out where the workshop is?" Jessie asked.

"Yes." Barker rubbed his chin. "Conrad mentioned having one, but he never said where. I should have asked."

"Go and ask him now," Sue suggested, wiping her hands on her apron. "Not everything needs to be this complicated."

"It's a little late for that," Barker said, his voice tight. "Not only has Conrad just fired me as his PI, I might have severed the one bridge I had with him."

"You're doing that a lot," Jessie pointed out.

Barker held out his hand until Jessie reluctantly handed him the old phone. He turned it over in his hands, his brow furrowing.

"Did you find out any more about Ethan?"

"Not yet," Jessie admitted. "I might have severed my own bridges with that couple. They weren't receptive to questions from the press. Or Mum, for that matter. She mentioned she overheard them in Fern Moore yesterday talking about getting away. Polly seemed eager to leave but Ethan wanted to stay to see the market out."

Barker hummed, a thoughtful expression settling on his face. "Ethan didn't seem too concerned to see Polly being led away by the police just now. And Melissa told your mum Ethan hated Wendy more than anyone."

"She ruined his business when his father was dying," Jessie reminded him. "But Conrad has hardly been straight with you." A flicker of doubt crossed her face. "Saying that, I didn't like Ethan one bit. Or trust him, but..."

"What is it?" Barker asked.

"Polly called Ethan 'weak'," Jessie remembered aloud. "I don't like him, but I didn't like that—it sounded like she was putting him down."

But Barker paced the small kitchen, the phone tapping up and down in his palm. "I need to find Conrad's workshop—if someone's planning to meet him there tonight..."

"What about the local business directory?" Sue suggested as she finished the washing up, only half-listening. "*Yellow Pages*? Most craftsmen list their workshops, don't they?"

"It's worth a shot," Jessie agreed.

Barker nodded, though his attention had shifted to peering through the beads as Julia and Moyes continued their chat at the counter.

Jessie lingered by the beaded curtain as Barker strode through to the café and handed the old phone to

DI Moyes. Her stomach clenched when he explained where it came from, but he didn't mention Jessie's involvement.

"This could help," Moyes said, turning the phone over. "We've got Polly at the station now. We're working on getting a confession about the threatening notes or at least a DNA sample to confirm the match. That hair you found might be the key."

"You might want to check for bruises," Jessie suggested, the frozen peas still pressed to her back. "Whoever posted that note hit the ice like a sack of spuds."

Before Moyes could respond, the bell chimed and Evelyn swept in, her flowing black kaftan rustling.

"Ah, this kills two birds with one stone," she announced as she glanced between Moyes and Julia, her eyes sparkling with urgency. She looked past them to Jessie. "Remember when I was meditating and you asked if I saw Ethan running past the B&B?" She waited for Jessie to nod. "Well, I mentioned it in passing to my grandson just now, and Mark said he saw someone matching Ethan's description *inside* the B&B coming from the direction of Wendy's room."

"Are you certain about this?" Moyes straightened.

"Mark was quite sure—said he even smelled like croissants."

"That sounds like Ethan," Jessie said, her mind racing. "Maybe poisoning the tea at the office wasn't his first plan?"

Without waiting for a response, Jessie ditched the peas and ran through the back door, sprinting towards

Ethan's pastry van. Her boots slipped on the icy cobbles as she approached, but she caught herself with his van before she fell. Ethan was already packing away.

"In a hurry to go somewhere?" Jessie asked.

"Clear off," he snapped when he spotted her. "I'm done with this crappy market."

"I know you were at the B&B," Jessie said, her voice steady despite her racing heart and sore spine. "Right before Wendy was poisoned. You were seen."

Ethan's hands stilled on a box. His gaze met hers for a long moment, guilt written across his features. Then he slammed the van's shutter down with a metallic clang, jumped into the driver's seat, and sped away from the market, leaving Jessie alone in a cloud of exhaust.

"The more you try to hide," Jessie muttered to herself as she stood where the van had been, "the guiltier you look."

14

*T*he bitter winter wind whipped around the empty market stalls as Barker huddled deeper into his coat. He positioned himself behind a wooden pillar, watching Conrad's desperate attempts to sell one last clock.

"Look at the craftsmanship—solid oak case, brass fittings. I'll give you half off. That's practically stealing it from me."

The potential customer, a middle-aged woman in a puffy red coat, shook her head. "It's lovely, but—"

"Fine. Clear off and stop wasting my time." Conrad's polite mask cracked, and the woman scurried away as Conrad slammed the clock into a box as he continued packing up.

Barker's jaw tightened. This volatile man bore little resemblance to the broken figure who'd first approached him after Wendy's death. Each new interaction revealed more cracks in his carefully constructed victim narrative.

Conrad loaded the last of his boxes into his old Volvo's boot, movements sharp with frustration. But rather than climbing in, he set off on foot towards the village green. Barker counted to thirty before following, keeping to the shadows.

"Oi, Barker! Fancy a drink?" DI Moyes' voice cut through the darkness as Barker rounded the corner. She stood in the pool of light spilling from the café doorway. "Polly's lawyer's got her maintaining complete silence. I need an hour or two to think about anything else but this case."

"Sorry, I can't. Have to be somewhere." Barker continued, scanning the village for any sign of Conrad. "Later."

"Where are you off to in such a rush?"

"I'll explain later."

He rushed up the street past The Plough and the B&B, but Conrad had vanished. He was about to give up when he heard car tyres screeching on Mulberry Lane and ran towards the sound. He rounded the corner just as Conrad reached the bottom of the street, a car speeding away, its driver shaking their head at Conrad in the rearview mirror. Conrad, in his haste, had nearly been run over.

As Barker passed the salon, Katie turned the key in the lock and tried to catch his attention.

"Have you called your brother yet?" Her voice held that familiar note of concern that made his jaw clench. "Barker?"

"Not now, Katie," he snapped, instantly regretting his tone when he saw her face fall. "Sorry."

He hurried on, his footsteps quickening. There wasn't time for pleasantries, not when Conrad could be about to meet with someone connected to Wendy's murder. If it wasn't him, it was whoever had sent that text message.

Outside the antique shop, Brian was red-faced. He struggled with an oversized Victorian chair, the wooden frame threatening to slip from his grasp.

"Ah, Barker, give me a hand, will you?" His father-in-law's voice carried expectation. "This thing is going to throw my back out."

Barker ignored the request, scanning the darkening street. "Did you see which way that man went? Mid-forties?"

"Down there," Brian called, readjusting his grip on the chair with visible strain. "Are you going to help me with this chair?"

"I'm working, Brian."

Barker hurried down the overgrown, dark path beside the disused builder's yard. He couldn't believe he'd waited for hours to follow Conrad, only to lose him immediately.

He reached a fork in the road—one path leading to the allotments, the other to Howarth Forest. Had Conrad cut through the allotments to take a shortcut to Riverswick? The only wood workshop he'd found was there, run by an old man named Rodger who'd never heard of Conrad when Barker called him earlier. Since the forest was mostly deserted and looped back to the village, he decided to risk it and headed towards the allotments.

The gravel crunched under Barker's feet as he entered the allotments. Winter had stripped the plots bare, leaving only skeletal remnants of last season's growth. A robin pecked at frozen soil near an upturned wheelbarrow.

And then the last people he needed to see, Dot and Percy, emerged from behind a ramshackle shed, pushing a rusty wheelbarrow.

"What are you doing here?" he demanded.

Dot's lips pursed. "Taking care of *your* allotment. I know you like to forget this place exists since you handed us the keys, but *someone* needs to keep it in order during these harsh winter months."

"Hush now, Dorothy." Percy placed a weathered hand on his wife's arm. "We enjoy the gardening, and it gives us some space from Ethel." He leaned closer to Barker, lowering his voice. "She's making a limited edition Wendy gnome after seeing how well that lady's book sold."

Barker blinked in disbelief as Percy launched into an animated description of their recent activities, searching for any signs of Conrad.

"We've been digging up beds, haven't we, Dorothy? And mulching. Thinking about turning the carrot patch into rhubarb this year." Percy rambled on. "Do you think Julia could make use of it at the café? I love the stuff, but it's not to everyone's taste."

"Possibly," Barker replied, scanning the rows of bare earth for any movement. "I don't suppose you saw a man come down this way?"

Dot's eyes narrowed. "What man?"

"I'm looking for Conrad. He might have come down this way on his way to a workshop."

"Workshop, is it?" Percy tapped his chin in thought. "I don't suppose you mean that chap three plots down from us? Hammering and sawing night and day. Pleasant enough but keeps himself to himself."

"That might be him." Barker waited until Dot and Percy returned to their gardening before approaching the fenced-in allotment.

The plot was quiet—almost too quiet.

Barker gripped the padlock, giving it a frustrated rattle. The metal chain clinked against the gate but held firm. Something about this didn't sit right.

Moving along the perimeter, Barker ran his hand across the wooden panels until one shifted under his touch. He pressed harder, and the panel gave way enough to squeeze through, his coat catching on a protruding nail.

The overgrown plot stretched before him, winter-dead vegetation crackling under his feet. A shed huddled in the far corner, soft light seeping through its grimy windows. This had to be it—where else would Conrad disappear to at this hour?

Drawing closer, Barker tried to peer through the stained glass, but he could only make out vague shadows within. A wooden sign hung crooked on the door: 'Conrad's Sanctuary' carved in flowing script.

He grabbed the handle, expecting resistance, but it shifted under his grip. Pushing harder, the door creaked open a few inches. Through the gap, Barker's breath caught in his throat.

Conrad lay sprawled on the sawdust-covered floor, blood pooling around his still form. The metallic smell hit Barker's nostrils as he shouldered his way inside.

"*Conrad*?" His fingers pressed against Conrad's neck. His skin was still warm, but he searched for a pulse that wasn't there.

Cursing under his breath, Barker fumbled for his phone with trembling hands. He'd lost sight of Conrad, and now his former client had slipped through his fingers. Conrad, like his ex-wife, was dead.

15

*B*arker's stomach churned as he stumbled out of the workshop, bile rising in his throat. He pressed his back against the rough wooden wall, its splinters catching on his coat.

"Moyes, you need to get to the allotments," Barker struggled to say into his phone once the detective picked up. "There's been another murder."

Clutching his phone to his ear, Moyes bombarded him with questions that he couldn't process. The image of Conrad's lifeless form burned behind his eyelids. All afternoon, he'd been watching the man sell clocks at the market, desperate to make money to sort his life out.

"Just get here!" he barked, hanging up.

The cold seeped through his clothes, but Barker barely noticed. He looked back through the gap to Conrad's body, bleeding into the sawdust. He should wait for Moyes to secure the scene—he knew the procedure, but his feet carried him back to the workshop door.

Inside, the air hung thick with the sharp tang of blood and fresh sawdust. Half-finished clocks lined the workbench, their faces frozen at different times. The soft tick-tock of dozens of the timepieces broke the silence. Moyes wouldn't take long; she couldn't find him lurking around the scene like this.

But Barker needed to know what had happened—he needed justice.

Scrubbing his eyes with his sleeve, he took in Conrad's workspace.

Barker forced himself to focus, letting his investigative instincts take over. The workshop held answers. It had to. His gaze swept the space methodically, searching for signs of violence beyond Conrad's body.

Nothing seemed disturbed. The bench remained pristine, tools arranged with strict precision. A clock sat half-assembled in the vice, its gears exposed like an incomplete puzzle. The craftsman would never get to finish his final piece.

Something nagged at Barker's attention. The wall above the workbench displayed an array of tools, each outline carefully traced in white pencil—a place for everything and everything in its place, except for one gap. The hammer's silhouette stood empty against the wall.

Metal creaked outside, the gate's hinges protesting. Barker's heart jumped to his throat. He squeezed back through the workshop door, nearly stumbling in his haste.

DI Moyes stood at the gate with PC Puglisi, her expression grim. "An ambulance is on its way. How did you get in?"

Barker moved to the fence, demonstrating the loose panel. "Here. I've contaminated the scene, but whoever did this likely came and went the same way."

Moyes ducked through the gap, Puglisi following close behind. She held back the panel, jerking her head for Barker to leave, and he didn't need to be told twice.

Barker slumped against the allotment fence, his legs weak beneath him. The winter night pressed in, broken only by the flash of blue lights bouncing off frost-covered sheds. Dot and Percy's footsteps crunched across the gravel.

"What's happened?" Dot clutched Percy's arm. "We heard sirens."

Barker's throat tightened. The words stuck like thorns. "Conrad. He's dead."

"*Dead*?" Percy gasped, dabbing his bald head with his handkerchief. "But we only saw him at the market this morning."

"I *knew* there was something fishy about him." Dot pressed a hand to her chest, edging close to the fence to peek through. "It could have been us, Percy. We were right *here*, three plots away. What if the killer—"

"No." Barker shook his head. "This wasn't random—someone planned this."

The wail of approaching sirens grew louder.

Paramedics soon rushed past with their equipment, guided by PC Puglisi's torch beam. The allotment gate creaked open as DI Moyes emerged, a set of keys jangling in her grip. Her expression hardened as she spotted Barker.

"Found them on a hook," she explained, swinging them around on her finger. "Seems he locked himself in, so he wasn't expecting someone or—"

"He was," Barker interrupted. "Haven't you looked through the phone I gave you?"

"I've been a little preoccupied with the ginger hair stuck to the note threatening your wife," Moyes replied coolly, arching a brow. "Care to explain what brought you here, Brown?"

"I was trailing Conrad—been watching him all day. Something felt off about his behaviour. He fired me, and I knew he was hiding something, but..." His voice cracked and he said, "... if I'd been faster, got here sooner—"

"Then you might be lying next to him." Moyes cut him off. "This isn't your fault. And it certainly wasn't your job to prevent it."

"But it's *yours*!" Dot's shrill voice pierced the darkness as Percy tried to hold her back. "What are you doing about it, Detective Inspector? There's a murderer on the loose and it seems anyone connected to Wendy is on the hit list. That includes *Julia*! Which, by extension, means *us*!"

"Alright, dear." Percy patted her hand, his voice gentle. "Let's give the detective some space."

The forensics van pulled up, its headlights cutting through the fog as Percy led a reluctant Dot away.

"Did you notice?" Barker asked.

"The body on the floor?" Moyes replied drily. "Funnily enough, yes."

"The missing hammer. From what I could see, it's the only tool not where it should be, and given how much blood was pooling around his head, Conrad was whacked with some force."

"Then we might have a murder weapon," she said, turning back to look at the allotment as the forensic officers got on with setting up flood lights. "I need to get on. This was the last thing we needed tonight."

"I suppose I was wrong about it always being the ex, huh?" Puglisi remarked, scratching his chin.

"Alright, Puglisi." Moyes shot him a sharp look. "Back to work. We have a hammer to find."

Left alone in the biting cold, Barker felt untethered. He'd spent days looking sideways at Conrad, building a mental case against him based on all the strange titbits, convincing himself his client might be the murderer.

Now, Conrad lay dead on his workshop floor, and Barker was back to square one. All his theories, all his suspicions—they'd led him to his former client's dead end.

~

Julia curled into the armchair, the heat of the fire washing over her as she studied her notepad. Her theories sprawled across the pages in a messy web, arrows connecting suspects and motives. Conrad, Melissa, Polly, Ethan, or Prudence. It *had* to be one of them. Mowgli purred on her lap, kneading her legs as she tapped her pen against the paper.

Despite Polly being the one at the police station, every thread led back to Conrad. His payments to Wendy, the kiss behind his Volvo, the threatening messages, the violent outbursts with his cooking students. Even his rekindled relationship with Melissa raised questions. But something didn't add up.

The front door clicked open, though she didn't hear it close. Mowgli darted off her lap and disappeared under the sofa as Barker stepped into the living room, rain dripping from his coat. His face was ashen, hands trembling as he stood in the doorway, the wind howling behind him.

"You're shaking." Julia rose from her chair, crossing the room to help him out of his sodden jacket. "Barker, what happened?"

"Conrad." His voice cracked. "He's dead."

The word dropped through the air like a lead balloon as Julia straightened his jacket before hanging it on the coat rack. She pushed the door shut, unable to believe what she'd just heard.

"Dead?" she confirmed.

"Murdered. Blunt force trauma to the back of the head." He ran a shaking hand through his damp hair. "I followed him to the allotment, and he was there to meet whoever sent him that message. They threatened to end things, and they did, and I was too late to save him."

Julia wrapped her arms around him, drawing him close. She couldn't remember the last time she'd seen him this shaken. He pulled away abruptly as she stroked his back, trying to offer comfort.

"I need to talk to Prudence," he said, rushing to the back door. "No more hiding."

Julia watched Barker stride across their rain-soaked garden towards Prudence's van, his shoes squelching in the mud. The red camper sat silent and dark.

"I don't think she's in," Julia called through the downpour, pulling her dressing gown tighter. But Barker continued, rapping his knuckles against the van's metal door.

"Prudence, if you're in there, open up now. We need to talk."

"Barker, I told you—she's not here." Julia stepped onto the wet grass, shivering as rain peppered her face. This time he turned, finally registering her words.

"I bet she's hiding," he said, scanning the garden. "The timing's too perfect."

"That's not fair." Julia folded her arms. "She opened up to me this morning—told me everything about her connection to Wendy. How Wendy manipulated her, got her fired from her own show—"

"Which only gives her *more* motive," he cut in. "Conrad admitted he was there through all of it, watching from the sidelines while Wendy took over Prudence's show. If she's held onto that hatred for Wendy all these years, why wouldn't she feel the same about Conrad? He stood by and let it happen, and now he's dead."

Julia blinked rain from her eyes. "You're not thinking clearly. You're upset about Conrad—"

"I'm thinking perfectly clearly. He's dead because I couldn't protect him."

Julia flinched as footsteps squelched through the wet grass behind them. Prudence rounded the corner of the cottage, plastic bags from the greengrocer's on Mulberry Lane swinging from her arms. Her grey hair hung in damp tendrils around her face, but she didn't seem to mind.

"Where have you been?" Barker's voice cracked like thunder.

Julia placed a gentle hand on his arm, but he shrugged it off. "Barker, please—"

"*Answer* me!" His shout echoed across the garden. "Conrad's dead, and you conveniently disappeared."

Prudence's weathered face hardened. Without a word, she climbed into her van and slammed the door with enough force to rattle the windows. Julia waited for the familiar strains of Karen Carpenter to blast through the walls, but only an unsettling silence followed.

A cry pierced the air from inside—Olivia, startled awake by her father's outburst.

"I'll go," Julia said, squeezing Barker's shoulder. "You need to calm down."

Julia carried Olivia into the kitchen, her daughter's sleepy weight warm against her chest. She settled Olivia into her booster seat, smoothing down her bedhead curls. The kitchen felt oddly still after the chaos outside.

Opening the fridge, Julia stared at its contents without really seeing them. Leftovers, eggs, milk—nothing registered. The back door clicked softly. Barker's footsteps crossed the tiles, and his lips brushed her cheek as he passed. She didn't turn away from the bright interior of the fridge as he filled a glass at the sink. The water ran, then stopped. He gulped it down in long swallows.

"My judgment is clouded." His voice was barely above a whisper. "My instincts... they're not sharp. I suspected Conrad—my own client who came to me for *help*. And I used his temper as a motive." He set the glass down with a quiet clink. "But how am I any different right now? I'm sorry, Julia."

She closed the fridge, turning to face him. "I understand why you're upset, but you handled that wrong with Prudence. She's shy, and maybe she is hiding something, but she's also been through a lot."

"I know." He slumped against the counter. "I've handled all of it wrong."

"Then we give up." Julia pulled open the drawer containing their collection of takeaway menus. "We let the police deal with this from now on."

"Is that what you want?"

"No," she said. "But maybe it's the right thing to do."

Barker mulled it over for a moment before he said, "One more day. For Conrad's sake, and before anyone else gets hurt in Wendy's fallout, we put a stop to this tomorrow."

"That," Julia replied, returning the kiss, "I can agree with."

~

Jessie's fingers hovered over her laptop keyboard, the blank document mocking her attempts to write Conrad's eulogy. The half-eaten pizza beside her had turned cold hours ago, but she couldn't bring herself to bin it. Through her bedroom window, the market square lay abandoned, the only sound coming from the teenagers squeaking on the swings, braving the cold.

The words wouldn't come. How could she write about a man who'd been both victim and villain? Each attempt at an opening paragraph felt either too harsh or falsely sympathetic.

The door buzzer's harsh ring jolted her from her thoughts. She ignored it, but it blared again. And again. She hopped over the mountain of clothes sprawled across her floor, no clue which was the clean pile anymore.

The intercom crackled as she lifted the phone. "Who is it?"

"Finally!" Veronica cried. "Can I come up?"

Jessie pressed the entry button, hearing Veronica's footsteps thundering up the stairs moments later. Her editor burst into the small flat, face flushed and glasses fogging with condensation.

"I've been trying to call you!" Veronica gripped the back of the sofa, catching her breath.

Jessie fished her phone from her pocket. The screen lit up with half a dozen missed calls and messages from Veronica. "Sorry, I put it on silent—I needed to focus." She slumped onto her worn sofa, rubbing her temples. "I needed no distractions, but if you're here for that article, I'm struggling."

"Forget the article for a moment." Veronica's hands trembled as she pulled an envelope from her pocket. Her fingers shook like leaves as she perched on the sofa next to her, spreading out a note on the coffee table crafted from magazine cut-out letters across the coffee table: 'SEARCH THE VAN FOR AN EXCLUSIVE...'

"This was slid under the office's door." Veronica's voice shook as much as her hands. "I wouldn't have found it until the morning if I hadn't left my glasses there."

Jessie stared at the crude letters, each mismatched in size and font—the same style as the threat her mum had received. Her heart thumped against her ribs as she traced the edges of the paper.

"They must mean Prudence's van." Jessie mulled it over, her mind racing through the possibilities. "Is Polly still at the station?"

"According to my contact, yes. What do we do?" Veronica asked, almost in a whisper. "Do we take it to the police?"

"And let them take the credit? We do exactly what the message says. We search her van."

"We could be being sent on a wild goose chase." Veronica pushed her glasses up her nose. "Or worse... we could be walking into a trap."

"*Or* we could be about to get the exclusive our newspaper desperately needs," Jessie said, crossing the flat to the small kitchen area at the back. Filling the kettle at the tap, she turned back and said, "We need to wait until Prudence is out tomorrow, and then we catch ourselves our next front page."

16

*T*he hum of the fridge filled the kitchen, a low, steady drone that did nothing to quiet Julia's thoughts. She stared at the chipped edge of her mug, the steam from her tea curling into the air like a question mark. Through the kitchen window, her gran's dogs darted across the grass, their playful barks muffled by the glass, while Prudence's van loomed like a relic from another time.

"It *must* be her." Dot's breath fogged the window as she spied on Prudence. "From what you've just told me about Wendy stitching her up with the studio executives, it doesn't sound like the woman has ever moved on."

Julia joined her gran at the window as Prudence hung freshly washed underwear on a makeshift line strung between the van and the oak tree. It was a scene so ordinary, yet it felt anything but. Prudence shouldn't have been there, but Julia still didn't know what else she was supposed to have done.

Squinting through the morning mist, Prudence seemed more than aware she was being observed. With a shake of her head at the dogs, she retreated into her sanctuary.

"I mean, *look* at her." Dot's nose wrinkled as she swirled her tea. "She probably doesn't even know what day it is, let alone what she's done. Her mind might have gone around the time of her decency."

"Her mind is still sharp," Julia corrected. "And there are other suspects to consider. Melissa, for one. She knew about the flowers, and she's known Wendy and Conrad longer than Prudence." She paused to sip her tea, the taste sweet but the thought of Melissa killing Conrad bitter on her tongue. "Then there's Polly and Ethan. Polly hasn't let go of her vendetta against Wendy, and Ethan was seen at the B&B not long before Wendy was poisoned."

"A regular old Sonny and Cher double act," Dot said with a sniff.

Julia narrowed her eyes. "I don't think they killed anyone."

Dot tapped her nose. "That we *know* of."

Pursing her lips at Prudence's van one last time, Dot spun away from the window and let the dogs in. Their muddy paws skittered across the kitchen tiles as she bent down to scratch behind their ears.

"Well, we know it wasn't Polly," Dot announced, clipping the leads to their collars. "She was still at the police station when someone whacked Conrad, and she's telling anyone who'll listen that she was framed."

"You've seen her?"

"She's at the market with a fresh batch of those books." Dot rummaged in the handbag hanging from the crook of her arm. "I thought you'd want a copy before they all sell out again—I bet there'll be a mountain of them in the charity shop by the end of the week."

Dot placed Polly's book on the breakfast bar: *My Decade Working Under the Wicked Witch*. The cover featured a stark black-and-white photo of a woman with a pixelated face, devil horns jutting from her forehead. The glossy cover was thin and curling at the edges—no doubt self-published, and only a little thicker than a holiday brochure.

"It's no L. Frank Baum, but from skimming through a few pages, it's certainly scandalous." Dot gathered up Olivia's bag and ushered the dogs out of the kitchen. "Right, Liv, time for an afternoon with Great-Granny Dot. We'll continue our poker lessons."

"Gran..." Julia arched a brow and added, "... please don't teach my toddler to gamble."

"Just a little joke, dear," Dot said, forcing a laugh and tugging at her stiff collar. She leaned down to whisper to Olivia, "Dominoes, it is."

Julia wandered into the sitting room with the book, disturbing Mowgli's nap under the radiator by the window. She watched them leave down the garden path—Olivia skipping ahead, the dogs straining at their leads. The cottage fell silent, suddenly too still. She flipped through the book, glancing at last night's scribbled notes in her pad on the side table. A maze of dead ends and question marks.

She'd intended to offer Prudence an olive branch to smooth things over after Barker's accusations. But would Prudence even listen? Julia doubted it. Not a morning person, she guessed, and likely even less inclined to chat after last night's drama.

The book tempted her—reading it might uncover helpful intel. She scanned some of the chapter titles: *Falling Under Her Spell, The Recipe for Disaster, The Witch's Brew, The Crumbling Empire, Breaking the Spell...*

But Julia snapped the book shut. Her first stop had to be Fern Moore. Melissa was the closest thing Conrad had to family, and she wouldn't be taking news of his murder well.

With one last glance at Prudence's van, Julia slipped the book into her bag and stepped into the crisp morning air. It was time to get some answers.

∿

The ticking of Conrad's clock taunted Barker in his office. He couldn't tear his eyes away from the thing as he tried to compile his evidence to confront Ethan. The clock wouldn't let him. The guilt wouldn't. But he couldn't sit there all day, wallowing in the feeling that he hadn't done enough. He needed to act, and now. Leaving his fragmented notes behind, he strode out of his office and into the market.

The damp market square was quiet, the air bitingly

cold. The pastry van's window stood propped open despite the chill, and Polly lingered behind a fold-out table piled with copies of her book. There were even fewer browsers today than before—perhaps the second murder had scared off the last of the curious shoppers willing to give the new market a chance.

Ethan's movements were robotic as he wiped the chalkboard clean, slashing prices and scribbling new offers in bold, uneven strokes. His eyes stayed fixed on his task, but his jaw was tight, his shoulders stiff. Behind her book-laden table, Polly pretended to reorganise her display, but Barker caught her inching closer, her ears practically pricking up like a cat's.

"Go away," Ethan snapped. "I have nothing to say to you."

Barker gritted his teeth. "A man died yesterday. Murdered."

"I'd heard." Ethan looked away, avoiding Barker's accusatory stare. "So what?"

Ethan was trying to get under Barker's skin, and he hated that it was working. He'd barely slept, the image of Conrad lying in the sawdust haunting him every moment since he'd left the workshop. He took a steadying breath, reminding himself why he'd decided to talk to Ethan first.

"I know you were at the B&B," Barker stated, keeping his voice low enough that only Ethan could hear. "The morning Wendy died."

Ethan's hand froze mid-stroke, the chalk hovering over the board. "I... I wasn't."

"A witness saw you. You smelled of fresh baking."

"Lots of people smell of fresh baking." Ethan's fingers tightened around the chalk, his knuckles whitening. "Must've been a funky-smelling aftershave."

Barker's nostrils flared. "This isn't a game."

"No?" Ethan choked out an unconvincing laugh. "I'm having fun."

"The B&B owner's grandson saw you there," Barker pressed. "You can't deny it. The question is: why? What were you doing near Wendy's room?"

"I deliver pastries to the B&B every morning." Ethan's voice wavered. "That's not unusual."

"No, you don't," Barker countered. "I know Evelyn well enough to know she doesn't serve pastries at her B&B, and if she did, she'd buy them from my wife."

"Yeah?" Ethan's hand trembled as he crushed the chalk against the board, leaving a jagged line. "You think you know it all?" His eyes darted between Barker and Polly, who had abandoned any pretence of arranging her books. "Clear off."

"I think I know enough," Barker said, refusing to back down. "Your father was ill—it's no surprise you were struggling to keep it all together. Then Wendy came along and destroyed what little you had left. It's no wonder you hated her."

"She tried to ruin me at my lowest," Ethan hissed, leaning across the counter. "I told her I wasn't interested in becoming the next Mr Wendy, but do you think that would stop a viper like her? And you know what she did when she'd brought my business to its knees?" He leaned back into the shadow of the van, folding his arms across his chest. "She made me a lowball offer to buy the bakery. She tried to play the saviour, but I'd have rather let everything crumble than give her a single crumb of what I'd worked for."

Barker's mind raced. Was that what Wendy had been trying to do to Julia with the nail in the cruffin—destroy her reputation so she could swoop in and take over the business? Julia would've let that happen over her dead body.

"Sounds like a motive for revenge to me," Barker pushed. "For Wendy *and* Conrad."

Polly abandoned her charade, drifting to the van like a moth to a flame.

"The reviews must have stung," Barker pressed. "And it didn't help that Conrad joined in too." He narrowed his eyes. "Why would he do that?"

"Because he could never quite let Wendy go—no more than she could let him go. They were made for each other." Ethan's voice cracked as he glanced at Polly. "You don't know what you're talking about."

Barker noted how Ethan's defensive stance had morphed into fear. "I bet after you left the B&B, you followed Wendy to the newspaper office. You confronted her. Things got out of hand—"

"*I* didn't kill her!" Ethan's fist crashed against the metal counter, the sound echoing across the empty market square. "Melissa warned me this would happen. She said people would point fingers at me because of my history with Wendy."

The mention of Melissa caught Barker off guard. "Melissa? When did she warn you about this?"

"Don't answer him," Polly cut in, wedging herself

between them. Her auburn hair caught the weak winter sunlight. "He's trying to twist your words."

"Melissa said it was only a matter of time before suspicion fell onto me," Ethan pressed on, speaking over Polly's shoulder. "She said—"

"Shut up!" Polly spun around, her face inches from Ethan's. "You don't have to tell him a thing. He's not with the police. He's trying to stitch you up. I bet it was you who put my hair in your wife's hate mail." Her cheeks flushed crimson as she turned back to Barker. "Back off!"

Barker's heart raced. Those words—the same as the threatening note pushed through the café's letterbox. He watched as Polly stormed across the cobbles, abandoning her book display. Ethan watched her go, the same detached stare he'd had when she'd been arrested yesterday. Polly had an alibi for Conrad's murder, secured at the police station. But Ethan didn't.

"Your girlfriend seems upset," Barker remarked.

"She's not my girlfriend." Bitterness laced Ethan's words. "I'm done. Once I've made my pitch fee back, I'm moving on, and she can do whatever she wants. She's no different to Wendy, and I'm not about to become Conrad."

"Where were you last night?" Barker asked. "About six?"

But the van's shutter came down with a metallic bang, leaving Barker alone with his thoughts spinning in new directions. His certainty about Ethan's guilt had wavered, replaced by fresh questions.

～

Julia sat on the edge of the floral-print sofa as Melissa's sobs echoed through the small flat, her shoulders heaving as she clutched a damp tissue. The scene transported Julia back twenty-three years to the college canteen, where she'd held Melissa through similar tears over Conrad.

"I *loved* him," Melissa wailed, her mascara leaving dark trails down her cheeks. "I loved him *so* much."

"I know." Julia placed a gentle hand on Melissa's arm. "I could see that."

"Conrad didn't want to be more than friends," Melissa's voice cracked. "But I would have... I might have been able to stop him dying if he'd let me back in, somehow... some way..."

"That sort of thinking won't help." Julia kept her voice soft, though she wasn't just there to console Melissa. "When did you last see Conrad?"

Melissa dabbed at her eyes. "At The Comfy Corner. When he got that horrid text message." The tissue shredded between her fingers. "When you were spying on us."

The accusation took Julia by surprise, yet she couldn't deny that she had been spying, in a way. "I went to clean up Olivia's spill. I wasn't expecting to see you there."

Melissa's face hardened, the grief vanishing like stage makeup wiped away. "I suppose you think that makes me suspicious? That I killed Wendy out of jealousy, then hit Conrad with a hammer?"

Julia sighed. "I didn't say that."

"But you're *thinking* it. Just like you're probably thinking about my stolen flowers."

"Melissa, I need to know everything about Conrad. How long had he been getting those messages?"

"A few weeks." Melissa dabbed at her eyes, smearing more mascara across her pale skin. "But it could have been longer. He didn't tell me everything." Her face contorted, anger flashing through her tears. "He didn't tell me about the kiss with Wendy on the morning of the market."

Fresh sobs wracked Melissa's body as she collapsed against Julia's shoulder, her tears soaking through Julia's cardigan. The familiar weight of Melissa's grief pressed against her, just as it had all those years ago in the college canteen. Only this time, Conrad wouldn't be coming back.

The flat door burst open, making Julia twist in her chair. Polly stood in the doorway, her hair wild from the wind. Her eyes landed on Julia, and she shook her head with evident disgust before marching past them into the kitchen.

Julia's brow furrowed as she turned back to Melissa.

"Polly and Ethan are staying in my spare room while the market is on," Melissa explained as she plucked a fresh tissue from the box. "I usually flower arrange in there, but I didn't mind giving it up for the week."

"You never said."

"Yes, I did." Melissa's forehead creased. "Last time you were here, I told you I had guests staying."

"Right." Julia nodded as the memory surfaced. "You did."

Melissa stood, smoothing down her skirt. "Excuse me, I need to go and freshen up."

Left alone in the sitting room, Julia wandered through to the tiny kitchen at the back of the flat. Polly stood at the counter, shoulders rigid as she waited for the kettle to boil. Her knuckles were white where they gripped the worktop edge, her gaze fixed on the linoleum. The usual sharp-tongued confidence had crumbled, replaced by something raw and desperate.

"I didn't realise you were so close to Melissa," Julia ventured, staying in the doorway. "You met through the crafting scene, right?"

"What?" Polly's head snapped up, eyes blazing. "We met years ago, at the studio."

"The TV studio?"

"No, the music studio when I was recording my hit album." Polly rolled her eyes sarcastically. "Yes, the TV studio. You want to know the truth? Buy my book like everyone else. Chapter 2. I'm not saying any more to anyone, so tell your husband and your daughter to—"

"Back off?"

Polly rolled her eyes again and stormed out of the flat, leaving the kettle to reach its boiling point and click off in her wake.

Melissa returned from the bathroom, her eyes puffy and red as she dabbed at them with a crumpled length of toilet roll.

"Have you noticed anything strange with Polly and Ethan while they've been here?" Julia kept her tone casual, though her heart hammered against her ribs.

Melissa twisted the toilet paper between her fingers. "They have been arguing quite a bit."

"About what?"

"I try not to listen." Melissa shrugged. "But Polly was at the police station when Conrad..." Fresh tears welled in her eyes.

"What about Ethan?"

"He wasn't here." Melissa's narrowed eyes scanned the flower-filled flat. "He came back hours later in an awful mood and locked himself in the spare room. Then I saw about Conrad on the Peridale Chat group and..." Her face crumpled as she dissolved into tears once more.

Julia wrapped an arm around Melissa's shoulders, her mind racing. Why had Melissa lied about how she'd met Polly? What else wasn't she telling them?

"I'll make us more tea." Melissa shuffled towards the kitchen, still dabbing at her eyes. "I'm sorry about being... all over the place." She dropped her head, unable to look at Julia. "I think it's the grief."

Once alone, Julia pulled Polly's book from her bag and flipped to the second chapter. The section contained brief anecdotes with bold headlines detailing Wendy's early TV career after taking over *Culinary Delights*. One heading caught her eye. Gulping, Julia read:

The Haunted Heckler

Wendy's rise to fame wasn't as smooth as she'd like everyone to believe. Oh no, there were cracks in her perfect little empire, and one of them came in the form of a persistent thorn in her side—someone from her past who never quite got over being wronged by Wendy.

This person, whose identity I'll keep to myself (for now), had a knack for showing up at the studio at the most inconvenient times. They'd arrive in different disguises—sometimes a delivery person, other times a studio intern—and always managed to slip past security. Once inside, they'd heckle Wendy during filming, shouting things that made her face turn the same shade of red as her infamously inedible beetroot soup.

It was hilarious. Wendy, the queen of composure, would unravel in seconds. The crew would scramble to cut the cameras, and Wendy would storm off set, muttering under her breath about 'unprofessionalism' and 'sabotage.' But the best part? She never could figure out who it was.

I, on the other hand, found the whole ordeal endlessly entertaining. I even struck up a friendship with the heckler—anonymous as they were. They'd slip me notes backstage, little jibes at Wendy's expense, and I'd laugh until my sides hurt. It was a game, a way to poke holes in Wendy's carefully constructed charade.

Looking back, I suppose it was a bit mean. But then again, so was Wendy. And if there's one thing I've learned, it's that karma has a funny way of catching up with people.

Julia's grip tightened on the book as Melissa returned with two steaming mugs. The cups clattered against their saucers as Melissa froze, her eyes fixed on the chapter title visible beneath Julia's thumb.

"Why did you lie to me about how you met Polly?" Julia's voice remained steady despite her racing heart. "You told me you met in the craft circles."

Melissa's hands trembled as she set the cups down, tea sloshing over the edges. "I... I was embarrassed." Her voice trembled. "I'm not proud of that time of my life. I was still hurting, and she... Wendy... she had everything handed to her. She didn't deserve it, and I just wanted to throw a spanner in the works."

"Melissa," Julia leaned forward, the book heavy in her lap. "What else haven't you told me?"

The softness vanished from Melissa's face, replaced by something harder, colder. Her eyes narrowed as she stared at Julia. "That's all, Julia." Her voice carried an edge Julia had never heard before. "You... you don't believe me, do you? I thought you were *different*. I thought we were friends."

"Melissa, I just want—"

"You should go. I need to lie down."

Before Julia could respond, Melissa had crossed the room and opened the door, her message clear. Julia gathered her belongings, an unsettling feeling crawling up her spine as she stepped out onto the bitter walkway. Melissa slammed the door behind her, leaving Julia wondering how things had turned so frosty.

17

*M*elissa's erratic behaviour at the flat had Julia's mind churning as she pushed open the door to her cottage. The grief seemed genuine enough, but something felt off about her defensive reactions and shifting stories. The lies about meeting Polly nagged at her particularly.

The familiar scent of chocolate cake stopped her thoughts cold. Rich cocoa perfumed the air.

Someone was baking in her kitchen.

And it smelled good. Really good.

She dropped her bag and hurried into the kitchen, where every surface bore signs of Prudence's presence—from the dusted flour footprints tracking across the floor to the parade of mixing bowls and measuring cups lined up with military precision. Even the light seemed different, softened by the clouds of cocoa powder hanging in the air.

"*Oh!*" Prudence startled, nearly dropping the

wooden spoon. "I thought you'd be out all day. I... I should go back to the van." A flush crept across her weathered cheeks. "It's just... it's been so long since I've used a proper, homely kitchen."

Julia's eyes fell on her mother's old recipe book propped open on the counter, its pages worn and spotted with years of use. The familiar slanted handwriting caught her eye—her mother's distinctive cursive words flowing across the stained pages. Little notes crowded the margins: 'Add extra vanilla!' and 'Watch temp - burns easily' followed by a row of her characteristic tiny stars she used to mark her favorites. Julia could almost hear her mother's voice in those hastily scribbled tips. The sight of Prudence working from those cherished handwritten recipes warmed her through.

"Please, stay," Julia said, rolling up her sleeves. "Mind if I join you? Baking helps me think."

"Me too," Prudence admitted. "I go into a sort of autopilot mode."

Julia smiled. "I've always thought the same."

She washed her hands at the sink while Prudence continued measuring with precise movements, flipping ingredients into the bowl in a way that might look haphazard but she didn't waste a drop.

"Is this your recipe book?" Prudence asked, running a finger along the faded writing. "It's quite comprehensive."

"My mother's," Julia replied. "Apart from a few pieces of jewellery, it's all I have left of her. The recipes aren't anything special—just simple home baking."

Prudence turned the pages with careful reverence. "But it *is* special," she said. "It's real. Honest." Her voice grew quieter. "Beautiful, even."

"Yes," Julia agreed, watching the former TV chef handle her mother's recipes with such genuine appreciation. "It is."

Prudence's finger traced along the pages until she paused at a recipe with a jagged tear down its centre, held together with browning tape.

"Julia's Birthday Cake," Prudence read aloud.

Julia's throat tightened at the sight. "Wendy ripped that page. Back at college." She touched the edge of the torn page. "I couldn't prove it was her, but I knew."

"Jealousy." Prudence ran her finger across the yellowed tape. "It's an illness."

"She was always like that, wasn't she? Even as a child, from what I've heard."

"Her mother died during childbirth with her." Prudence's hand stilled on the page. "That's a shadow that lingers, whether you admit it or not."

"But I thought she was a middle child?"

"She was. Her father remarried." Prudence closed the recipe book with careful movements. "Before she turned on me, we had a night at the studio bar. After a few too many glasses of sauvignon blanc, she opened up about her pain." She exhaled, her gaze drifting to the steamy window. "Oh, it was *deep* pain. Her father always blamed her for his wife's death. And her stepmother— she resented how much Wendy reminded her husband of his dead wife."

The revelation about Wendy's mother dying in

childbirth settled uneasily in Julia's stomach. It cast Wendy's fixation on Julia's own motherless state in a new light—had she recognised something of herself in Julia?

The thought that they shared that deep wound made Julia's certainty waver. Not enough to excuse Wendy's cruelty, but enough to make her wonder what might have been different if they'd connected over their shared loss instead of letting it divide them.

"Children need to be *nurtured*," Prudence continued, her voice softening. "She was ignored. I felt so sorry for her that night. I thought I could be like a mentor to her. Perhaps not a mother, but... maybe a teacher." Her shoulders dropped. "Perhaps that's why the betrayal hurt more. I never understood it."

Julia's hands stilled on the whisk. "An explanation, perhaps. A sad one. But not an excuse for what she did to people."

Prudence watched Julia's technique with the chocolate mixture, stepping closer to adjust her wrist position. "Here, like this. More fluid."

Julia followed the correction, marvelling at the sensation of being taught rather than teaching. After years of instructing others in her café, the role reversal felt oddly refreshing.

"No, you're right. It's no excuse," Prudence agreed, dabbing at her eyes with her sleeve. "You're fortunate your mother left you this book. It set you in good stead." She traced the edge of a well-worn page. "She must have taught you everything she knew."

"Her and someone else." Julia caught Prudence's eye

with a knowing smile. "I really was a huge fan of yours growing up."

Prudence's weathered face softened as she patted Julia's cheek, her flour-dusted hand leaving the faintest mark.

"It's been a long time since anyone's said that to me. Rather nice to hear, actually." She straightened her apron with renewed purpose. "Thank you for showing me kindness, even if your husband hates me."

"He doesn't *hate* you," Julia said. "He's just... stressed." She paused her whisking, the case pushing back to the forefront of her mind. "Prudence, do you know Melissa?"

"Who's that?" Prudence turned away, busying herself with flipping through the pages. "Now, I didn't find cruffins in here, so you're going to have to walk me through them." A ghost of her old TV smile flickered across her face. "Just when you think you know it all, there's always something new to learn."

Prudence's swift deflection to the cruffins wasn't subtle, but it was telling. The same woman who'd just opened up about Wendy's tragic past now couldn't meet Julia's eyes at the mention of Melissa. Julia filed away the reaction. The former star might project an air of isolation, but she clearly knew more about the other players in this drama than she was willing to admit.

Julia sighed, but she wouldn't turn down the request. She understood Prudence enough now to recognise when she was avoiding talking about something she didn't want to. Jessie had said Julia could be the same, and if it was always this frustrating being on the other end, she owed Jessie a thousand apologies.

"What are you hiding, Prudence?" Julia whispered to herself as she dug more flour out of the cupboard.

∼

Jessie crouched around the corner of the cottage, ignoring Veronica's nervous fidgeting beside her. Through the kitchen window, she could see her mum and Prudence absorbed in baking, a cloud of flour hanging in the air between them.

"Maybe this isn't such a good idea," Veronica whispered, adjusting her glasses. "Breaking and entering isn't exactly ethical journalism."

"We're not breaking anything." Jessie peered around the bush. "I used to live here. And the note said to look in the van. Don't you want to save the paper?"

Veronica fidgeted, dead leaves crunching beneath her feet. "Well, yes, but—"

"Then keep watch." Jessie darted across the garden, ducking beneath the washing line where Prudence's mismatched clothing hung like limp flags in the winter air.

Jessie hesitated, her hand hovering over the van's door handle. What if Prudence caught her? What if she found nothing and wasted everyone's time? But the thought of the newspaper—and the mystery—pushed her forward. She couldn't just sit back and do nothing.

The hinges protested with an ear-splitting screech as she eased the door open. Jessie froze, but the baking lesson continued undisturbed. The entire van groaned as she hauled herself inside, the metal floor creaking beneath her weight.

Her heart thundered as she waited for Prudence to come storming out of the cottage, wooden spoon raised like a weapon. When no angry chef appeared, Jessie allowed herself to breathe.

The van's interior felt smaller than it looked from outside. Boxes of sauce bottles competed for space with stacks of old VHS tapes. Where would someone hide evidence of murder in this chaos?

"If I were a clue," Jessie muttered to herself as she began rifling through the nearest box, "where would I be?"

∾

Julia watched Prudence work the whisk with skilled movements, but she couldn't hold back the question burning in her throat any longer. "Prudence... did you...?"

"I didn't kill Wendy." Prudence's voice remained steady, though her whisking faltered. "I didn't like her any more than you did, but I didn't kill her. And believe me, I wanted to many times." She shook her head, silver hair catching the kitchen light. "And I certainly didn't kill Conrad. I... I knew they weren't going to last, but it was clear she drained the life from that man. Listen, Julia," Prudence's movements slowed, her voice dropping. "There is something I haven't told you—"

The opening notes of *We've Only Just Begun* burst

through the kitchen window, cutting her off. Prudence's face darkened as she abandoned the whisk with a clatter. She charged towards the back door, surprisingly spry for her age, with Julia close behind.

The sight that greeted them stopped Julia cold. Veronica stood awkwardly by Prudence's washing line, surrounded by drying undergarments, while the music drifted from the open van door where Jessie fumbled with the vinyl player needle inside. The record scratched to silence.

Prudence hauled Jessie from the van and tossed her onto the muddy grass. "How *dare* you!"

"Alright, lady!" Jessie cried. "I'm sorry."

When Prudence turned to Julia, the betrayal in her eyes cut deep. "This was all a set-up, wasn't it? Get me out of my van so you could go snooping?"

"Prudence, I had no idea—" Julia started, but the van door slammed shut with such force the whole vehicle rocked. "You came into the kitchen on your own." Julia's heart sank. She doubted she'd get another chance to reach the real Prudence hiding beneath those defensive layers.

"We got this note," Jessie explained, scrambling to her feet as Veronica produced the crude magazine cut-out message. "We thought... well, it doesn't matter. I didn't find anything. Complete waste of time."

Julia studied the familiar style of lettering, identical to the threats she'd received. The blissful bubble of their baking session had well and truly burst.

"Why send this to the newspaper instead of the police?" Julia wondered aloud.

"They're playing games with us." Veronica pushed her blue frames up her nose. "We thought we'd play along."

Jessie followed them into the cottage, wiping her muddy boots on the mat. "What did they expect us to find?"

"This is getting out of hand," Veronica said, her voice sharp. "We're not detectives, Jessie. If the murderer is toying with us, we're walking right into their trap. We need to think this through before we do something reckless."

Julia read the note again, something nagging at her mind. "It says search the van, but... *which* van? There's more than one at the market."

Veronica's eyes widened behind her glasses. "You don't think—"

"Guys?" Jessie's voice cut through their speculation. She held up a delicate white flower, its petals crushed and muddied. "I'm no expert, but is a lily of the valley a little white thing like this?"

"Yes." Veronica nodded. "My old neighbour used to have them everywhere. She always joked about killing off her husband if he ever misbehaved."

"It was stuck to my shoe," Jessie said quietly, glancing back at the bottom of the garden. "I must've picked it up."

Prudence's van roared to life, the washing line snapping as she trundled down the side of the cottage, speeding off to who-knew-where.

Julia's stomach turned to lead. "Oh, Prudence. Not *you*."

18

*B*arker pressed his palms against his desk, studying the mess of papers spread before him. The steady tick of Conrad's clock seemed to mock him from the corner.

He picked up his notes on Polly and Ethan. The timeline was there, the motive clear as crystal: Polly's book sales would soar now that Wendy was dead, unable to block its publication. And Ethan? He'd finally be free of the woman who'd destroyed his business when he was already down.

"The puppet master and her puppet," he muttered, sketching out the relationship on a fresh sheet of paper. But something had changed. Ethan's behaviour at the market... he'd grown distant from Polly, almost resentful. Had he cut his strings? Tired of doing her bidding?

Barker began mapping their movements on that crucial morning:

10:30 AM - Wendy's nail in the cruffin
11:00 AM - Dot's photo showing Ethan and Prudence absent
? - Ethan spotted at B&B
11:30 AM - Last confirmed sighting of Wendy
12:00 PM - Body discovered at salon

The ticking of Conrad's clock grew louder, demanding his attention. Barker lifted his gaze to study it—such beautiful craftsmanship, even with its maker's flaws. Conrad had poured his soul into these timepieces while his life crumbled around him.

If Polly and Ethan were behind this, Barker was missing something. A way to prove it conclusively. The threatening notes pointed to Polly, but with her in custody when Conrad was killed... unless that's exactly what they wanted everyone to think.

The rain drummed harder against the basement door. Somewhere out there, Ethan was still manning his pastry van, going through the motions. But for how much longer? If Barker's theory was right—if Polly was the puppet master—then Ethan's apparent break from her control made him dangerous. A loose canon.

Barker wanted to bang his head against the table. What was he missing?

∽

"It doesn't make sense." Jessie paced Veronica's sitting room for what felt like the hundredth time, wearing a path in the rug. "We must have gone to the wrong van."

Veronica leaned against her dining table, surrounded by open newspapers and half-empty coffee cups. Rain drummed against the windows, matching Jessie's restless energy.

"We found the flower, Jessie," Veronica said, defeat thick in her voice. "The poison flower that killed Wendy. Right there on your shoe after snooping in Prudence's van."

"But—"

"Think of the headline." Veronica's eyes lit up with an enthusiasm Jessie hadn't seen since before Wendy arrived. She grabbed a notebook, already scribbling. "'FORMER TV CHEF'S SLOW-COOKED REVENGE.' The story practically writes itself, and we get to break it here, in Peridale. First Wendy steals her show, then years later—"

"My mum let her live in her garden." Jessie's boots squeaked against the wooden floor as she turned. The sound grated on her nerves, but she couldn't stay still. "Julia wouldn't have done that if Prudence was guilty— her instincts wouldn't have let her. You know what she's like with people."

"I'm sure Julia has been wrong before." Veronica's pen stilled on the paper. "She's not a murder mystery oracle."

"But never *this* wrong." Jessie collapsed onto the worn leather armchair by the fire, only to spring up again seconds later. "This doesn't add up."

"Look, it's over." Veronica dropped her pen and sank

into her chair with a weary sigh that seemed to age her ten years. "I should never have told you about the higher-ups wanting to cut circulation. It's made you reckless, running around breaking into vans, chasing stories that aren't there—"

"It's made me want to fight." Jessie planted her hands on Veronica's table. "Remember that feeling, Veronica? Wanting to fight for what's right?" Her voice softened as she studied her mentor's face. "Maybe you should have told me sooner about the paper's troubles. You used to want to keep me in the loop. This... hiring Wendy without asking what I thought..." Her voice hardened again. "What else aren't you telling me?"

Veronica wouldn't meet her eyes. "Jessie, please—"

But Jessie was already halfway to the door, yanking it open to let in a blast of heavy rain. The weather matched her mood—dark and troubled.

"Where are you going?" Veronica called after her, rising from her desk. "*Jessie!*"

The rain soaked her to the bone in seconds as she plunged into the downpour, but she didn't care. Her instincts were telling her this wasn't over, and if Julia had taught her anything, it was to chase that feeling.

"To make sure we found the right van," Jessie said to herself.

~

The rain hammered against the cottage windows as Julia curled deeper into her armchair, trying to ignore the steady drip-drip-drip down the chimney. That sound always meant trouble—another thing that needed fixing —but how could she think about having workmen in when her mind was spinning with suspects?

Polly, Ethan, Melissa, Prudence... where had it all gone so wrong? And that flower in Prudence's van. Her childhood idol. The thought made her stomach clench.

A sharp knock at the door jolted her from her thoughts. Finally—she'd been waiting for DI Moyes for over an hour.

But when she opened the door, only another magazine-cut note greeted her on the doorstep. The paper was sodden, but the message was clear: 'THIS IS YOUR LAST WARNING!'

Julia yanked the door open, her heart skipping a beat. The rain lashed against her face as she squinted into the darkness beyond her porch light. Empty path, empty garden—only the slight glow of Veronica's cottage across the lane.

"Whoever you are..." Her voice cracked, barely carrying over the wind. She swallowed hard and tried again. "... I'm not scared of you!"

But her legs wobbled, betraying the lie. The same person who'd killed Wendy and Conrad could be watching her right now from the shadows. The thought sent ice through her veins.

She slammed the door shut, fingers fumbling with the lock. The click of the deadbolt offered little comfort as she hurried to the kitchen, nearly slipping in her wet socks. Her hands shook so badly she dropped the phone twice before managing to punch in Dot's number.

The dial tone stretched on forever as Julia pressed

herself against the wall, watching the windows. Why wasn't her gran picking up? She always answered, even at this hour. Unless—

"Is Olivia alright?" The words tumbled out before her gran could finish saying hello. "Is she safe?"

"Of course she is, dear." Dot's voice carried its usual calm assurance. "We're having a lovely tea party with Ethel's gnomes. They don't make the best company, but we're getting by. Why?"

"Just... lock the doors, alright? And don't go out." Julia pressed her forehead against the cool fridge. "Have you seen Prudence's van anywhere?"

Another knock interrupted Dot's reply.

"Gran, I have to go—"

This time, DI Moyes stood on the doorstep, rain dripping from her coat. "What's so urgent?"

Julia ushered her in, words failing as she handed over the fresh note.

"For heaven's sake." Moyes' face darkened as she read it. "I'll send it with the others for testing, but whoever's doing this must be wearing gloves. We got nothing useful from the previous ones, except for that hair."

"And?" Julia's voice caught.

"DNA confirms it does belong to Polly, but with her being in custody when Conrad was killed—and no proof she sent any of the others—we can't be sure if she actually sent the notes or if someone's trying to frame her."

Julia wrapped her arms around herself, the kitchen's warmth doing little to chase away the chill of fear. DI

Moyes' words about Polly's DNA twisted her thoughts in new directions. If someone was framing Polly, that meant the murderer was clever enough to plant evidence.

"The hair could have come from anywhere in the market," Julia said. "Polly's been selling her books there all week."

"Exactly." Moyes pulled out her notebook. "Listen, I know you won't want to, but why don't you get out of the village for a few days? We're going public tomorrow with an appeal about the hammer. It might turn up in someone's garden or bin." She tried for an encouraging smile. "Then everything might get wrapped up."

Julia stared at the rain streaming down the window, remembering how just hours ago she'd been baking with Prudence in her kitchen. How quickly everything could change. How wrong she could be about people.

Julia's fingers trembled as she reached into her apron pocket. "I didn't call about the note." She pulled out the clear sandwich bag containing the delicate white flower. "Jessie found this earlier today in Prudence's van."

The crushed lily of the valley's tiny bell-shaped bloom looked almost innocent, hiding its lethal nature. Julia's stomach churned as she handed it to DI Moyes.

Moyes' expression hardened as she examined the flower through the plastic. "Prudence's van?"

Julia nodded. "I called as soon as we found it. It was on Jessie's shoe."

"And where is Prudence now?" Moyes' tone sharpened.

"I don't know." Julia backed into the oven, the

kitchen suddenly feeling colder. The cruffins were still inside, uncooked and abandoned. "She drove off before we could ask her about the flower."

"Running, more like." Moyes shoved her notebook away after jotting down the details. "That lines up with the sighting that was reported this morning."

"Sighting?"

"On Mulberry Lane," Moyes said, pulling open the door to the rain. "Your stepmother's apprentice decided it was the perfect time to remember that she saw a 'sort of bag lady' in the salon around the time Wendy was killed."

"Bag lady?" Julia repeated. "Prudence?"

"Who else?" Moyes rolled her eyes as she stepped out into the rain. "Lock up behind me, and think about what I said about getting out of Peridale."

Julia's hands shook as she turned both locks and slid the bolt across. The rain hammered harder against the windows, and somewhere in the darkness, a murderer was loose—perhaps the same person she'd welcomed into her kitchen just hours ago.

She pressed her back against the door, the wood solid and reassuring behind her. But what now? She considered taking Moyes' advice and packing a bag but that felt too much like running away.

The dripping from the chimney grew louder, each drop echoing like a ticking clock counting down to something just out of reach.

She couldn't bear the sound any longer. She snatched her raincoat from its hook and grabbed her car keys.

The windscreen wipers of her old car struggled against the relentless downpour as she sped through Peridale's winding streets towards Mulberry Lane. A jagged streak of purple lightning split the sky, casting an eerie glow over the deserted roads. She slammed on the brakes outside the salon just as thunder cracked overhead, its deep growl echoing through the empty street.

Inside, she found Katie and Clarice sharing sandwiches at the reception desk.

"Julia! You look absolutely frazzled." Katie jumped up, reaching for her arm. "I think it's time you let me tackle those eyebrows again. It's the least I can do. Sit down, let me make you a cuppa—"

"No time." Julia turned to Clarice, who shrank back in her chair. "I spoke to DI Moyes. Tell me about this woman you saw. The bag lady."

"Bag lady?" Katie echoed, putting down her sandwich. "Are you talking about Mrs Coggles because she'll never let it go if you—"

"No, not her." Clarice's fingers twisted in her lap. "I... I didn't think much of it at the time. She was just some woman."

Julia moved closer, lowering her voice. "What kind of woman?"

"Wearing lots of layers." Clarice's voice grew smaller. "I thought she was homeless... confused. She came in asking for Wendy, but I didn't know anyone called Wendy then, so I couldn't help..."

"Where did she go after that?"

A blush crept across Clarice's cheeks. "That prawn

madras really did a number on me. I had to run off to the bathroom. She might've left."

"Or she might have gone upstairs," Julia finished what Clarice couldn't admit. "This was after Wendy came back from the market?"

Clarice nodded.

"Well, that settles it." Julia's chest tightened as she slumped down into a chair. She shook her head at Katie as she reached for the threading string. "Prudence killed Wendy, and probably killed Conrad to finish getting her twenty-year revenge. And now her and that red camper van have gone and they could be anywhere."

～

Jessie huddled behind Ethel's gnome stall, watching Ethan's van through the curtain of rain. He'd been parked there for hours despite the empty market square. Only a few determined stallholders remained, huddled beneath dripping awnings.

Through the drizzle, Jessie watched Ethan take another sip from his water bottle. His fingers drummed against the counter, looking out for non-existent customers.

Ethan's leg bounced with increasing urgency. Nature would have to call eventually—the new public loos were across the market by the post office. Jessie's muscles ached from crouching, but she forced herself to stay still. Just a bit longer.

Finally, Ethan hopped down from his van, keys jangling as he locked up. The moment his figure disappeared around the corner, Jessie sprang into action. Her heart pounded as she tried the van's back door—locked.

Refusing to give up, she circled to the front. The metal shutter groaned as she tested it, then slid upward with surprising ease. She pulled herself up, her shoes slipping against the slick metal as the van rocked. She couldn't give up. Not now. With a final heave, she hauled herself over the counter and dropped down.

The inside was a disaster. The kind of mess that would fail an unannounced visit from a health inspector. *One star—do not eat here.* The man had clearly given up.

She had to move fast. Ethan wouldn't be gone long, and she needed answers about his connection to both murders. Jessie began rifling through drawers and cabinets, searching for anything suspicious.

Jessie's fingers trembled as she pushed aside trays of stale pastries. The van's musty interior reeked of rancid butter and desperation. Nothing suspicious in the food—of course not. What had she expected? A signed confession tucked between croissants?

She yanked open a cupboard beneath the counter, finding boxes stacked haphazardly. Her heart raced as she rifled through their contents. Old receipts, delivery notes, a stack of bad reviews printed from various websites. Then her hand brushed something cold and wet.

Jessie pulled out a plastic carrier bag, heavy and dripping. Her stomach lurched at the dark red stains seeping through. With shaking hands, she unwrapped a sodden rag, revealing what lay within—a hammer, its metal head crusted with blood.

The click of a key in the lock behind her made her blood run cold. Jessie clutched the bag to her chest, frozen in place as the door creaked open.

Rain poured in as the door swung wide, silhouetting Ethan against the grey afternoon. Water dripped from his hair, running down his face like tears, but his eyes blazed with fury as he took in the scene—Jessie, the hammer, and nowhere for her to run.

He stepped inside, the door slamming behind him with horrible finality.

"You shouldn't be in here..." His quiet voice carried more menace than any shout.

19

"*A*nd you're sure Olivia's alright?" Julia asked for the third time.

"Right as rain," Dot replied. "Though speaking of rain, it's finally easing off. Have you found that red van yet?"

"No."

"I *knew* it was her." Dot's voice rose with vindication. "Didn't I tell you there was something off about that Prudence woman. Clearly lost her marbles. I'll get out with Lady and Bruce—we'll find her in no time."

"No!" Julia's sharp tone surprised even herself. "Just stay there with Olivia. Doors locked."

"Right." Dot's enthusiasm dimmed. "Oh, Julia, I don't like how scared you sound. Is this what it was like? Back when Wendy was bullying you?"

Julia's throat tightened as she considered the question. The notes weren't just bullying—they were something darker. Like the ones sent to Wendy before she died, they were meant to frighten, to unsettle. And it was working.

Katie appeared in front of her, waving to get her attention. Julia seized the chance for an escape.

"Katie," Julia said, pocketing her phone, "if you're about to thread my eyebrows again, I really do like their natural—"

"It's not that." Katie thrust her phone in front of Julia. "I put out a call on social media, like last time. We found those clues in the pictures before."

"Those were red herrings," Julia said wearily. "Conrad and Wendy kissing didn't matter in the end."

"Well, this might." Katie tapped a nail on the screen. "*Look.*"

Julia's heart skipped a beat. There, timestamped just minutes ago, was a photo of a familiar red camper van parked on the outskirts of Fern Moore. She grabbed her jacket and ran for the door.

～

Barker pulled off his reading glasses, pinching the bridge of his nose as if it might squeeze clarity into his thoughts. He was going in circles, trying to connect the dots without the string.

The sudden thundering of footsteps on the basement stairs jerked his head up. Jessie burst into the room, chest heaving, and slammed a plastic bag onto his desk with such force that the clock toppled. Its rhythmic ticking cut off abruptly, the silence ringing louder than the clatter.

Barker blinked away the shock. "What's that?"

"The murder weapon," Jessie said, breathless. "Conrad's hammer."

Barker noticed Jessie wasn't alone. Ethan lingered in the doorway, his eyes darting around the office like a cornered animal.

"What's he doing here?"

"I found it," Jessie explained, "in his van."

Barker rose from his chair, fumbling for his phone. "And he just came with you willingly?"

"Of course he did." Jessie's voice carried an edge of triumph. "Because Ethan didn't kill anyone. And if we can prove his alibi for the time of Conrad's death..." She nodded encouragingly at Ethan.

Ethan swallowed hard, his Adam's apple bobbing. "I was at The Plough all night, drowning my sorrows at the bar. The barmaid I was desperately flirting with will vouch for me." He bowed his head. "I didn't take the hint she wasn't interested the first time. Made a fool of myself, truth be told. It's... been a rough week."

Barker's sceptical gaze shifted between Ethan and the bloody hammer. He'd never seen the man so vulnerable, so cornered—but it could still be a trick. He tried to imagine this version of Ethan, a boy lost in a man's world, lifting a hammer to strike Conrad down in his workshop. But the image wouldn't come.

"Why were you at the B&B?" Barker demanded, his voice sharp.

Ethan flinched, then sighed, running a hand through his dishevelled hair. "I only went to confront Wendy, to give her a piece of my mind. Polly was having a go at me all morning for the way Wendy snubbed her stall. Made me feel like I should've done or said something, but I didn't want anything to do with Wendy. I was happy to be snubbed. I didn't want to be on her bad side again, and if that made me *weak*, so be it. She'd only just left me alone, but Polly wouldn't stop poking and poking, so I stormed off to go and find Wendy." His eyes met Barker's, pleading. "You're right, I *did* go to the B&B, but she wasn't there, so I went back to the market. Even now, I don't even know where the newspaper office is, and I wouldn't even know where to begin with poisoning someone."

Barker studied Ethan, weighing his words. The man's usual evasiveness was gone, replaced by a raw honesty that felt out of character.

"Think about it, Dad," Jessie urged, spreading a note on the desk assembled from cut-out magazine letters. "This came to the office. If Ethan was behind this, why would he send a note telling us to look in his van if the murder weapon was sitting in there?"

"Maybe Polly sent the note?" Barker suggested, keeping his eyes trained on Ethan, who seemed more terrified than threatening. "There's a million explanations for—"

"Polly didn't send the note." Jessie planted her hands on the desk, staring firmly at Barker with more conviction than he'd ever seen from his daughter. "She was in the police station then, just like when Conrad was murdered. I don't think she sent any of the notes—not even the one with the hair."

"She didn't," Ethan said, shaking his head. "It's not her style."

Jessie nudged Ethan, dragging him into the light of Barker's desk lamp. "Tell him, Ethan," she urged. "Tell him whose flat you've been staying in."

～

Julia barely registered the drive to Fern Moore, her Anglia bouncing over speed bumps as the grey tower blocks loomed ahead. She circled the estate twice, scanning every corner, but the red van remained elusive.

Finally, she pushed open the door to Daphne's. The café was empty.

Daphne rolled her neck at the sight of Julia. "Something tells me you're not here for a sandwich?"

"I need your help." Julia approached the counter, keeping her voice low despite the lack of customers. "If your café is anything like mine, you'll know what's going on around here. I'm looking for a red camper van. The woman inside—she might hold answers to what's happening in the village. She... she might be a murderer."

Daphne's expression hardened. "We don't snitch around here."

"I know," Julia pressed on, "but I need to know where she is. Café owner to café owner, if that means anything, I need to know... I..."

Daphne exhaled, her lips pursing as she studied Julia's face. Just when Julia thought she wouldn't help, Daphne's stern expression softened.

"Alright, just calm down," she said, sucking her teeth. "You Peridale folk are always so dramatic." She jerked her head at the far wall. "She's round the back. Wanted to plug into the café's electric, if you can believe it." She shook her head. "Does she know how much it costs these days?"

Julia released the breath she'd been holding.

"Be careful, yeah?" Daphne called after her. "If you're not back in here in two minutes to let me know you're alright, I'm calling the police."

Julia managed a smile over her shoulder. "Make it five. She doesn't like to get to the point right away. Thank you, Daphne."

"I suppose us 'café owners' should stick together, right?" Daphne said reluctantly as she pulled a cigarette out of a packet. "Even if I do rent."

Julia hurried around the side of the building, skidding to a halt at the sight of the familiar red van parked in the shadow of the café. And there was Prudence, crouched beside an old metal bin, trying to coax life into a struggling fire while the wind and rain mocked her.

She spotted Julia from the corner of her eye, her expression hardening as she straightened up. The flicker of firelight cast shadows across her features, hollowing out the aged skin clinging to her once-sharp cheekbones.

"What do you want?" Prudence muttered. "I thought I'd made myself clear."

"We need to talk."

"I've nothing more to say to you," Prudence declared,

turning on her heel and marching back towards her van. She tried to slam the van door, but Julia caught it with the tip of her shoe. "How dare you!"

"I dare," Julia said, meeting Prudence's gaze. "I respected you. I looked up to you, and you—" Her voice caught. "You killed Wendy, and Conrad. I know she had it coming, but—"

"Hold your horses!" Prudence fanned her hands in front of her. "I told you already, I didn't kill anyone. The only thing I've killed is my pride."

"Jessie had a flower stuck to her shoe after she left your van." Julia's voice hardened. "I know she shouldn't have been snooping like that, but it was the same flower used to poison Wendy. Lily of the valley." She waited for Prudence to react, but the woman offered nothing more than a slight arch of her eyebrow. "And now that I think about it, Shilpa from the post office said she saw you skulking off around that time. A fresh eyewitness came forward, placing you in the nail salon right before Wendy would have been poisoned upstairs." Julia tossed her hands out. "You can't keep lying, Prudence. I know it was you."

Prudence's glare made Julia's certainty waver. She wasn't just looking at the face she used to see on TV anymore—she was staring at someone she realised she'd never known at all. All that warmth through the screen had been Julia's own projection, looking up to a woman who reminded her of her mother, someone she'd wanted to become... had become.

"You might be a good baker, Julia," Prudence said softly, "but you don't know everything." She stepped back from the door. "Now, do you want to come in for a cup of tea?"

"Skip the tea," Julia said. "Tell me everything."

"Fine."

Prudence struck a match and tossed it into the bin. The flame caught with help from several squirts of lighter fluid, casting dancing shadows across the weeds jutting out of the cracked paving stones. She settled onto an upturned milk crate in the fire's glow, but Julia remained standing.

"I'll admit it," Prudence began, her face haunted in the firelight. "I went to the nail salon. I even followed Wendy to the office." Her voice dropped to barely above a whisper. "I don't know what came over me, but after seeing her up to her old tricks with that obviously planted nail in your cruffin, I finally wanted to give her the piece of my mind I'd been holding back for twenty years."

She stared into the flames. "But someone beat me to it. I went upstairs and found her on the floor, gasping for breath. Her last breath." Prudence's hands trembled. "I saw the life fade from her eyes as she stared at me, begging me to help, to save her, and then... I left. I didn't call for help. I just left her there to die, like she left me to die all those years ago."

"Oh, Prudence."

Tears glinted in the firelight. "And even after everything she did to me, I haven't been able to sleep a wink since. I keep thinking about that girl who never had a mother... that girl who felt left out, powerless..."

Julia sighed, not knowing what to believe anymore.

"That's a convenient way to put yourself at the scene without admitting to anything. How did that flower get into your van if you didn't put it there?"

"Because I didn't leave Mulberry Lane alone." Prudence's voice carried a weight Julia hadn't heard before. "I tried to tell you earlier when your daughter rudely interrupted us. I told you I had something important to tell you."

"You did," Julia remembered, still wincing about that interruption. "So, tell me."

"I left the salon and went back out on the street. I was in such a daze, I didn't know what to do, so I decided I'd just have to carry on as normal. I knew she was dead, and it would only be a matter of time before the police found a hair or something. You know what they're like with DNA these days, so I knew I had to keep going. I'd get back to selling my sauces. That's all I could think to do. I suppose I was in shock, but that's when I saw that woman. That florist."

Julia frowned. "Melissa?"

Prudence nodded slowly. "She told me she was coming back from her florist shop."

Gulping, Julia said, "Melissa doesn't have a shop. She arranges flowers from home and works part-time in a garden centre."

"Then that explains why she was shaking and sweating," Prudence said. "I invited her into my van for tea, and we waited there until someone announced they'd found Wendy dead." She poked at the fire with a stick. "And then we never spoke again, and I never asked her any questions. Wendy had ruined enough lives without ruining another, but I knew. Deep down, I knew it had to be her. But it was that man that confused me... Conrad..." Her voice cracked. "Melissa wouldn't kill him. She loved him. I'd see the way she'd look at him when she'd turn up at the studio when Wendy first joined the show. And again at the market. She wanted him."

Julia narrowed her eyes, staring past the café towards Melissa's flat, seeing those rooms full of flowers in her mind's eye. Melissa's words from her last visit echoed back: I loved him so much, and if he'd have let me back in, he might not have died.

"Melissa wanted Conrad back," Julia said slowly, the truth crystallizing. "That much was obvious..."

The pieces were falling into place, each revelation clicking with horrible clarity, when DI Moyes rushed around the corner, breathless.

"Got a call from the station about you confronting a murderer," she panted, waving for Julia to step back from Prudence and the fire. "Then Barker called saying they've found the murder weapon."

"Murder weapon?" Prudence asked, standing.

"The hammer. Found in Ethan's van, but he's claiming he's been set up." Moyes looked past Julia to Prudence. "You found her then."

"Thank Katie and the power of social media," Julia said, standing between Moyes and Prudence, "but she's not behind this. She was at the salon, but so was someone else."

Moyes sighed, planting her hands on her hips. "Who?"

"The same person who's been sharing a flat with

Polly and Ethan. She had access to Polly's hair, she would have known where and when to plant a hammer in Ethan's van, and most importantly," Julia's voice hardened before she said, "she knew all about the poisonous flowers."

"Melissa?" Moyes frowned. "But she's so... quiet. Isn't she your friend?"

"She was," Julia confirmed, her voice tinged with regret. "We were good friends in college, but we never stayed in touch. It's like you said before, Laura." She levelled with the DI on a personal note, her tone softening. "When you meet people you haven't seen in years, sometimes they're not who you want them to be. We're never how we remember each other years down the line, not really... but sometimes, things do stay the same." She looked to the floral flat again as Melissa closed the curtains. "Melissa has hated Wendy and Conrad for two decades. And in those two decades that I haven't seen her, the seeds of that hatred have bloomed into something dark and ugly."

Moyes studied Julia, her expression shifting from scepticism to reluctant understanding. "You really think she's capable of this?"

"She's hiding," Julia said. "From us, and from herself, I think."

"But none of the evidence..." Moyes started. "This isn't going to be easy to prove."

"Then we don't prove it." Julia rounded the corner of the café, her gaze fixed on Melissa's window, where she could see her former college friend watering her plants, all trace of earlier tears gone. "We catch her in the act."

She turned back to them, her mind racing ahead. "Prudence, I need you to write a letter to Melissa, and I need you to move your van back to the market."

Moyes didn't look convinced. "What's that going to achieve?"

"Melissa's still out there delivering threatening letters, trying to scare people off." Julia's voice carried steel now. "It's time we play her at her own game. Tomorrow, at the market, we'll see how things unfold." She met Moyes' uncertain gaze. "Tomorrow, this ends."

20

The next morning, Barker hung back as Julia moved through the familiar routine of opening the café: chairs scraped against the floor as she set them down, lights flickered on, and the scent of freshly brewed coffee mingled with the faint aroma of Sue's baking from the kitchen. He watched her from the counter, his hands wrapped around a steaming mug of black coffee he couldn't stomach.

Julia paused to wipe down a table, her fingers tracing the grain of the wood as if grounding herself. She hadn't touched her own peppermint and liquorice tea.

"There has to be another way," he said, not for the first time that morning. "DI Moyes could—"

"No," Julia said. "It has to be me."

"You're not trained for this." Barker set his mug down, trying to plead with a stare his wife refused to meet. "What if something goes wrong? She's more unpredictable than you give her credit for."

Julia set down her cloth, the soft thud of it against the table punctuating her words. "She won't hurt me, Barker."

"You don't know that."

"Don't I?" She twisted her wedding ring. "She had the opportunity to poison me when I had tea at hers, and she didn't. Even though Melissa is jealous of what we have. And not just us—anyone who found their happily ever after. The one she wanted to have with Conrad. The one she cried about when we were eighteen in that canteen, how she planned to split Wendy and Conrad up, to win him back, to prove to him that she was worthy of being his girlfriend."

"An obsession."

"Love," Julia corrected.

"Is there a difference?"

She arched a brow in a way that let him know she thought he was being silly. "Melissa loved Conrad, but it warped into something dark, and him walking back into her life at the garden centre all those years later by accident gave her a glimmer of hope that never came." She cast her gaze out the window as Ethel ferried her latest batch of gnomes across the green in cardboard boxes. "If Melissa was going to hurt me, she could have. She tried to frame Polly and Ethan, when I was right here. Wendy embarrassed me at that market launch. I would have been an easy target."

"But the letters—"

"Harmless bits of paper."

"Threats, Julia."

"She could have struck at any moment!" Julia tried to

laugh, but the sound rang hollow around the café. "I wish I didn't, but I understand her, Barker. Even after everything, she still looks at me like I'm that girl who supported her all those years ago. She's been trying to hide behind me, to pull the wool over my eyes, but—"

Barker sighed. "But you've never been this close to the truth before."

Julia turned to face him, resting a hand on his cheek. "It has to be me. I understand her in a way nobody else does. I know how loss can eat away at you, how resentment can fester." She touched her mother's old recipe book on the counter, its torn page still held together with yellowing tape. "Some people lash out because they're hurting. Others do it because they learn to enjoy the power. Melissa started as one and became the other."

"All the more reason to let the police handle this."

Julia shook her head. "It has to be someone she trusts, someone she thinks she knows." She squeezed his hand. "Someone who once shared in her pain, or she'll just go on lying."

"And what if you're wrong?" Barker's voice cracked. "What if that connection isn't enough?"

"Then we've badly misread everything." Julia attempted a smile that didn't quite reach her eyes. "But I don't think we have." She glanced at the clock—nearly time. "Trust me, Barker. Please."

He pulled her close, breathing in the familiar scent of vanilla that always clung to her clothes. "I do trust you. It's her I don't trust."

She stepped back, squeezing his hands one final

time before gathering her coat. "I need to go. The others will be waiting." She paused at the café door. "Go and check on Olivia at my dad's shop if you want to be useful. Otherwise, stand back and wait for the show to begin."

Barker could only nod, watching his wife step out into the bitter morning. The hum of the coffee machine on a self-cleaning cycle filled the silence, steam rising like a ghost in the winter light, but he couldn't bring himself to make another cup that would go cold.

Instead, he reached for his phone.

BARKER

This better go off without a hitch.

MOYES

I've got every officer in the county in plain clothes waiting at the market.

BARKER

That's not what I said...

MOYES

I know, but you couldn't talk her out of it anymore than I could. You know she has a point.

BARKER

I just wish there was another way.

MOYES

We need that confession or the case falls apart. Julia is right. We CAN catch her out. You know it's a sound plan

BARKER

I know :/

If Julia was right, this would all be over soon. And if she was wrong... he pushed the thought away, unable to finish it.

∿

Jessie's fingers cramped around her fourth cup of coffee as she hunched over her laptop in Daphne's. She'd positioned herself perfectly—clear view of Melissa's flat while appearing absorbed in work. The morning rush had dwindled to a few regulars, leaving the café wrapped in an uneasy quiet broken only by the gentle clink of cups and the hum of the ancient heating system.

"Another refill?" Daphne's voice carried a hint of concern as she approached with the coffee pot. "Or maybe something stronger? Got a bottle of brandy out back."

"Just coffee." Jessie managed a weak smile. "Thanks."

Daphne lingered, wiping down the already spotless table. "More trouble brewing, is it?" She lowered her voice. "First that Wendy business, now this. Fern Moore's got enough problems without—"

"It'll be over soon," Jessie cut in, though she couldn't quite meet Daphne's eyes. "One way or another."

Through the streaked café window, Jessie watched Melissa move between her beloved plants, misting leaves with a spray bottle. Anyone looking would see a quiet woman tending her indoor garden. But Jessie knew better. For as sweet as she came across, Melissa was as fake as Wendy.

Her phone buzzed.

DAD

Updates???

JESSIE

Nothing yet. Normal routine. I told you that I'll text when she leaves 👀

DAD

IF she leaves

JESSIE

She will. CHILL OUT.

DAD

👍

JESSIE

😵😵‍💫😑

With her phone still in her hands, she swapped to the gallery app. She pulled up the picture of Wendy and Conrad kissing. Both dead, but it was the stall next to it that she hadn't noticed before—Melissa's flower stall, conveniently empty. She'd no doubt been off somewhere, crushing and brewing her poison to add to Wendy's tea the first chance she got.

"What's that you're looking at?"

Jessie jumped. Daphne had returned, settling into the chair opposite with her own cup of coffee.

"You've been watching that flat all morning."

"Just... research." Jessie tried to sound casual. "For an article."

"Must be some article." Daphne's eyes carried a knowing look. "That Melissa keeps to herself mostly. Moved back here about a year ago—right after her mother passed. Inherited the flat." She stirred her coffee thoughtfully. "Seemed nice enough, but there was always something... what's the word?"

"Off?"

"Distant. Like she wasn't really here." Daphne glanced at the flat. "Started having those guests stay, though. The angry couple. Caused quite a stir with their arguing. I know Shelly upstairs hasn't been too pleased. I saw that fella they found dead in the workshop visit a few times. She ran after him once, apologising. She was all red, her lipstick smudged, and he was wiping his mouth. Do you think she made a pass at him?"

"Dunno," Jessie replied, but movement in the flat caught her eye. Melissa had appeared at the window, checking her watch. "Come on," she urged under her breath. "Take the bait."

"What is it with your family?" Daphne said, shaking her head as she left the table. "Never can mind your own business. Must be in the blood."

"I'm adopted."

"A funny gas leak at your house, then."

"We don't live together."

"Know-it-alls, too!" Daphne said, planting her hands on her hips. "There's no end to you lot."

But Jessie wasn't listening. Melissa had vanished from the window. Moments later, she burst from the flat's entrance, fumbling with her keys. Her composed mask had slipped completely now, replaced by barely contained panic as she scanned the courtyard, as though she knew she was being watched. Her frantic gaze drifted right by the café.

Jessie was already pulling on her coat. She dropped a twenty on the table, far too much for the coffee, but she didn't have change and had no time to wait.

"Watch how you go." Daphne's voice followed her to the door. "Whatever you're mixed up in."

Outside, the bitter wind stung Jessie's face as she followed Melissa's hurrying figure. Her target moved with single-minded purpose, barely noticing the treacherous ice beneath her feet. At the bus stop, Melissa checked her watch again, then her phone, then her watch. She took a moment to clutch her side, as though nursing a bruise.

Jessie's back still hurt from that fall—she'd been so close to catching her then.

Melissa wasn't going to get away so easily this time.

The bus appeared as a soft blanket of swirling snow started to drift down, right on schedule. Jessie counted to five before climbing aboard, keeping her hood up. She chose a seat near the back, heart thundering as Melissa's fingers drummed against her handbag four rows ahead.

Jessie watched Melissa's reflection in the window, noting how her formerly pristine posture had crumpled, how her hands shook as she checked her watch yet again. Dropping her head, Jessie pulled out her phone.

JESSIE

The eagle has flown 🦅Mum was right. Prudence's letter worked!!

DAD

266

JESSIE

That's all you have to say old man...

DAD

I don't know what to say... I'm...

JESSIE

Freaking out?

DAD

Yep 👍

JESSIE

Me too 👍👍👍👍👍👍

Before she pocketed her phone, she sent one more text she knew she wouldn't get a response to.

JESSIE

Hope you're comfy Mum. She's on her way 💀😹⚒

The bus wound its way towards Peridale, and Jessie couldn't shake the feeling that they were all hurtling towards something none of them were truly prepared for.

21

*J*ulia lay still in Prudence's van, forcing her breathing to remain deep and even. The scents of garlic and herbs couldn't mask the underlying mustiness, nor calm her racing heart.

Outside, the market square had fallen strangely quiet. It was busy—heaving, even—and Katie had been giddy at the sight of the people flocking in that morning. Julia hadn't had the heart to admit she knew they were undercover police officers, all with Melissa's description memorised in case things didn't go as Julia had predicted.

But they would.

Melissa had come this far.

Yesterday's final warning letter to Julia proved she still thought she could get away with her crimes, even after everything. Knowing what she knew now cast Melissa's erratic behaviour at the flat in a different light. A woman scared she was about to be rumbled, but she'd still let Julia slip through her fingers, even knowing that Julia could 'sort things out.' Though this was a little more important than planted cake boxes, a stolen school bag, and a broken teenage heart.

She checked her phone for the time in the dim light filtering through the van's curtains. Half past eleven. She didn't risk replying to Jessie, not wanting to move too much. Melissa would always arrive ten minutes early to every class, perching on the edge of her seat like a bird ready to take flight.

She'd been so eager to make something of herself. Who would she have become if she hadn't let her heart distract her?

Too late to find out.

Only one future stretched out in front of Melissa now, and it involved His Majesty's court and barred windows.

But the memory of the younger Melissa brought an unexpected lump to Julia's throat. That scared girl seemed worlds away from the woman who'd poisoned Wendy, who'd struck down Conrad in his workshop.

Yet somehow, they were the same person.

Julia had spent the night wondering how she'd missed it back then—or if she'd known all along that something was off about Melissa and simply chosen not to see.

Melissa had been too eager to cling to Julia. Too eager to try and rope Julia into her plans to split Wendy and Conrad up. Julia had refused.

Tossing and turning all night, she'd tried to remember the last time she'd seen Melissa before she turned up in her café, full of bright smiles and ready to reminisce about the past. It wasn't easy to recall. She'd never consciously decided that Melissa wouldn't be part of her life going forward. It was true they'd drifted apart, but after digging into her memories, she remembered the exact day.

They'd gone to a little country pub—converted into flats, last time Julia drove past—to celebrate finishing college. Julia had been relieved that Wendy hadn't gone along, not that she'd had any friends left. Like when she'd left Auntie Shelly, Wendy had spent their final day proclaiming she was going to make something of herself, letting them all know she thought they were beneath her.

That suited Julia fine.

After convincing Mr Jackson to let her take her final exams, he'd decided to chalk the whole cake box incident up to a misunderstanding, and though that hadn't felt like justice, Julia had gone along with things to not provoke Wendy further.

Melissa had been at that pub, though. And at first, all had seemed well. The people on the course were all talking about their futures. Some were going off to work in family bakeries, others to university to study further, and Julia had talked about how all she wanted to do was open a little café in Peridale. A dream that had taken her another decade and loose change to realise, but she'd got there.

And Melissa... Melissa drank too much and spent the night, once again, sobbing about Conrad, blasting Wendy, and as usual, Julia had been left with Melissa, the only person on the course still willing to offer a shoulder to cry on. She could see the faces of the other students now—pitying Julia for being the one stuck with the girl who never stopped crying; embarrassed about how Melissa didn't seem to notice or care that everyone in the pub was staring at them; oblivious to the fact it was supposed to be a celebration.

A small part of Julia had hated those looks, wishing they understood Melissa's pain the way she did. Then maybe they'd want to help her, to make things right... except Julia did remember the last time she saw Melissa. And though the moment might not have been a conscious goodbye at the time, she'd known in her heart of hearts she couldn't continue by Melissa's side.

It had been close to eleven, and Julia had been trying to make her apologies so she could go home. Dot had already called the pub twice to make sure Julia was fine, but that excuse hadn't been enough for Melissa. She'd clung to Julia—physically and emotionally. And when Melissa cried that it had been six months and she'd never get over it, Julia, after one too many half-pints, had snapped that maybe it was time she did try to get over it.

"You can't carry on like this forever," Julia had said. "It's taking over your life!"

"I thought you *understood*!" Melissa had wailed. "I thought you were my *friend*!"

Melissa had stormed off into the night, and every instinct in Julia's body had told her to go after her—to make sure she was all right, to see that she got home safe. But Melissa had left Julia standing in the dark outside the closed pub, without a care for her.

So Julia let her go. And in the taxi they'd planned to share, she'd felt relieved to be moving on to whatever came next.

A part-time job at a bakery, marriage, working in a factory in London, separation, then her dream café, and the rest—and she'd never given Melissa much of a second thought until she'd shown up on the morning of the market launch.

Julia had been so happy to see someone from her past, she'd forgotten the rest.

A shadow passed across the van's window. Julia's chest tightened as soft footsteps approached, crunching against the fresh blanket of snow fluttering down. The door handle turned with aching slowness, letting in a blast of winter air that made Julia fight not to shiver.

She kept her eyes closed, maintaining the illusion of sleep as the van's ancient springs creaked under new weight. A pause, then the soft rustle of fabric—a pillow being lifted. Julia forced herself to remain still, counting her heartbeats. One. Two. Three—

The pillow descended swiftly but not violently. Even now, Melissa was trying to be gentle. Julia's hands shot up, pushing the pillow aside as she sat up.

"Hello, Melissa," Julia said. "You're right on time."

Melissa stumbled backwards, nearly falling through the van's door. The pillow dropped from her trembling fingers as confusion replaced determination on her face. "Julia? But... Prudence..."

"I'm sorry for the deception." Julia kept her voice steady despite her racing pulse. "But we needed to be sure."

"We?" Melissa's eyes darted towards the door. Her face hardened as understanding dawned. "You've set me up?"

"Like you set up Polly?" Julia watched hurt flash across Melissa's features. "And Ethan?"

"You don't understand—"

"I think I do." Julia shifted forward. "You're not going to hurt me, Melissa. Not after everything we shared." She paused, measuring her next words carefully. "And not with everyone watching."

Before Melissa could respond, Julia reached for the van's curtain. She drew it back slowly, revealing the circle of witnesses. Plain-clothes officers positioned in a strategic circle around the van. No escape, nowhere to run. Barker stood with DI Moyes. Jessie, notebook in hand. Prudence, Ethan, and Polly—all the players in Melissa's elaborate game gathered to see its end.

"How long have you known?" Melissa's voice had lost its warmth, becoming something harder, colder.

"Deep down? Since I caught you in the lie about how you met Polly." Julia shook her head. "Such a small lie, but it was the thread that made everything else unravel. The 'haunted heckler'—showing up in different disguises, desperate to spoil Wendy's moment in the spotlight." Julia leaned forward. "You let your pain take over your life so much that I don't think you've ever truly lived."

"I... I..."

"You had it all planned, didn't you?" Julia continued, sitting up fully in the bed that wasn't hers. "That first morning when you were in my café. The way you ran off when Wendy turned up. Ran off to prepare your poison?" She tilted her head to meet Melissa's eyes. "Nobody stole your flowers, did they? You were just trying to get ahead of the story."

"I had to be careful," Melissa whispered. "It had to look natural."

"The perfect murder." Julia's voice hardened. "Heart failure in a woman known for her sharp tongue and high stress. Nobody would question it." She pulled out the sandwich bag containing a pressed flower. "Did you plant this in Prudence's van to cover your tracks, or did you not know you had one stuck to your shoe?"

Melissa's fingers twitched, as though longing to touch the preserved bloom. "Such a beautifully tragic flower." Her voice carried a dreamy quality. "Did I ever tell you they were the first flower Conrad gave to me on our first date? I still have one pressed at home."

"You never tried to get over him."

"He wasn't hers to take." The words burst from Melissa like they'd been waiting years to escape. "He was mine. My special love. He chose me. The best-looking guy on our course."

"Melissa, he... tried it on with every girl."

"But he chose me," Melissa cried, extending a finger to Julia. "And she took everything from me just because she could. My love, my future, my chance at happiness—"

"So you took her life?"

Tears spilled down Melissa's cheeks, but these weren't the theatrical sobs from her flat days. These were real, raw, decades of pain finally breaking free.

"She never loved him," she choked in a whisper. "When I saw him at the garden centre, it was like my life had come full circle. I'd been waiting to see him again, to talk to him, to hold him... I knew it would happen one day. Destiny. And he was just... there, looking at plant pots." She laughed, wiping her tears. "He was looking for something to brighten up his workshop, and it was like no time had passed. I still loved him, and I could see how sorry he was. He invited me out for a drink, and he told me about the cooking school, about Wendy bleeding him dry." Her voice cracked. "He looked so broken, so lost. Just like I'd been all these years. I knew I had to do something to help him. We had our second chance right in front of us, I just had to reach out and grab it."

"By killing her."

"She couldn't get away with it again." Melissa's teary-eyed stare begged Julia to understand. "I had a chance to set things right, so I hadn't wasted my life for nothing. I called Polly to ask where Wendy was these days, and she mentioned Wendy was moving back here, trying for the newspaper job. It was too perfect—too easy." A bitter laugh escaped her. "Everyone Wendy had hurt over the years, all in one place."

Prudence cleared her throat. "It was you," she called through the window, her jaw gritted. "You slipped that flyer about this market under my windscreen wiper."

"And you invited us to come and stay with you," Polly said, shaking her head. "We were just pawns in your sick game."

"I needed suspects." Melissa's gaze drifted to the

watching crowd, searching for someone who understood. "People with better motives than me. I'm sorry, but Wendy wronged all of us. I couldn't be the only one."

"You tried to frame me!" Polly cried, beating a fist against the glass. "You planted my hair—"

"You were never my real friend," Melissa spat back. "You only kept in touch with me when you wanted someone to complain about Wendy to. Didn't you ever think about how that affected me? Dragging up my past, writing about me in your silly little book? It was too easy to frame you."

Julia sighed. "But Conrad figured it out, didn't he?"

Something dangerous flickered in Melissa's eyes. "He said he had a feeling I was the one sending him those texts, trying to scare him. I just wanted a reason to comfort him—he wouldn't let me in again. But he put the pieces together, and when you saw us at The Comfy Corner, he said he was going to tell everyone. Said I needed help." Her hands clenched into fists. "After everything I'd done for him... Wendy's death was supposed to free him. Free us both. But he couldn't see past her, even then."

"So you killed him too."

"I didn't mean to!" Melissa cried. "I didn't plan it. I gave him a choice."

"Shut up and be your boyfriend again or die?" Julia asked, unable to stop her head shaking in disapproval. "That wasn't much of a choice, Melissa. What sort of life would that have been?"

"We would have been together."

"Out of fear?" Julia said, pleading. "You murdered him out of rage. You loved him so much that you hated him for not loving you. Pure, blind passion."

"The hammer was just there." Fresh tears fell. "I didn't mean to. But he wouldn't stop talking about her. About how sick I was, how I needed help. He said he was going to the police." Her voice dropped to a whisper. "I couldn't let him ruin my life again."

"And Prudence?" Julia asked softly. "If she was in the bed right now, you would have smothered her?"

"She sent me a letter—"

"Telling you that she was going to the police if you didn't hand yourself in by noon?" Julia finished for her, nodding. "Yes, I know. That was my idea. She kept quiet about seeing you that day, after Wendy."

"I would have made it gentle. Like going to sleep."

"Please!" Prudence cried from outside. "This woman is worse than Wendy. At least Wendy knew she was a rotten egg."

Julia thought of that scared college girl, desperate to be loved. Of the woman that girl had become, twisted by obsession and grief.

"You always saw through me, didn't you?" Melissa didn't resist as DI Moyes approached from behind with handcuffs. "Even back then?"

Julia watched her former friend being led away, snow swirling in thick swathes, dusting the market square in clean, forgiving white. She remembered their shared cups of tea, their whispered confidences, their mutual understanding of loss.

Some wounds, she realised, never truly healed. They

just grew deeper, darker, until they changed you into someone you never thought you'd become.

Like that night when Julia had been left alone outside that country pub, watching Melissa run off into the dark, Julia let out a sigh of relief as Moyes and her officers rounded the corner.

The market square slowly came back to life around her. Stallholders emerged from their hiding places. Barker approached, wrapping her in a tight embrace. Jessie's pen scratched across her notebook while Veronica took pictures of everyone and everything, recording the final chapter of their latest mystery.

But Julia's gaze remained where Melissa's flower stall had stood, remembering the friend she'd lost not once, but twice—first to obsession, and now to justice.

∽

Later that afternoon, the café hummed with activity, the clatter of knives and forks and the hiss of the coffee machine creating a comforting backdrop to the conversation. With Sue manning the counter, Julia sat at the kitchen island, picking at a day-old cruffin, not yet ready to face the questions from her regulars.

"You should be proud, Julia," DI Moyes said, leaning against the counter. "You cracked this case wide open. Without you, Melissa might still be out there."

Julia shook her head, her gaze fixed on the crumbs scattered across the stainless steel. "I didn't do it for praise. I just wanted the truth."

"Well, you got it," Jessie chimed in, her thumbs flying

as she jotted down notes on her phone. "And now I've got the scoop of the year. This article's going to blow the lid off everything."

"Just make sure you get the facts straight," Barker said, his tone dry as he sorted through a stack of case files. "Conrad's family deserves that much."

Jessie rolled her eyes but didn't stop typing. "Relax, Dad. I'm a professional."

Barker shot her a look but didn't argue. Instead, he turned to Julia, his expression softening. "You did good, love. Really good."

Julia smiled faintly, though her eyes remained distant. "It doesn't feel like a victory. Not really."

Moyes pushed off the counter, her tone brisk but not unkind. "That's because you're in the wrong line of work. You've got a knack for this, Julia. I could use a woman like you on my team."

Julia laughed, the sound warm but tinged with weariness. "Thanks, but I'm quite happy where I am."

"Suit yourself. But if you ever change your mind, you know where to find me." Moyes checked her watch and straightened. "Right. Time for a date night with Roxy. I think I've earned it."

"Go on," Julia said, waving her off. "Don't keep her waiting."

As the back door swung shut behind her, Jessie locked her phone and stuffed it into her pocket. "Right, I'm off to start this article. Veronica's deadlines wait for no one."

"Don't forget to eat," Julia called after her, but Jessie

was already halfway out the door, her mind clearly elsewhere.

Barker pressed a kiss to the side of her head. "Conrad's case is officially closed, but there's still paperwork to finish. Not that anyone checks, but old habits die hard."

"Go on. I'll be fine."

He hesitated, his gaze searching hers. "You sure?"

"I'm sure," she said, offering him a small smile. "I'll see you at home."

"I'll cook?"

"No," Julia said, her smile tight. "It's alright. I don't mind."

Barker laughed, kissing her again before heading out. The kitchen fell quiet, the sudden absence of voices leaving only the hum of the café beyond the beads.

Julia took a sip of her tea, the warmth spreading through her as she sank onto the stool. It was over—the case, the mystery, the chaos. But the bittersweet ache in her chest remained, a reminder that not all endings were happy.

Still, as she listened to the familiar sounds of her café—the chatter of customers, the clink of cutlery, Dot somehow taking credit for everything by proxy—she felt a quiet sense of peace. This was her place, her purpose. And for now, that was enough.

∽

The squeak of the swing chains pierced the evening silence as Julia pushed herself back and forth. The snow had melted, leaving the playground damp but not icy, and the air carried a faint promise of warmer days ahead. Sue sat on the swing beside her, her feet scuffing the ground as she rocked lazily.

"Forecast says it's going to be warmer next week," Sue said, breaking the quiet. "Can't wait to pack away these thick coats."

Julia nodded, her gaze fixed on the market square in the distance. The stalls were empty but no longer ominous. The snow hadn't stuck, and the ground was soft underfoot, as though the earth itself was ready to move on.

"It feels like this winter has dragged on forever," Julia agreed.

Sue glanced at her, her expression thoughtful. "Do you think it's really over? With Melissa, I mean."

Julia let the swing slow to a stop. "She confessed. It's done."

"But do you think she'll ever really understand what she did?" Sue pressed. "Or why?"

Julia shook her head. "I don't know. I don't think she ever really understood herself. She was so consumed by what she lost—Conrad, her future, her sense of self— that she couldn't see anything else. Not even the damage she was causing."

Sue kicked at the ground, sending a small spray of damp wood chips into the air. "It's sad, really. All that pain, all that anger... and for what? Conrad wasn't worth it. Wendy certainly wasn't."

"No," Julia agreed. "But to Melissa, they were everything. Conrad was her first love, her 'special love,' as she called him. And Wendy... Wendy was the villain in her story, the one who took everything from her. In her mind, she was just setting things right."

"By becoming a villain herself."

Julia didn't respond. She didn't need to. The truth hung heavy in the air between them, as undeniable as the chill of the evening.

"Do you think Melissa ever really loved Conrad?" Sue asked, as though reading her thoughts.

After a moment, Julia said, "I think she loved the idea of him. The idea of being chosen, of being special. But love... real love... it's not about possession. It's not about control. And it's certainly not about revenge."

Sue nodded, her expression thoughtful. "And Wendy? Do you think she ever loved anyone?"

Julia hesitated. "I don't know. Maybe she loved herself. Or maybe she was just so broken that she didn't know how to love anyone else."

Nearby, Katie played with Olivia, Vinnie, and the twins. Their laughter echoed across the playground, a stark contrast to the sombre mood of the adults. Katie had been quiet since Melissa's arrest, but now she seemed lighter, as though a weight had been lifted from her shoulders.

"Do you think the market will recover?" Sue asked, following Julia's gaze to the square.

"I hope so," Julia said. "If a murder and bad weather kept people away, solving it before the sunshine returns should bring them back. At least, that's what I'm counting on."

Sue smiled faintly. "You've always been an optimist."

"Someone has to be," Julia replied, returning the smile.

They sat in silence for a while, the rhythmic creak of the swings the only sound. The laughter of the children drew their attention back to the climbing frame. Katie was chasing Olivia, her face alight with joy. For a moment, Julia allowed herself to believe that everything would be alright—that the market would thrive, that the village would heal, and that they would all find a way to move on.

As the evening deepened, the playground emptied, the children's laughter fading into the night. Julia and Sue stayed on the swings, the quiet companionship between them a balm to the day's turmoil.

"Tomorrow," Julia said, breaking the silence. "We'll start fresh tomorrow."

Sue nodded, her gaze fixed on the horizon. "Tomorrow."

And for the first time in what felt like forever, Julia allowed herself to believe that tomorrow might just be better.

22

*J*essie passed through the salon on her way to the office upstairs. Every client cradled a copy of the paper between manicured fingers, their faces absorbed in the story that had gripped the village. 'HAMMER TIME FOR POISONOUS LOVE RIVAL: The TRUE Story of Wendy and Conrad Michaels' Murders.' Even Mrs Coggles hadn't found fault with a single word.

Jessie pushed open the door to find Veronica surrounded by stacks of fresh papers, a rare smile lighting up her face behind those enormous frames— green, this week. The usual chaos of her desk had been replaced by neat columns of numbers.

"Don't just stand there," Veronica beckoned her over. "Come see what you've done."

"What *we've* done," Jessie corrected, crossing to the desk. She studied the figures, hardly daring to believe them. "Is this right? Best-selling issue in almost a year?"

"Since the Twisted Tree Murders. People couldn't get enough copies." Veronica tapped the front page, where Melissa's mugshot photograph stared back at them. "But it wasn't just the sensationalism of it all. You showed the human side—how obsession can corrupt even the quietest soul. Made people think about their own relationships, their own buried resentments. Wait till you see the comments online!"

"I learned from the best." Jessie settled into her chair, the leather creaking beneath her. "Though you did try to hire the worst person for food critic."

Veronica's smile faltered. "Lesson learned. Trying for a quick fix instead of trusting what we already had." She pulled an envelope from her drawer, the official letterhead visible through the thin paper. "Speaking of desperate measures..."

"More restructuring threats?" Jessie didn't need to see the letter to know what it contained.

"They're impressed by this week's numbers." Veronica removed her glasses, polishing them with practised movements. "But they want to see sustained growth. In their words, 'adapt to modern media consumption habits.'"

"Then we keep giving the people of Peridale what they want to read about," Jessie said firmly, refusing to give up. "This story proved people still want real journalism—stories that matter to their community." Her fingers flew across her phone as ideas formed. "We follow this up with a series on local businesses reinventing themselves. Start with the market—how it's bounced back after everything. Profile Barker's book launch—"

"The buzzards won't wait forever," Veronica warned, but her smile was returning. "We need to prove ourselves every week, not just when murder rocks the village."

"Then we'll find the stories that matter." Jessie met her mentor's gaze. "The ones that remind people why local papers matter. Why community matters." She grinned. "Besides, have you seen how many letters we've had about Ethel's gnomes? There's a feature right there."

Veronica laughed, the sound echoing off the mural-covered walls. "You never give up, do you?" The sound of an incoming email pinged from the computer, sending Veronica wheeling back to her screen. She peered over her glasses, reading for a moment, her eyes growing wider with each word. "I... I don't believe it."

Jessie's head snapped up. "What?"

Her editor's fingers hovered over the keyboard, a rare mixture of excitement and disbelief crossing her face. "I think you need to get back to Fern Moore. There's a story brewing, and oh, it's a doozy."

"Veronica," Jessie pressed, "what is it?"

"Just received an anonymous tip. A couple at Fern Moore has won the lottery." She turned her monitor slightly, allowing Jessie a glimpse of the email.

"How much?"

"One point two *million* pounds."

"Shut up." Jessie laughed. "For real? That's going to change their lives."

"Or ruin it," Veronica muttered as her fingers flew across a reply email. "But it seems like you have a new story to chase. There's only one thing people love reading about more than murder..." She paused, peering over her glasses before adding, "...and that's a rags to riches story."

"I think we've got our next headline sorted," Jessie said, grabbing her bag and heading for the door. "Who said this journalism job was difficult?"

"Don't get cocky now."

"Me?" Jessie winked back at her editor before slipping out the door. "Never."

∽

Barker stood at the back of St Peter's Church, watching the small crowd gather for Conrad's funeral. The wooden pews were barely half full—a handful of fellow craftsmen, some market regulars, a few faces he didn't recognise. No family. No one to mourn the man Conrad might have been, if time hadn't run out.

"Thought I'd find you hiding back here." DI Moyes appeared beside him as the vicar began speaking. Her voice was barely above a whisper. "Got the sentencing recommendation for Melissa back this morning."

Barker held his breath. "And?"

"Life, most likely. Premeditated murder for Wendy, voluntary manslaughter for Conrad." She shifted her weight, leather shoes creaking against the stone floor. "We found a scrapbook at Melissa's flat. Pages and pages of obsessive notes, going back years. She followed Wendy's entire career, cutting out pieces from magazines and papers, adding her thoughts. That alone was enough for the CPS."

Barker's gaze drifted to the simple oak coffin at the altar. Conrad would have appreciated the craftsmanship, even if he'd moved on to different materials. "He was always chasing something just out of reach, wasn't he? Some version of happiness he couldn't quite grasp."

"Not so different from Wendy in that way."

"But different where it mattered." Barker watched as the vicar spoke about new beginnings and fresh starts— words that felt hollow in the cold church. "Wendy took what she wanted, damaged everyone around her. Conrad just... got damaged. Let himself be used until there was nothing left."

"Speaking of damaged people..." Moyes kept her voice low as the congregation bowed their heads in prayer. "Polly and Ethan have split. She's headed north for some publishing deal; he's taken his van south. Clean break."

"Probably for the best." A shaft of winter sunlight streamed through the stained glass, casting coloured shadows across the coffin. "I'd hate to see them end up like Wendy and Conrad one day."

"All that wasted time," Moyes mused. "All those chances to change course, to choose differently. And in the end..."

"In the end, time runs out for everyone." Barker straightened as the service concluded. "It's what we do with it that matters."

"Speaking of time..." Moyes checked her watch. "Don't you have somewhere to be? Heard there's quite a crowd gathering in the market square for your book launch already."

Outside, weak winter sunlight bathed the churchyard. Through the wrought iron gates, Barker could see the market square coming alive with morning crowds. Time marching on, as it always did. Even for those who spent their lives measuring it.

~

Julia climbed the familiar concrete stairs to Shelly's flat, fresh magazines tucked under one arm and a covered cage held carefully in the other. The building felt different now—less oppressive somehow, as though Wendy's shadow had finally lifted from its walls.

Shelly's face lit up at the sight of the magazines. "You remembered!" She ushered Julia inside, clearing space on her cluttered coffee table. "Though I hope there's nothing too exciting in these ones. I've had enough excitement lately to last a lifetime."

"I promised I'd replace them." Julia set down the cage, her heart fluttering with nervous anticipation. "And I brought you something else."

Shelly's eyes widened as Julia lifted the cover, revealing a small brown-and-white rat washing its whiskers. "Oh my..." Her weathered hands trembled as she reached toward the cage. "He looks just like—"

"Frank," Julia finished softly. "I know he can't replace him, but when I saw this little guy at the pet shop, I thought maybe you could give him a home."

"All these years," Shelly whispered, her eyes welling

with tears, "I thought I'd imagined how much that rat meant to me. Silly, really."

"It's not silly at all." Julia helped Shelly open the cage, watching as the rat sniffed curiously at her outstretched fingers. "Sometimes the smallest things carry the biggest pieces of our hearts."

Shelly gathered Julia into an unexpected hug, her thin frame surprisingly strong. "If Wendy had had a friend like you," she said against Julia's shoulder, "maybe things would have worked out differently."

The words hit Julia hard, making her think of Melissa—of all the times over the years she could have reached out, could have seen the darkness growing. She hugged Shelly back, trying to push away the guilt. Some choices, she knew, belonged to others.

"What will you call him?" she asked as they separated.

Shelly watched the rat exploring his new home. "Frank the Second," she declared with a watery laugh. "Frankie, for short."

~

The sun hung low in the sky as Julia made her way through the cemetery gates, a bouquet of her mother's favourite flowers cradled in her arms. White lilies. Poisonous to cats, but not to dogs or humans—Julia had checked, just out of curiosity. Frost crunched beneath her Oxfords as she wound between the gravestones, their shadows stretching in the fading light.

She stopped short at the sight of a familiar figure

already standing at her mother's grave. Prudence's silver hair caught the sunlight as she arranged her own small posy of flowers.

"I hope you don't mind," Prudence said without turning. "Seemed right somehow, paying my respects."

Julia moved to stand beside her, taking in the weathered stone, the dates that still made her heart ache. "She would have liked that."

They stood in comfortable silence for a moment, watching their breath mist in the cold air. Finally, Julia reached into her bag. "I bought you something. It's not much, but..."

Prudence's hands trembled slightly as she accepted the blank recipe book, its leather cover smooth and unmarked.

"It's never too late to start fresh," Julia said softly. "To begin again."

Tears glinted in Prudence's eyes as she ran her fingers over the empty pages. "Thank you," she whispered. Then, clearing her throat, she said, "I've been thinking about staying, you know. In Peridale."

Julia's heart lifted, but Prudence was already shaking her head.

"But I won't." She squared her shoulders. "The road's in my blood now. But I'll do things differently this time. No more hiding, no more shortcuts." A smile tugged at her lips. "Prudence White is back—not that she ever really went away."

Julia was glad to hear it. "Where will you go first?"

"There's a food festival in Yorkshire next month." Prudence's eyes lit up with something Julia hadn't seen before—hope, maybe. Or peace. "Thought I might try my luck there. Properly this time, with all the right permits."

Julia squeezed her hand. "They won't know what hit them."

As the sun dipped lower, Julia watched Prudence walk away, recipe book clutched to her chest, and felt something settle in her own heart. Some chapters had to close before others could begin.

23

The sun drifted over the horizon as Barker signed his name one last time. His wrist ached from the hundreds of signatures he'd penned throughout the day, but seeing the eager faces of his readers—both old and new—had made it worthwhile. The other stallholders seemed to share his contentment, their smiles genuine as customers browsed—and bought—their wares with renewed interest.

"Best launch yet, Mr Brown." PC Puglisi clutched his freshly signed copy of The Man in the Field, practically bouncing on his heels. "Can't wait to start reading."

"I hope you enjoy it, Jake." Barker managed a tired smile. "And you were right, by the way."

"About what, Mr Brown?"

Barker chuckled, shaking his head. "You said it's always the ex. Not always, but this time it was—we were just focused on the wrong ex."

Jake grinned, already thumbing through the pages as

he hurried away to begin reading. Barker began gathering the remaining books, his movements slow and tired. The book was finished, and he'd yet to start the next one. Maybe he'd start that night. Or tomorrow. Or next week. He wasn't sure what the next one would be about. He'd thought about writing about Melissa, Wendy, and Conrad, but it felt too close to home.

"Not running off, are you?" Katie's voice cut through his thoughts as she approached his stall. Her pink suit seemed to glow in the fading light. "Can I have a quick word?"

He hooked his thumb over his shoulder. "Actually, Katie, I was just—"

"You can't avoid looking for your father forever." She placed a notepad and pen on his table with deliberate care. "What are you so afraid of?"

Barker's hands stilled on the stack of books. "What if he's already dead? What if I won't want to know him? What if—" His voice caught. "What if he won't want to know me? I'm scared, Katie."

"I know." Her voice softened as she pushed the pen closer. "So was I, and I didn't like what I found, but I'm better off knowing." She met his gaze, her eyes full of understanding. "One day, you'll be too old for it to make a difference. Don't get to your deathbed regretting that you never tried." She tapped the notepad. "Write to your brother—write to Casper. If anyone knows something, it's him."

Barker nodded, the words sticking in his throat. "I will."

But after Katie left, he could only stare at the blank

paper before him. The market square emptied around him as traders packed away their stalls, but still the pen remained untouched. He screwed up the paper and tossed it into the box before dragging it back to his office.

In the quiet of his basement, his mother's final words echoed in his mind: Promise me, Barker, promise me you'll be okay not knowing.

He'd made that promise over a decade ago, watching her slip away in that sterile hospital room. The memory remained sharp enough to cut.

His gaze drifted to the framed photograph on his desk, positioned next to Conrad's clock—his mother's smile forever frozen in time, her eyes holding secrets she'd taken to her grave.

"Sorry, Mum," he whispered, and picked up the pen and a fresh sheet of paper.

～

The first morning of February dawned crisp and bright, a welcome respite from the dreary grey that had cloaked Peridale for weeks. Katie burst into the café, her cheeks flushed with excitement. "It's official! The market is finally a success! Another day of people showing up to shop."

Julia smiled as she wiped down the counter, the warm scent of freshly baked cruffins wafting from the kitchen. "I knew it would. And look, the weather has brightened up too. For the first time all year, spring is in the air."

Katie leaned in. "Speaking of things in the air, did

you hear the rumour about the young couple winning the lottery at Fern Moore?"

In the corner, Dot, Percy, and Ethel looked up from their tea, their eyes wide.

"It's going to ruin that poor young couple's lives," Dot declared. "Look at how money ruined your life, Katie. Mark my words, it always does."

"That much money, that young... it's not the blessing it seems," Percy agreed, shaking his head. "Does anyone know who they are?"

"They've decided to remain anonymous," Katie said. "But there'll be signs... it'll leak."

Julia let their chatter wash over her, glad the café was back to its usual hum. In the kitchen, Prudence was baking one last time before heading off to her next adventure. Julia gathered up the empty cups and plates scattered across the tables.

"Good luck to that couple," she declared, "whoever they are."

"I wonder if they'll go public with it," Evelyn mused from her spot by the window.

Shilpa looked up from the crossword. "I'd keep my lips sealed."

"I'd sneak off into the sunset," Ethel said with a wistful sigh. "Somewhere nice and hot."

Percy chuckled. "I'm surprised you haven't already, with your gnome earnings. You sold out!"

"I know," Ethel said, flexing her fingers. "But when I minused off the pitch fee and the costs and the time... and my arthritic wrists. I'm hanging up my crafting hat, for now."

"Me too," Amy declared, tossing down her lumpy knitting. "I don't even know what this is supposed to be."

"It's February, dear," Dot declared. "New Year's resolutions are *so* last month."

Evelyn closed her eyes, a serene smile on her face before she swirled her tea leaves. "I sense great things for that couple."

Dot snorted. "That's a bad omen if ever I've heard one."

Shaking her head with a smile, Julia carried the stack of cups and plates into the kitchen to check on Prudence, but the room was empty, the ovens cooling. Julia wasn't surprised; Prudence didn't seem like one for long goodbyes.

But she had left something on the kitchen island: the old cookbooks dug from Dot's attic, tied with a bow, next to a plate of perfectly golden cruffins. With curious fingers, Julia untied the ribbon and opened the cover. There, in Prudence's looping script, was an inscription: 'To Julia. Keep baking. All my love, Prudence.'

Julia laughed, the sound bright and warm in the quiet kitchen. She picked up a cruffin, the pastry flaking apart in her hands, and took a bite, the sweet, rich flavour bursting on her tongue. They were absolutely perfect, and Prudence was right—she had used too much jam in hers. What a funny week it had been.

Outside, the sun broke through the clouds, casting the market in a soft, hopeful light. The dark days of winter were finally coming to an end, and Julia had a feeling that, for Peridale, the sunshine would bring better days.

~

**Thank you for reading, and don't forget to
RATE/REVIEW!**

~

Julia and Peridale return **SPRING 2025**
in...

MILLIONAIRE'S SHORTBREAD AND MURDER
PRE-ORDER NOW

*A young Fern Moore couple has won the lottery, but what
should be the start of a great new life for them is only the
beginning of their downfall...*

~

Sign up to **AgathaFrost.com** to never miss a release!

THE PLOT THICKENS - CHAPTER ONE

READ THE FIRST CHAPTER FROM THE PLOT THICKENS, THE 2ND BOOK IN MY NEW MEADOWFIELD BOOKSHOP MYSTERIES SERIES (OUT NOW)

*E*llie Swan knew she was about to be buried—she'd tugged a little too hard, but how could she not? She'd already stripped a quarter of the shop's walls, and no piece had come off this easily before. The massive sheet of wallpaper was too heavy, though, and as it tore free, it collapsed over her head, covering her brunette hair and pale face in a thick layer of dust.

"Lovely," she spat, brushing off the flakes of plaster clinging to her skin. So much for making this look easy. "What does DIY stand for again?" She stepped back, wondering if she should turn off the steamer and throw in the scraper. "Destroy It Yourself?"

"Talking to yourself? First sign of madness," Granny Maggie called as she emerged from the back room, on her way to the front door—it must have been lunchtime already. "Blueberry or chocolate muffin?"

"Blueberry," Ellie said, picking at the layers of gloopy

paper stuck like a cast around her fingers. "And I *am* mad if I thought I could renovate this bookshop."

"*We*'re mad," Maggie corrected, dragging open the heavy front door. "But it's under control—"

Maggie tripped over the rotting doorframe—the one responsible for the limp she now tried to hide ever since breaking her hip during a burglary gone wrong months earlier—catching herself just in time with a quick grab at the doorframe. Ellie glanced up from her work, pushing fixing that chunk of decaying wood to the top of her cluttered mental to-do list. Maggie straightened, brushing off the moment with a wave.

"Everything's fine!" she grinned, the door slamming behind her.

Alone with only the creaking floorboards underfoot, Ellie kicked the fallen strip aside, jamming the scraper under the next stubborn corner. The old wallpaper clung to the walls like a second skin, refusing to budge. She wiped her brow, shaking her head at the irony— she'd spent the last decade as a continuity expert in a television studio, paid to focus on every tiny detail. Yet here she was, struggling with something as simple as peeling wallpaper.

Of course, the studio had merged last year, and authentic historical drama wasn't prompting people to click thumbnails on streaming services these days. Now she was back in her home village, her knees aching from hours spent on the hard floor of the old family bookshop.

Her inexperience was obvious—her hands, covered

in grime and torn wallpaper, moved with a clumsy rhythm, a far cry from the confident strokes she had imagined. Still, the shop needed it. Six layers of wallpaper had to go, revealing the lime plaster beneath, one strip at a time.

Ellie recognised at least three of the patterns, each a relic from her childhood spent with Granny Maggie. The green-and-white floral design took her back to being a ten-year-old girl, spreading paste with one hand while holding an Agatha Christie paperback in the other. Maggie hung the paper with a book balanced on the top step of the ladder, only half-invested in giving Meadowfield Books its fresh coat, always caring more about the stories in the pages than the look of the shop.

But customers had changed, even in a small Wiltshire village like Meadowfield. Along with the burglary and all the collective minor problems that had surfaced—never mind the dwindling profits, or lack thereof—a breath of fresh air wouldn't be enough. Maggie might pretend everything would work out, but Ellie could hear the death rattle creeping through the empty shelves with its clear warning.

Breathe new life into the old place, or hear its last gasp.

Ellie paused, sitting back on her heels to survey the progress. The shelves, once overflowing with books of every size, shape, and genre, now stood empty, their contents packed away in boxes hidden upstairs. In three months, they'd made slow but steady progress, yet they were still a long way from reaching that end goal: curling up by the fireplace with a Jane Austen novel in the finished, thriving shop. Between here and there, dozens of tasks awaited, each broken down into smaller steps, which fractured into even tinier tasks. Sweating the big stuff into the small stuff had always been a skill of detail-orientated Ellie. Maybe that's why she'd thrived in television production for so long—a world where every project felt like it would win a BAFTA, until the end product failed to make the studio money and was tossed aside, rendering all their hard work in vain.

That wouldn't happen in the bookshop, though; they were inching toward that end goal, and she wasn't stumbling through it alone—her phone, with an internet connection, was a lifeline, and thanks to the likes of Handy Steve, she had help, albeit virtual.

She brushed away fallen strips of wallpaper, their dusty remnants trying to cling to her phone screen. With a tap, she resumed the video she'd paused just moments before the eight-foot-long, intact strip tried to bury her.

"And *that's* when Debbie left me," Steve said, his sigh so deep that Ellie couldn't help but join in. They were on video 18 of 293 in his *Decorating for Beginners* playlist—also known as Episode 18 of the *Steve and Debbie Divorce Show.* "You can't smooth over some cracks, can you?" He sighed again, dunking his trowel into the plaster mix he'd prepared in the previous video using lime, sand, and horsehair. "But if you used the correct ratio, those surface cracks should disappear in no time." Another even deeper sigh. "Be careful of those deeper, structural cracks, though—the ones you don't realise are there until it's too late. Then suddenly, they're telling you it's not working and that the yoga instructor you weren't supposed to worry about? You *should* have been worrying about them. I should have seen it coming when—"

"*Ellie!*" Maggie gasped, returning from The Giggling Goat café further down South Street, laden with paper bags. "Did you skip from papering to plastering without me? And who's the 'yoga instructor'?"

"New character. And sorry, Gran. I couldn't resist."

"Hmm. Has poor Steve explained why Debbie left him yet?"

"Not yet," Ellie groaned as she rose, her lower back protesting after a morning spent squatting. "But his talent for shoehorning divorce details into every DIY video has kept me—and about twelve hundred other people—captivated since he first posted the videos eight years ago."

"Well, I can't wait to hear how it ends," Maggie said over her shoulder, her limp noticeable as she powered through it. "Still, you *are* skipping ahead. We can't plaster until we've stripped all the wallpaper, and you'll only want to rush ahead to see if Steve gets Mr Bean in the divorce. Given what his solicitor said, though, Debbie will take the cat when she moves to Kettering." She paused at the door to the back room, shaking her head as if the cat's fate was to be decided now and not almost a decade ago. "Back to it. You keep peeling, I'll plate up lunch."

Ellie glanced at the paint scraper in her hand, wondering how she had got here. Just a few months ago, after losing her TV job in 'the big reshuffle', she'd been serving lattes in a busy coffee shop across the bridge in Wales, scrolling through TV job listings with no luck. Now, thanks to Steve's cheerily saying, 'And remember, DIY is for everyone' at the end of each video, she believed she could rebuild the entire shop. But here it was, the first day of autumn, and the hope of reopening by the end of summer had whooshed past, much like Ellie racing through a good book.

"Halloween opening?" she mused aloud as she teased off another satisfying chunk of encrusted wallpaper. It jumped away like it had been waiting to reveal the wall underneath. "Pumpkins on the doorstep, horror novels in the window..."

"Very Stephen King," Maggie called above the clatter of plates. "That's why you'll make a better custodian of this place. I never notice Halloween's happening until it's already passed."

"You've always been in your own world, Gran."

"*Other* people's worlds," she corrected. "Who cares what the season is when you're five hundred pages deep into *Wuthering Heights*?"

Ellie almost wanted to fact-check her, sure the book was closer to four hundred pages, a fact she knew from working on a low-budget adaptation that one critic described as 'Wuthering Lows.' Still, they'd praised the historical accuracy of the sets and costumes, a win Ellie had clung to after fighting the set designer's urge to buy everything from IKEA.

Outside, the faint chime of the bell at St. Mary's

Church drifted through the open windows, announcing noon to the village—and making Ellie's stomach growl in response. Eggs and soldiers in Maggie's garden seemed longer than a few hours ago, but back then, there had been a full wall of wallpaper. Now, only a rectangle the size of a single mattress—like the one she slept on at Granny Maggie's— remained.

She froze mid-scrape, her breath catching as a dark patch emerged beneath the paper. Her nerves tingled with unease as the dark stain grew with each pull of the wallpaper.

"Please don't be black mould," she whispered, the air around her seeming to grow colder. She crouched, nostrils flaring for the telltale sweet musty scent of decay Steve had warned about. But there was nothing—just the familiar aroma of reactivated wallpaper paste. No dampness.

Her fingers, thick with layers of wallpaper remnants, brushed over the surface. Too smooth for mould. Her heart still pounded as her eyes narrowed. The dark spot wasn't spongy, as she'd feared. On a film set, it could have passed for mould, but up close, the splatter marks gave it away. Spray paint.

"For a moment," she chuckled to the splotch, "you *almost* ruined my day."

"*Muffins!*" Maggie called from the back room as she emerged with two plates. "Oliver didn't have blueberry, but your brother suggested lemon drizzle, so I grabbed that instead..."

But the black spray paint had Ellie too fixated to hear

the rest of her gran's café-chat. She forced more of the paper away, and the dark splotch formed into an arrow —or maybe a mountain? Another scrape of metal against the lime plaster, and more paper came off, revealing a shape that morphed into something deliberate. Her breath caught again as the sharp lines of a letter appeared—*W*.

While Ellie wondered what was happening on the wall, life continued as usual outside on South Street. Sylvia Fortescue's refined voice—so posh, she wouldn't have sounded out of place in a period drama—carried from the cheese shop next door, loudly regaling the delivery person about her recent food award. "You simply must try the new Wiltshire Loaf, darling. It's so perfectly crumbly and deliciously nutty, I'm not surprised the judges awarded me gold."

Young PC Finn Walsh's excited cricket chatter followed. "Did you see that last over? Six runs off the last ball! Brought me to tears."

Inside Meadowfield Books, Ellie scraped away the wallpaper in the vigorous manner Steve had warned against, but she wasn't thinking about pulling a muscle at that moment. Each scrape revealed more letters, more of the cryptic message hidden beneath the layers of time.

"*Saw*," she read aloud as the first complete word appeared. "Saw *it*..."

"Are you going to eat this?" Maggie called from the counter, her back to Ellie. "Even Michelangelo took a lunch break, dear."

"Gran…"

Ellie stepped back, her breath catching as the words pulsed on the wall, seeping from the lime plaster as though they were trying to grab her. She tripped over Steve, still paused on the phone screen, unable to tear her eyes away from the chilling phrase.

'WE SAW IT ALL…'

"…*Gran*?" Ellie's voice wavered, still fixated on the message. "Forget the muffins and look at this…"

"*Forget* the *muffins*?" she mumbled through a mouthful. "I'll tell your brother you said…" Her words trailed off as she joined Ellie in front of the wall. She swallowed, then licked her lips, her crumb-coated lips tightening. "Saw what?"

"That answers my first question—you've never seen this before."

Maggie shook her head, backing away as if the words had grown roots, trying to latch on. "The shop was my sister's before mine, and our mother's before that… but I remember my sister, Vera, putting on that bottom blue layer with the white daisies. She talked about stripping the wallpaper back. I offered to help but she told me in no uncertain terms that our mother left the shop to *her*, so she'd be taking care of it… until she couldn't, of course."

"Year?"

Maggie hummed for a moment. "Your mother had already had you, still dragging herself to auditions with a pram. Vera fell out with me for a week when I said you'd be as much my grandchild as Oliver." She smiled apologetically. "Your Great-Aunt Vera had old-fashioned views about babies, marriage, and decorating, so we can rule her out." She sighed. "I'm sorry, love. I don't know where this came from."

"Don't be sorry."

"But I *am*," Maggie said, hugging her knitted beige cardigan tight. "I wish I knew what it meant. Do you think it could be builder slang?"

Ellie shrugged, turning back to the wall. She'd halved the remaining rectangle of wallpaper, but another strip still clung beneath the message. One tug confirmed Ellie's suspicion that they'd only uncovered half the story.

"Why go to the trouble of telling us they saw *something*," she muttered, letting the paper fall from her crusty fingers, "without telling us what they saw? 'We saw it all. Meredith Fenton killed Tim Baker.' Gran?" She turned to find Maggie bumping into the counter, rattling the plates. "You know these names, don't you?"

"A *cruel* joke."

"Did Tim Baker die in the 1990s?" Ellie pressed.

"1994," Maggie confirmed, her wide eyes glued to the words on the wall. "And if you don't know Meredith Fenton, you know her husband."

"Mr Fenton?" Ellie's eyes widened at the memory of him. "The 'other' history teacher. People groaned when they got Mr Fenton instead of you. His lessons were... monotonous."

"I'm flattered, but George Fenton was a fine teacher, got great GCSE results despite his delivery, and *is* a dear friend." She paused, tucking her arms tight against her cardigan. "As was Meredith. She suffered horribly from those vicious rumours the first time around, but I will say this once and *only* once: Meredith Fenton is not a murderer." Her wide eyes flicked from the wall to Ellie. "She was a sweet woman, a little on the... kooky side. But being odd doesn't make you a killer, no matter what people in Meadowfield thought in 1994."

Ellie barely registered her grandmother's mix of present and past tense, her gaze already sweeping across the rest of the shop. What other secrets might lurk beneath the remaining wallpaper?

"What do we do?"

Maggie shook her head, her brow furrowing deeper. "Nothing. It's leftover, incorrect gossip from thirty years ago. Maybe whoever my sister hired to decorate thought it was funny."

"But who? And why? This isn't casual graffiti. It's *murder*."

"Eleanor," Maggie said, exhaling after the emergency breakout of Ellie's full name. "This isn't like what happened with the Blackwood family and *The Last Draft* manuscript riddle when you first came back to the village. There's no mystery for you to dig into."

"But how can you be so sure?"

Maggie hesitated, her gaze dropping to the floor. "What happened in 1994... the frenzy that took over the village after the hauntings..."

"H-hauntings?"

She sighed, rubbing her temples as if warding off a headache. "Ellie, I'd rather not dredge all that up. Paint over the wall, leave it alone..."

"But Gran," she pressed, unwilling to let the accusation slide, "if there's a chance this is true, shouldn't we check? For Tim Baker's sake?"

"Ellie..." Maggie exhaled again, letting whatever she'd meant to say float away. "Tim's fall was nothing more than an accident, and everyone—or should I say, most rational people—around here know it."

Ellie hated the dismissal, but the pain thick in her gran's voice was hard to ignore. She wished they could go back to talking about Handy Steve and Oliver's low stocks of blueberry muffins at The Giggling Goat.

"What do we do?" Ellie asked again.

"You can call the police," Maggie said, glancing at the wall one last time before retreating to the back room. "Or you can paint over it and forget you ever saw it. Some ghosts are best left undisturbed."

As the door to the back room closed—another oddity—Ellie stared at the black splotches, and something within those words stared back, like dark eyes peering out from an unexplored, dense forest. More than she wanted to uncover the history behind how these words ended up underneath the wallpaper at Meadowfield Books, she needed to understand why her gran was comfortable sweeping an accusation of murder under the rug, as though there was no way to read between the lines:

WE SAW IT ALL...

MEREDITH FENTON KILLED TIM BAKER.

And all Ellie wanted to do was dig between those lines.

~

Continue reading in **THE PLOT THICKENS** on Amazon

NEW TO THE SERIES? Start with the first book, **THE LAST DRAFT**. Only 0.99!

Thank you for reading!

DON'T FORGET TO RATE AND REVIEW ON AMAZON

Reviews are more important than ever, so show your support for the series by rating and reviewing the book on Amazon! Reviews are **CRUCIAL** for the longevity of any series, and they're the best way to let authors know you want more! They help us reach more people! I appreciate any feedback, no matter how long or short. It's a great way of letting other cozy mystery fans know what you thought about the book.

Being an independent author means this is my livelihood, and *every review* really does make a **huge difference.** Reviews are the best way to support me so I can continue doing what I love, which is bringing you, the readers, more fun cozy adventures!

WANT TO BE KEPT UP TO DATE WITH AGATHA FROST RELEASES? *SIGN UP THE FREE NEWSLETTER!*

www.AgathaFrost.com

You can also follow **Agatha Frost** across social media. Search 'Agatha Frost' on:

Facebook
Twitter
Goodreads
Instagram

ALSO BY AGATHA FROST

Meadowfield Bookshop (NEW)

Join Ellie and her Granny Maggie in their Meadowfield bookshop for more murder mysteries...

Peridale Café

There's always a cup of peppermint and liqourice tea and a murder to solve in the Peridale Café...

Claire's Candles

Head to Northash to join Claire as she solves mysteries from her candle shop...

Printed in Great Britain
by Amazon

61512100R00190